NO
GODS,
NO
MONSTERS

BOOKS BY CADWELL TURNBULL

The Lesson

NO GODS, NO MONSTERS

A NOVEL

CADWELL TURNBULL

BLACK
STONE
PUBLISHING

Copyright © 2021 by Cadwell Turnbull
Published in 2021 by Blackstone Publishing
Cover and book design by Kathryn Galloway English

Printed in the United States of America

First edition: 2021
ISBN 978-1-9826-0372-4
Fiction / Fantasy / General

1 3 5 7 9 10 8 6 4 2

CIP data for this book is available
from the Library of Congress

Blackstone Publishing
31 Mistletoe Rd.
Ashland, OR 97520

www.BlackstonePublishing.com

To all the ones we've lost.

A FOREST OF WORLDS

Tanya meets me at our usual spot in Cameron Village, and we sit outside under a patio umbrella, the North Carolina heat cooling to a low simmer in the setting sun. I haven't told her why it's so important we meet. We order drinks—me, a Corona because I'm basic as fuck; Tanya, a house cider—and we start talking about work and the adjunct professor struggle. We both know I'm dancing around something. Every few minutes, she looks at me as if to say, "You gonna spill it, or what?" But I just keep on asking questions about her students as if I hadn't heard about them a thousand times already.

We're splitting a plate of fries when I tell her.

A french fry rests on her lip at the exact moment I say it. She holds it there with her fingers as if she were about to light up a cigarette. "For the summer?"

I shake my head. "I gave my notice. I won't be back in the fall."

Tanya puts the fry all the way into her mouth and chews. Her

eyes stay on me the whole time, weighing the information. "So this is permanent, then?"

"Maybe. Don't know yet."

"Got a place set up?"

"I'm going to stay with a friend for a while."

Her eyebrows rise.

"No, nothing like that. Brian. You met him when he came to visit."

"I remember."

She is considering something, and I think I know what it is. Only the lime is left in my Corona bottle, but I have the urge to put the smooth glass to my lips out of nervous habit. I have to will myself not to pick the bottle up. "It wasn't an elaborate plan or anything," I say. "I decided last week."

"That's still a long time to keep it to yourself." She looks away. "Well, I'm assuming Brian knew, so not just to yourself. Does your mom know?"

"I told her this morning."

"How'd she take it?"

"Badly. She hasn't been home since what happened to Cory."

Tanya knows the whole story, so she lets it lie between us, unmentioned. She places a hand over her lips and stares off for a long time. The action somehow isn't strange. It's as if she's keeping something trapped inside, and we're both the better for it. Then she gets up, puts a hand on my shoulder, and says she's going to be right back. She heads for the ladies' room inside the bar.

She isn't gone long. While she's away, the server gives me another Corona. I've taken only a couple of sips by the time she comes back and sits down, looking normal—relaxed, even.

"I'm going to miss you," she says, picking up the conversation

as if no time had passed. "Your mom will get over it. Can't run from the past forever. Who knows? This might be good for the both of you."

I smile. This might have been what she was going to say, but it feels sifted through, the impurities removed.

We finish our drinks and the plate of fries, talking about Tanya's chances of becoming an assistant professor. She is feeling good about it. Hopeful. We leave, and I walk with her down the street to her apartment on Ossipee. We hug at the entrance, a little longer and a little tighter than usual.

"We'll be hanging out again before I leave. You not rid of me yet."

She lets go. "Was it ever going to happen between us?"

And there it is, low enough that I can pretend I haven't heard, but my face has already given me away.

"I want you to come up," she says.

"I don't think that's smart."

"You don't want to?"

"I do, but—"

"I'm a grown woman," she chides.

I let her pull me up the stairs. We have another drink and then make love on the couch. It is urgent and without grace. Afterward, we lie together, our limbs tangled, my head resting between her breasts. As we lie there, I listen to her breathing, her heartbeat, the soft human noises of her stomach. I run my fingers down her arm as she strokes the top of my head, her fingertips gently moving with the grain of my fade.

"You should've told me sooner," she says.

"I know. I'm sorry," I say.

"No, you're not."

I don't try to defend myself.

At some point, I fall asleep on top of her. When I wake up, I am still on the couch, my body stretched under a soft quilt. The smell of fried eggs and bacon wafts from the kitchen. Tanya turns when she hears me stir. "You know you sleep like the dead? I couldn't even wake you up to get off me."

I smile and sit up. I can feel the sweat between my thighs, under my pits, and it is uncomfortable. My clothes are on the coffee table, folded neatly.

"I'm making breakfast because I'm hungry," Tanya adds. "But don't think I'm going to be serving your ass. You better get up and get some."

I try putting on my underwear under the quilt but then give up, standing to get it done. Tanya watches, a lustful half smile on her face. "Seriously," she says, "I could have dressed you myself without you waking up."

When I'm finished, I come over to the kitchen. I give Tanya a hug but don't lean in for a kiss. I don't know what this is going to be, and I want to leave the decision up to her. She slaps me on the butt and points to the cabinet with the plates. I do as I'm told and get one for each of us, then pull some bread from the fridge to make toast. Neither of us broaches the subject of the night before. We eat quietly, and I leave.

I wait a day before texting her, and she takes several hours before hitting me back.

> I think I need some time to get over
> whatever this is. Don't worry, we cool.

> Okay. I really did have a great time.

She doesn't respond. A month later, when I'm getting on my plane, she sends me a goodbye text.

> Be safe. And let me know when you
> land.

I replay that morning with Tanya in my mind as I go through TSA, thinking, if things had gone differently, if we'd been straight with each other sooner, would it have been different between us? I was going home no matter what, so it is a useless exercise. I am tired of visiting St. Thomas only in my dreams.

On the airplane, I sleep like the dead.

I was in my twenties when I read *The Unbearable Lightness of Being* for the first time. I found it among Cory's things, worn and yellowed. On its cover, a bowler hat hovers in midair, nothing under it but a dull brick road. For a long time, I felt a personal connection to that image—a hat without a body, an absence. It remains on my bookshelf even after so many years.

Don't get me wrong. My love for the book isn't without criticism. This statement in its opening chapter, for example:

> Putting it negatively, the myth of eternal return states
> that a life which disappears once and for all, which does
> not return, is like a shadow, without weight, dead in ad-
> vance, and whether it was horrible, beautiful, or sub-
> lime, its horror, sublimity, and beauty mean nothing. We
> need take no more note of it than of a war between two
> African kingdoms in the fourteenth century, a war that

altered nothing in the destiny of the world, even if a hundred thousand blacks perished in excruciating torment.

The *we* here is meant for all of us. We all agree, right? Wars in African nations and hundreds of thousands of dead Blacks have altered nothing in the world. No great minds perish in Africa. No Caesars or Alexanders. No great mass movements start there to inspire the world. No empires, no utopias. History is never altered by Africa, in this timeline or any other.

The narrator goes on to say that, in contrast, the French Revolution is of note, and the certainty of this statement drips off the page. It's just facts, people.

The first time I read this shit, I just glided right over the bit about African kingdoms. That first reading, the idea of eternal return stirred something in my mind. It is only briefly referenced in the quote, but the hovering nameless narrator of the novel goes on at length about it. Eternal return is a central theme of the book. The concept is this: The universe and the history of everything are on repeat—a vinyl record spinning forever. Every action happens an infinite number of times, from the big bang to the heat death and back again.

That first time, I misread eternal return as historic recurrence, thinking the narrator meant that world events repeat themselves with minute variation. Both concepts were new to me. I'm not as bright as Cory—I've never read Nietzsche—so I don't catch my mistake until years later. But I read that book at least five times that first year, seeing my brother in it, seeing myself. I return to it now, knowing the difference between the two concepts and believing in both.

Every moment is eternal. Every story carries a bit of the past

with it, like a long poem, with stanzas and breaks and refrains. The same is true across timelines, too. If the world is born a billion times in parallel, all those iterations will spring up like a forest of the same wood, repeating themselves up into their leaves and across the whole forest of worlds.

For someone standing in that forest, there would be no way out—in all directions, a mirror.

3

I'm going to tell you a story. And, like so many stories, this one begins with a body.

THE BLACK HAND

LAINA CALVARY
SOMERVILLE, MASSACHUSETTS

TWO WEEKS BEFORE THE FRACTURE

It is October 2022, and Lincoln is dead.

Laina stands over her brother's body, looking at the thin white sheet that covers his lower half. The sheet looks more real than the man, though she can't say why. Perhaps it's because she is used to seeing life in her brother, and now there is only this dead outer covering. Lincoln's skin looks like dried wood now, his nose and lips taking on the quality of wax. All signs of something lost that cannot be touched, noticed only in its absence.

Her brother is filled with holes. The ear canals and nostrils and pores are all useless now, but familiar. The punctures along his arms are also familiar, markers of a time when Laina was close enough to see the damage he was doing to himself. But now there are two new holes, large and unfamiliar. One is just below his heart, the other above his right brow. Either would have killed him easily, but there they are, a constellation of two to show that the job was properly done.

How long has she been in here alone, looking at these holes? Laina asked to be alone with the body, and the coroner obliged. She wants to go to the door and call the coroner back in, but she can't pull herself away. She looks the body over again, from feet to head. She focuses on his overgrown beard once more. This was the other thing that had stopped her from identifying him quickly. The beard and the lifelessness. Before this, she'd seen him at their mom's funeral seven years ago, standing under a naked tree, its fingers branching to the pale sky. He wore large sunglasses over his face and a torn winter jacket. He was far away, but it was him all right. Facial hair, sure, but not this ugly thing. And then she saw him again on the Red Line, on her way home to Somerville, maybe three years past? Something like that. On that occasion, she got a good look at him, exchanged words. His beard was long then too, but still manageable.

He was naked when he died, the coroner explained—running through the street as bare as on the day he was born. It must have been an episode, she thinks. High out of his mind, but not dangerous. Right? He clearly couldn't have been armed. He had nowhere to hide a weapon. Laina feels a surge of anger at this thought. *Don't do it*, she tells herself. *Don't go there, not now.* She sets the thought on fire and lets the smoke curl away to nothing before it can do any harm. Anger she will have to save for later, when it can be used.

It is the whole moment, really. Her brother's body on the slab, the subject of her thoughts. It feels so familiar, as if Cory were lying there too, dead and full of holes.

When they were children, Lincoln and Laina's cousin would come over to cut Lincoln's hair. Simone was nine years older than Laina, already out of high school and doing nothing with her life except for her hair-cutting side hustle. She cut Lincoln's hair for

free, but she charged all the neighborhood boys so she had spending money she didn't have to beg from Auntie Jane.

Simone liked to do her haircuts in the bathroom, sitting Lincoln on top of a wooden stool so that she could see the boy in the mirror as she did her work. This meant that Laina had to make sure to use the bathroom before she came over. She was shy, and something about Simone made her uncomfortable, so she tried to avoid her and the bathroom if she could.

But sometimes, even with all her planning, she still had to open the closed door, interrupt the haircutting—which Simone was never happy about—and grab her scrunchies or comb or brush or Blue Magic before slipping back out again. On those occasions, she planned meticulously, remembering in her mind's eye what she needed and where to find it. Then she took a breath, turned the knob, and opened the door, ready for a quick extraction.

The morning it happened, Laina had forgotten her vented hairbrush and was already late for school. She took her breath. She turned the knob. She flung the door open, revealing the crowded bathroom, her brother, and her cousin.

Simone pulled her hand away from Lincoln's lap. "What do you want?" she yelled, flicking off the hair clippers in her other hand.

Laina tried to make eye contact with Lincoln, but his head was lowered. He had a look about him, as if he were trying not to take up space, shrinking into himself. She couldn't decide whether it was him shaking, or her.

"This fucking girl . . ." Simone stepped toward Laina, mumbling something under her breath. Laina cringed in preparation, but Simone only reached out her hand and pulled the door shut, right in Laina's face.

Laina stood there. Around her, the cramped apartment held

its breath. Then the hair clippers buzzed to life again from behind the closed door. Laina reached again for the knob but held back. Her cheeks were on fire. She wanted to tell someone something, to say something, but couldn't put the words together.

Her mother had already left for work. Laina needed to get down to the bus. Simone had agreed to get Lincoln to school herself. All these thoughts, she knew, were connected somehow, but they floated rootless above her. Laina didn't remember a lot after that—only that her hair was messy that day and a boy at school had called her nappy-head. She cried and couldn't stop. She couldn't remember anything after that day, either. A haze swallowed the weeks and months of memories that followed. Simone continued coming over to cut Lincoln's hair, she knew, until one day she stopped. And eventually, that sick feeling went away, though she couldn't pinpoint when.

But here it is, back again, knocking on the old closed door in the back of her mind, returned to fill the silence left behind by those two bullets.

Laina keeps staring at the body, unable and unwilling to look away.

"You blame yourself," I say.

It isn't really a question, but Laina answers the way I always have: "How could I not?"

Our conversation ends there. The coroner comes back in and says, "Time to go." The words fail to catch Laina's attention the first time, and after a while standing next to her, the coroner says it again and guides her out.

The room lies quiet after they leave. Only machine hums and the mute dead.

5

The thing is, Laina had decided to use one of her sick days. The bookstore calls these "wellness days" to encourage their use more broadly. Laina wasn't sick, but she wanted to stay home and binge-watch *The Americans*. It was pure happenstance she wasn't at work when she got the call that the fingerprints of an unidentified person matched her brother's. Since her husband, Ridley, was already at work in the bookstore, he wasn't with her when she got the news. Laina made no conscious decision to keep it from him, but now, after seeing the body, calling him doesn't seem right.

Still in shock, she parks her car on Summer Street near their apartment and starts down the steep hill to Union Square. The square was once a recruitment and mustering site for the Union Army in the Civil War, hence the name. It's located at the intersection of Somerville Avenue, Prospect Hill, and Washington Street, just a fifteen-minute walk from Laina and Ridley's apartment—a huge convenience. Their store, Anarres Books, lies right at the

junction of the three streets. They started renting the space after a
Korean grocery moved to Medford. Laina didn't know Ridley when
the bookstore opened. It took her a year to discover the store, and
several months before they had an opening she could apply for.
Ridley and three others co-owned the bookstore at the time, and
within another couple of years, it had five worker-owners, Laina
among them. She had never worked at a cooperative, but she knew
she wanted to. She also loved books, which helped. Falling in love
with Ridley happened later. It was slow and easy, like wearing in
a good shoe. Ridley never liked that analogy, but that was what it
felt like for Laina.

When she walks into the bookstore, she's fine. She even greets
a few coworkers without getting any strange looks or questions.
But when she sees Ridley, they lock eyes, and she can't even get
to him before the tears start streaming out. He comes right to her
and pulls her into a hug.

"What is it, babe?"

She tells him.

"Oh God," he says. He holds her as they make their way back
through the bookstore, having to field questions from Madeline
at the information desk.

At home, they sit in the living room, his arm around her. She
can't speak, and he doesn't push her to. She falls into her own
thoughts, and when she comes out, a half hour has passed as if
by magic.

"Tea," Ridley offers. He just seemed to be waiting there, waiting
for her to come out again, so he could make the offer. She nods,
and he dutifully disappears to the kitchen.

In the living room, a bird of happiness hangs over the TV, its
thin wooden wings in perpetual flight. It is spinning, propelled by a

stream of air coming in the cracked window. The apartment is filled with similar objects, all Ridley's creations: a wooden bowl on a thin shelf, with pens in it; a varnished spoon that differs only slightly from the ones they use in the kitchen; a crude dragon wrapped around a wood stump. There is another bird of happiness in their bedroom, and several bowls, spoons, and spatulas in the kitchen; a small box in their second bedroom/office, heaping with rocks they've collected, some ordinary, some with embedded crystalline structures. And Ridley's most treasured possession: a wooden shelf, also in that second bedroom. An ugly thing, cracked and uneven, so that books fall over if they're not wedged in tight. But it was Ridley's first large project, so it remains. And Laina would never admit that she hates to look at it.

Ridley returns with a cup of steaming milk tea and sets it on the table. "Do you need me to call people?"

Laina thinks about that. Should she wait until she can make those calls herself, or let Ridley help with this too? The decision is easy.

"Call my aunt. She'll tell everyone."

There aren't that many people to tell, really. Lincoln cut ties with most everyone, and Laina, for her part, maintains only a few familial relationships.

Ridley makes a motion to stand, but Laina stops him. "In a minute," she says. "Sit with me." Her husband settles back down with her and puts a hand on the small of her back.

The tears begin again.

Over the next couple of weeks, Laina buries herself in funeral arrangements. Time blurs, and she makes no effort to keep track. She makes phone calls, pools the money from willing family members, pays for the casket, the viewing, the burial. Her husband's hands are on her back, stroking her arms, her shoulders. He is kissing her forehead. It is night and day and twilight as she stands at her bedroom window, staring out at clouds and sun and stars. Then she is walking down the center of some high-ceilinged church and there are whispers and someone hugs her and someone else tells her that he is so sorry for her loss. There is singing and the lowering of the casket. There's a man in robes saying words from the good book. Someone is putting her in the back of a car, and she is arriving at a reception hall with food and drinks and somber-looking people trying not to look at her. More people say more words and the audience makes soft murmurs of agreement, and then they ask her if she will speak. To this she shakes her head, and not a word is

required of her. She is standing by the ice bucket and water pitch-
ers when Ridley lets go of her hand and tells her he's going to the
bathroom and will be back soon. And somehow, Simone is there
as soon as her husband leaves.

"Fucking tragedy," Simone says. Her cousin is older now, gray-
ing. "I talked to one of the witnesses. They didn't even help the
boy. Just let him bleed out on the street."

Laina tilts her body to face Simone. The fog retreats.

"There's a tape," her cousin is saying. When Laina doesn't
respond, she adds, "I know some people. The cops are keeping it
real tight."

A smile almost touches Simone's lips when she says she knows
some people. But she keeps it down, fights it back, as a decent
person would, even though she isn't a decent person. The fog is
completely gone now, Laina's fire lighting again.

"He was a good kid. He was struggling, but everyone has their
share, you know? We all struggle. He was a good kid, though. It
was that cop."

Laina's husband is walking toward them. He slows and then
stops, worry on his face.

Simone shakes her head. "Loved that boy."

And it is as if Laina were watching it happen from somewhere
else. She sees Ridley start toward her but also sees Simone fleeing.
She watches herself grab the back of Simone's neck. She feels her
nails dig in. She hears herself: "Motherfucker." It isn't a yell. It is
calm, cold, lower than her own voice. It makes the hairs on her
neck stand up.

"What are you doing?" Simone is asking as she turns, her
hands raised. Laina clenches her other hand into a fist and punches
Simone hard in the ear. She feels the skin on her knuckle split as

she makes contact with the cubic zirconia stud in Simone's earlobe.

Ridley is there, holding her. "Stop," he says. "Baby, please stop."

Simone wrests Laina's hand from her neck. "What is wrong with you!"

Her ear is bleeding, and so is Laina's hand. Simone dances back away from Laina, but Laina lunges again, dragging Ridley with her. Simone is too far away, though, and others have come between them.

Simone makes her way across the room, looking back and swearing. Laina screams as if some animal trapped in her had finally been released. She claws at the air. Auntie Jane puts her arms around Laina. "Calm down, love," she says. "I know. I know."

"You *don't*," Laina says.

Auntie Jane looks at her with sad eyes. "Get her some fresh air," she tells Ridley.

"Let's go, baby," he says.

Simone, like the scared rat she is, has bolted out the front entrance, so Laina calms and lets Ridley lead her out the side exit.

Outside the open door, Auntie Jane tells one of her daughters to get a wet cloth napkin. When her youngest returns, Auntie Jane takes the cloth and wraps it around Laina's hand. A few people crowd by the door, staring out at her. Only then does Laina begin to feel the slightest bit of embarrassment.

The alleyway stinks of piss and garbage. She looks up at the sky, trying to control her breath through her mouth, and before long the nausea recedes. An expensive car buzzes by, and Laina realizes where she is.

Jamaica Plain has been sufficiently gentrified, but some of its prior harshness still remains: this alleyway, a reminder of its previous life and the desperation that underlies every large city. Nothing is

completely washed away. Not ever. She left the old neighborhood, going off to college and trying to stay away, but here she is again. Things change, but they always wrap back around on themselves, circles within circles. Her brother is dead, but his death is just a change of state really. How many times did she bury him already? How many more times will she have to bury him?

Time blurs again, and she is staring out her bedroom window, the night dark and starless, silent as if the mouth of a giant had swallowed the world.

When Lincoln was seventeen, he disappeared for a couple of days, and Laina had to go looking for him. She found her brother over at his friend Tomas's house in Roxbury. Their mom had called everywhere, but not there. Her mother did not know Tomas, and Lincoln never mentioned him. Laina had met him at Lincoln's last birthday party. He was twenty, though he looked at least a decade older, standing in the corner. It was more of a hang-out than a party—some music, some dancing, but mostly just teen-agers sitting around drinking and talking. Tomas looked as if he didn't belong, so Laina chatted him up. By the end of that first conversation, she knew the sort of person Tomas was. After the party, she had asked around about him, found out where he lived, just in case.

Lincoln didn't like people getting involved in his business. Laina learned how to get involved at a distance, which mostly worked out to learning things without Lincoln knowing she knew.

And so, in this case, she knew where her brother might be, once the obvious places were ruled out.

Laina had to knock several times before Tomas answered the door. When he did, she forced her way in to find Lincoln on the couch, sprawled out, his eyes half rolled back. The smell of burnt chemicals clung to the air around him. He didn't acknowledge her at all. He lay there as if stunned.

"Lincoln," she called, but then could find no words.

Laina turned to glare at Tomas. "Do you have anything to do with this?"

"This?" he repeated, and looked at Lincoln as if just discovering he was there. His eyes were wet. He was swaying. "He wanted to. It has nothing to do with me."

"You should hang out with people your own age," Laina said.

"Like you?" Tomas smiled, showing stained teeth.

"Wipe that smile off your face before I—"

"Leave him alone," Lincoln said. It was soft enough that, for a moment, Laina thought she imagined it. But when she looked at him, he was looking back at her, his eyes more focused than before, though he had trouble keeping his head from rolling back.

"You knew, didn't you?" he said.

The question came so out of nowhere that Laina looked at Tomas to see if she'd missed something. Tomas shrugged.

"Knew what?" she asked.

Lincoln laughed. It was weak and ragged, but there was no mistaking it. It ran along, dipping and rising again, his body hopping along the track with it, until the laugh descended into a trembling terrible enough to make Laina's heart sink with worry. And then it wasn't laughter. Lincoln shut his eyes tight as if he'd been hit, and his body rolled forward in violent sobs. He put his

hands to his face. His body was crouched over like a serpent eating its own tail. And then he toppled over to one side on the couch, still curled into himself, and continued crying quietly.

Laina felt that old feeling. She wanted to reach out and give him comfort, but the child in her was glued in place. The rock in her throat shifted. Her eyes burned.

How much time passed? Minutes? An hour? Tomas was on the floor now, in the same spot he had been standing, looking away with something like embarrassment. Eventually, the crying stopped. Lincoln uncoiled himself slowly. Then he reached for a Ziploc bag resting on the table, pulled out two pills, and crushed them with an ashtray. Just like that, his eyes on Laina the whole time.

"You doing that in front of me?" Laina asked, hoping he would stop even if just to consider the question.

Without a pause, Lincoln took a rolled-up dollar bill and sucked in hard. He wiped his nose. "You're no one," he said.

The statement had enough venom in it to reach across time and space and strike me in the chest.

Laina pursed her lips. "Kill yourself if you want. But I'm not going to be here when you do." She shot Tomas one last evil eye and walked past him, making sure to nudge him aside with her leg. "I'll tell Mom where to find you," she said before stepping out the door.

She didn't see him again for another three years.

Three days after the funeral, Laina comes back from work to find Ridley sitting in front of his laptop at the dining room table wearing his big over-the-ear headphones. When she enters, he looks up, tucks the right ear pad behind his ear, and mouths a noiseless *good night, my love.*

Laina can hear the voices coming from his headphones: another SEN Collective meeting. She smiles, mouths *shower,* and goes down the hall to the bathroom. She undresses and hops in the bath and takes a quick one, then spends several minutes standing in the tub, letting the water drip from her fingertips. The door is slightly ajar to let the steam out, so she hears when Ridley gets up from the table and stomps down the hall. The door creaks open. She rolls the shower curtain back just enough to see him poke his head in.

"You're home early," he says. "Bad day?"

"No, just not a good one."

He slips into the bathroom and stands by the light switch, giving her the silent nod to go on.

She sighs but relents. "Our coworkers stayed pretty much out of my way. They asked how the funeral went but didn't pry about Lincoln. I did my shift at information—a few out-of-store book requests and the usual stuff. I tried to be friendly, smile at the regulars, but I was off and no one bought it, and so they let me leave early, told me if I wanted I could try again tomorrow. So not too bad, not too good."

He leans his head back against the wall. "And will you be coming in tomorrow? I'm supposed to be on the afternoon shift."

Laina shrugs. "Maybe." She motions for him to give her the towel, and he pulls it down from the hook and hands it to her. As she dries off, she changes the subject. "How was the meeting?"

"Same old. They want the fall retreat to be three days, but I'm trying to get it down to two." He looks meaningfully at her.

Laina wraps the towel around her and steps out of the shower. "Take the three days," she says. "I'll be okay."

"You're sure?" When she nods, his shoulders ease just a bit, and he takes a breath. "So, is there any news on the investigation?"

Laina grunts and leans on the sink.

"I shouldn't have asked."

"It's okay." Laina shakes her head. "Nothing. No mention of a video, either." She doesn't want to admit it, but she feels tired. She wants it to be over. All that anger she wants to feel has been sucked out of her by the whole ordeal. "Can we just go to bed?" she asks. "I want to be held. I don't want to talk."

Ridley gives her a sad smile. "Okay, my love."

She gets dressed in her shorts and sleeping shirt and gets into bed. Ridley is there waiting for her. She snuggles up against his

shoulder and whispers, "You ever feel like there's a world beneath this one?"

"What do you mean?" Ridley's breath rises and falls, his heart beating steady as a drum.

Laina struggles for the words. "Like we are a speck on some larger thing that we only catch glimpses of."

He hesitates, then asks, "Is this about the investigation?"

"I guess. But more than that." She sighs. "I don't know. Never mind."

Ridley makes a sound as if he's going to talk again, but doesn't. Laina snuggles deeper into him, and he kisses her on the temple. He keeps his face to hers, so she feels his breath on her. This is reassuring. She is feeling shaky and needs his steadiness.

She tries to settle the matter in herself, but her mind frets on. She can't tell what she knows from what she doesn't, what she wants from what she only thinks she should want. Lincoln's toxicology report returned inconclusive, but that still doesn't explain why he was running through the street naked. Does she want people digging into his past, unearthing all the ugly, unsavory moments of his life to discredit him, diminish his humanity? She says she will fight for him, but if she decides not to fight, will it be to spare him that disgrace, or to spare herself? Will it be a gift, or just another betrayal? And if it is a bit of both, how much of each is permissible? Where is the line that would damn or redeem her? And shouldn't she know? Shouldn't she have the ability to unearth the truth of her own heart?

This is only part of what she wants to say to Ridley. The other part feels too strange, too terrible, too nihilistic to say out loud. She is feeling, deep inside herself, that none of it matters anyway. None of it matters, because none of it is real. An image comes to

mind. She is a ship, and so is everyone else: a cluster of ships on a dark sea. They are all packed tightly together for protection, but it is futile because at any moment, some black hand will pull one or two or all of them under, and everyone will see it, but no one will know what they're seeing or what to do about it. Not just dying, but something deeper than dying. The place that dying comes from— the vast and heavy nothing at the bottom of all things, returning to claim all things. Everything—her life, Lincoln's life, the movements of every life—is the mere useless stirrings on the surface of that nothing. The nothing is real. They are not.

The thoughts persist. Ridley is asleep now, and the quiet drumbeat of his heart keeps time as Laina's consciousness bobs along with no destination. Her restlessness dulls to the obsessive thoughts of someone on the verge of sleep, fighting against it with a relentless anxiety. But eventually, the thoughts turn to static, her anxiety softens, and without even realizing it, Laina inevitably slips beneath the tide.

• • •

Laina is on the subway platform for the Red Line to Alewife. The train is just arriving. She is standing just beyond the yellow line, where you're not supposed to stand. The hot wind hits her face, pushed ahead of the train as it comes through the tunnel and into the more open space of the station. It screeches to a stop. The double doors open with a clamor. Laina steps through.

It is late; hardly anyone is in the subway car. She takes her seat across from a man asleep under a dirty child-size blanket. She doesn't recognize him right away, but once she does, she spends the next few minutes staring at his sleeping face. A stop goes by, then

another, before her brother opens his eyes. The action is slow, as if he were in his own bed, stirred awake by a lover. His eyes focus on hers but with no recognition. She may as well be a stranger.

Everything is hyperreal, vibrant: the textured face, the yellowed and bloodshot eyes. His skin gleams with days of grime. His forehead has a smudge of dirt; his cheeks are cratered with pockmarks. At the next stop, someone sits near Laina, but they are out of focus, the hyperreality of Lincoln sucking the reality from everything else.

"What, you going to take me home?" As always, he says this as if they'd been talking all along.

"If you'd let me," she says. To her own ears, her voice sounds as if the volume had been turned all the way down.

"I got a place."

Laina looks at the weather-worn duffel bag at his feet, the child's blanket, caked with dirt, that he's using for warmth. "Please come home with me."

"Admit it," he says.

This time, Laina doesn't lie to herself. She knows what he is talking about—has always known. She thinks of saying, *How could I know?* Or, *I'm sorry.* Or, *I didn't see anything; you should have told me something was wrong.* A dozen more answers present themselves, all of them terrible.

Finally, she chooses the truth. "I knew *something*, but it scared me."

He laughs, that same laugh that has no joy in it. It turns to coughing. Then she notices that a darker patch on his covers is spreading. Was that there before? And with the logic of dreams, she remembers that he's been shot. That he is dying.

The world around them suddenly dissolves, until it is just them, and then even Lincoln is fading. Almost simultaneously, another

thing happens. Her brother is *peeling*. Slowly at first, quicker now, his whole body turning inside out from that dark wound. Inner flesh and fat expose themselves, the sound of it tearing at her eardrums, and then the space between them starts seeping into the black hole. She feels herself pulling apart too, strand by strand, the scream in her throat sucked out of her and into him. She is reaching her hands up to her neck and mouth, where she finds . . . nothing. A gaping hole where all her bits are spilling out into the open air.

Laina gasps awake. Her nightshirt is drenched in sweat. Around her, the room lies dark and silent. She puts a hand to her chest and takes enough slow breaths to settle her heart.

It is only after she relaxes that she has the feeling someone else is in the room. She doesn't have a reason to think this; there is no evidence other than the feeling. But then a voice comes, hovering just above her head, a whisper: "Do you want me to get the video for you?"

It is a woman's voice. Sweet. Not at all threatening. Laina is too stunned to speak.

I am just as shocked as she is. No one is there. No one has been there.

"I can get you the video," the woman continues. "Show you what happened that night. Do you want to know what happened that night?"

The voice sounds Caribbean. Laina has family from St. Lucia, and the woman's voice sounds something like that, but also different. I recognize the accent because I've heard it all my life. It isn't St. Lucian; it's St. Thomian. This woman, whoever or whatever she is, has a background similar to my own.

"I can find almost anything," the voice says. "The world is filled with secrets I've found. This is just a small thing."

"I want it," Laina hears herself say. Her right hand is inching toward the lamp next to her bed.

"What will you do with it once you have it?" the voice asks. It is closer now, right in her ear.

Laina trembles. "I don't know," she says. "I'll know once I have it." The thought occurs to her that she has just given her soul to the devil. "What do you want in return?"

"Nothing at all," the voice says. "Give me a day. I'll—"

Laina flicks on the lamp. And somehow, this is worse: to see an empty room in the light. Finally, she screams.

9

"Maybe I should call off today."

Laina tries on her best smile, kisses Ridley on the forehead, and lingers close to his face. "It was a bad dream," she says. "Really. I'm fine."

Ridley looks deep into her eyes but doesn't say a word, which tells her that her act hasn't worked, but she may still get away with it. "Okay," he says. "Call me if there's any trouble."

When he leaves, Laina finds herself alone in the apartment. It wasn't a bad dream. She's sure she was awake, sure she had escaped that terrible dream into a reality just as terrible, because suddenly Ridley was there with her, his arms around her in the very same moment she flicked on the light and screamed.

Quietly she entertains another possibility. The black hand. Perhaps, it has a voice as well.

Perhaps, I think as well, entertaining the possibility that there are stranger things in the universe than I.

As I follow, Laina checks every room several times before she settles in the kitchen. She kicks herself up onto the countertop. She has no idea why this feels like the safest place to be, but she stays there until a knock at the door stirs her. She hops down and approaches the front door as if nearing a cliff edge. She thinks, no one shows up at their apartment without invitation. All the people Laina knows intimately enough to call friends are at work. Maybe a neighbor? But why?

She doesn't want to think it could be a dangerous stranger or, maybe worse, the voice taken physical form.

She pushes through her fear and unbolts the door. When she opens it, a young woman is standing there.

"Good morning," she says. "My name is Rebecca. I was a friend of Lincoln's?"

Laina nods in answer to the unasked questions. Yes, she knows who Lincoln is. Yes, she is his sister. "Laina. Nice to meet you."

Rebecca has strong eyes. She is very attractive and well put together. Laina hates herself for observing that, for thinking that this could not truly be Lincoln's friend. And then she realizes she's spent an uncomfortable amount of time just staring at the woman. "I'm sorry. Please come in."

Laina leads Rebecca to the living room and then gets them each a glass of water. She places the glasses on the table between them, taking the love seat and giving Rebecca the couch to herself.

Rebecca gives her a disarming smile. "I called some family members and got your address. I hope that was okay."

It isn't, but Laina smiles back. "No problem."

"I don't know how else to say it, so I'll just say it."

Having said this, the woman, Rebecca, hesitates anyway. Laina is both amused and wearied. She waits as patiently as she can,

watching several expressions pass over Rebecca's face, none of them immediately telling since she doesn't know the woman.

Finally, Rebecca says, "Lincoln was coming to see you before he died." She reaches for her glass and takes a long gulp of water.

"That day?" Laina asks.

"No. Well, I don't know. Sometimes, a . . ." Rebecca stops herself. She seems to reconsider her wording and tries again. "No, but he was planning to come see you. He was killed before he could."

Was killed. A deliberate choice of words. Laina can detect some anger in them, too. Rebecca must have been really close to Lincoln to know so much, to feel so passionately about how he died. Laina decides just to be blunt about it. "Were you a lover?"

Rebecca laughs. Again, it is disarming, smooth like melted butter. "Oh, no. No, I'm not Lincoln's type. And he definitely isn't mine. Wasn't mine."

Laina frowns but presses on. "Best friend, then?"

"Maybe," Rebecca says. "He wasn't always in the mood for that."

Laina understands this. Her brother could be prickly, occasionally unkind. "So why was he looking for me?" she asks. Laina looks down at her lap. She is wearing blue sweatpants covered in fuzz balls. She pulls a few off, realizes what she is doing, and stops. "I suppose it wasn't good."

"I think it would have depended on the outcome."

"The outcome?"

"I don't know what you knew about Lincoln. He had a few rough years. Spent some time on the streets. He'd been using terribly for a long time, almost died."

Laina doesn't say anything, just waits.

"We met because he got hurt once when he was alone," Rebecca

says. "I'd gotten hurt the same. I was able to help him, introduce him to some support."

"Hurt how?"

Rebecca watches Laina. Those fierce eyes she glimpsed at the beginning have returned. "On the streets, misfortune finds you. No one is looking or caring. If you're vulnerable like Lincoln was, like I was when it happened, misfortune finds you faster." Her finger strokes her eyebrow, the gesture idiosyncratic and intimate. "You understand." Not a question, but a sharp line. *Don't ask any more questions*, Rebecca is saying. *I won't give any more answers.*

"I'm sorry."

"It wasn't you." Rebecca smiles again, and all the tension and anger is smoothed right out of her face as if it had never been there. "Anyway, we helped Lincoln get sober and helped him with the other scars too. He was coming to make amends."

"For what?"

Rebecca smiles. "Because trauma is an open door. We all have to make amends to all the people we let in."

This, of all things, Laina did not expect, and she feels stripped down to her essential parts.

Suddenly, Laina is standing in front of a closed door, the buzz of hair clippers in her ears. She is standing over a couch, on a subway platform, over a metal slab, over a coffin. She is standing in an alleyway, pungent smells filling her nose, her knuckles stinging, the blood bright on her hand, and Lincoln beyond a closed door, a crawling thing devouring himself. All those years of wounding him, of punishing herself. How he would get so angry at the tiniest offense. How he'd say just the right words to hurt her. And how she had used that torture to justify her rejection of him, the distance she kept. He must have felt it. And it must have made

him angrier. That she had the audacity to be hurt, to judge him, when she had turned her back so. What did any of it mean, now that she knows he wanted to apologize? What did it mean that she had never, not once, thought to do the same?

Rebecca is leaning in front of her, holding her hand as if in prayer. When did that happen? Why can't she catch her breath? When did she start crying? "You were ten," Rebecca is saying. "You were just a child." She knows so much. How dare she know so much! This is Laina's private shame. She has no right to it. No right.

Rebecca is still talking, the words flowing like warm water. Laina doesn't come back to herself right away, but when she does, Rebecca is sitting with her, hand in hand, tears in her own eyes. "It took him a long time to get there. Bad relationships. Bad choices. He went all the way down to the bottom. He was coming back up. And they took that from him." The fire is back in Rebecca's eyes. "We won't let them get away with it."

There is a span when no one says anything. Laina takes her time calming down. All the while, Rebecca is watching her, intense and empathic at the same time. Laina is afraid to ask what she means by "we" or "them," or what threat lies beneath the words, what action Rebecca is willing to commit to not "let them get away with it." Laina knows how these things go. It isn't up to them. It has never been up to them. Sometimes, if enough people scream loud enough, the combined effort might get into the head of someone power-ful. It might help that powerful person's career to give a little push to a popular cause. But that depends on a number of factors. She doesn't want to say it, but Lincoln might be too damaged for that sort of charity. They might be left to the whim of public opinion, which might also deem him too messy to be worth the effort. They will fight and fail, and everything will move on, leaving them bitter

and broken. Laina drinks some of the water she has let turn luke-warm on the table. She is no longer shaking. Her eyes and mind feel clear. She tests herself.

"What can we do?"

"We're planning a protest," Rebecca says. *You should come* is left unsaid, but Laina can read it plainly on her face and in the lingering silence Laina is meant to fill.

Laina says nothing.

Rebecca seems to understand. She pulls out a pen from her purse and writes something on a piece of paper, putting it on the table. Then she gets up. Laina follows with her eyes but doesn't stand.

"I should go," she says. "But that's my number in case you need it. I can see myself out." She gives Laina another warm smile, to end things on good terms, and walks out the way she came, clos-ing the door behind her.

In the following silence, Laina tries to make some decision about what to do with the phone number Rebecca has left. As before, she can't settle on any one thing, so she'll hold on to it by default. She gets up and quickly locks the door, partly to be decisive about something trivial, but also because she's started to feel vulner-able again, as if a threat is waiting right beyond what she can see.

When she returns to the living room, the slip of paper is where Rebecca left it, but right next to it is something else, which was definitely not there moments before. A chill crawls up Laina's back. She leans in for a closer look. The flash drive is a sleek and feature-less black tile, like a monolith in miniature.

Something tells Laina to look again at the piece of paper Rebecca has left, and when she does, the gravity in the room shifts, as if she were in a box someone has turned on its side. She has to

sit down to calm her sense of vertigo. She looks at the paper again. No, she didn't imagine it. Rebecca's number is written there in blue ink, but beneath it, scrawled in black, are words in an entirely different hand.

As promised, it says.

Laina waits until after Ridley is asleep before slinking into the living room with her laptop. She sits on the couch, types in her password, and stares at her desktop for a long time. Behind the clutter of documents and folders lies a Japanese-style painting of a carp, the scales intricately drawn like the tips of overlapping fingernails freshly polished in gold. Around the carp, splashes of watercolor bleed together, the edges of the painting fading to white.

The tiny monolith is so light in her palm. It should have more weight, be more substantial. She has tried all day to put the jump drive into the USB port and view its contents, but each time, all the doubts and fears rise up to block her path. This video might show her brother running through the streets in the midst of some episode or, worse, rushing toward a policeman, with violence in his eyes.

No, there has to be more. Why didn't they release it? Why were they so nervous?

Her palm is itching, her mouth is dry, her heart throbbing. Until she knows, she won't be able to go back to bed. She has to know.

She removes the thin cap from the jump drive and seats it in the port. The computer recognizes it immediately. No alarms. No sign of some virus ripping the guts out of her PC. The hardest step is done. Just a little further.

She clicks on the notification that appears in the upper right corner of the task bar. A small window opens, and she selects "open files." Like the drive itself, the contents are unassuming. The drive has only one untitled folder, and in it only one file, titled "Video001." Laina clicks on the file and puts on her headphones.

At first, she doesn't know what she is looking at. Everything is black. In her headphones, she hears labored breathing and then a man whispering that he is still in pursuit. On the screen, she sees movement and then realizes that the man, the cop, has been standing behind a parked car and is now on a sidewalk. Something flashes across the screen—a hand, most likely—and moments later a gun is in view, pointed ahead. Laina's breath catches in her throat and she leans forward, her hand to her mouth. This could be it: the moment her brother dies.

The body cam shakes as the cop begins running. "I see it," he says, and there is panic in the words. "It's big."

Laina inhales sharply and has but a moment to consider what "it" is before she sees it too, a few feet down the sidewalk. It turns as the cop approaches, bares its teeth and growls. The body cam shakes so hard, the image blurs. But she can still see the eyes of the thing reflecting light, the bright orbs turning to streaks as it surges forward. Three shots pop in Laina's ears, the thing howling as at least one of them hits its mark. The cop is back-stepping fast

but keeping his gun pointed at the thing pursuing him (doglike, Laina is thinking, although it is much bigger than any dog she's seen). When the hulking animal leaps into the air, the cop follows it with his gun, screaming and releasing four more shots all at once. A fraction of a second later, the animal collides with the cop from above, everything shaking now. The sky comes into view, starlight streaking by like thin comets, before a mountain of hair obscures the body cam. There's the cop's panicked breaths and more screaming before Laina catches sight of one of the cop's legs. Something scrapes against the pavement, like metal. She has to focus to make sense of what she is seeing: the cop dragging himself backward, the shuddering body of the huge beast revealing itself. The animal moans and whimpers, crawls forward. The fur around one eye is matted with dark blood. Laina can see the muzzle, the blood-stained teeth, and the long, pointed ears. And then, after a few more attempts to move, it collapses, the great furry head flopping to the pavement. With a final shudder, it stops moving.

The cop gets to his feet and radios that shots have been fired. He looks around a bit, the body cam shifting back and forth, taking in some of the world around. Next to the sidewalk, a line of parked cars stretches down the street in one direction; across the sidewalk, a block of residential homes. A woman comes out of her door and stands on her porch. She has a phone in her hand, and it is pointed down out of view, where the animal lies. The light from the phone is very bright.

"Go back inside," says the cop. "We'll dispose of it. Don't worry."

"Why would you say that?" the woman asks.

A moment passes. Laina can't really see the woman's face, but she recognizes the disbelief in her voice, the horror. The

cop must have too, because he doesn't answer the question but takes a couple of steps back. He is off the sidewalk now, standing between two cars. From that vantage, Laina can see the spot where the animal was slain, only the animal is gone and a naked man is in its place.

"I don't understand," the cop says.

Laina doesn't either.

A voice comes out of the darkness beyond her computer screen to make the leap that Laina's mind can't. "Your brother," the voice says, cutting through the noise in her headphones as if by strange magic.

"No," Laina says. "What?"

"I don't understand," the cop shouts again in her ears.

"That is your brother lying there," the voice says.

"I . . ." Laina feels dizzy.

The cop is screaming. "I don't understand. What is happening? Oh God, no!"

Laina pulls off the headphones and flings them. She slams the laptop shut. "I can't," she says.

"I hope I haven't broken you," the voice says. "This is what you wanted. What they kept from you. Now that you have it, what will you do?"

Laina feels as if she is rushing toward something at great speed, outpacing the reality she knows. She enters an open space so vast, she can't feel the edges. She's been blasted open and feels herself as wide as the universe. The question the voice asks seems far away, and Laina has to pull herself back to it, to focus on each word so that she can make some sense of this place that no longer makes sense. She combines the words and uses them as a place to plant her feet. Her lips form words, the muscles in her face and the nerves

in her throat bringing her blasted bits back into solid form. "I will make amends."

"Good," the voice says.

It is here that I stop time. The world around us slows, all matter falls still, and all sound stops. There is only the voice and me. I reach out to the formless thing, trying to access its mind, but finding nothing. In all my time traveling the fractal sea, this has never happened. Minds are always open to me.

"What are you?" I ask directly. "What is this?"

For a terrible moment, the voice doesn't answer, and for the first time, I feel a sense of danger I've never thought to feel.

"I've signed a contract," it finally says. "I am bound not to speak to you."

"By whom?"

"The universe," it says.

And the voice answers no more of my questions.

"What is this about?" Ridley asks as Laina sits him down in the living room. The television is already on, the sound low. Ridley takes one look at the screen and stops asking. The video has been playing periodically for at least an hour and will likely play on every channel for many days to come.

Ridley turns to watch her, his mouth a wordless question, and stares at the screen again. The sun is beginning to rise, and a littlest bit of early morning light cuts through the window behind the television. She hears footsteps in the apartment above, and people walking down the halls, knocking on doors. Her cell phone buzzes on the coffee table. She imagines the whole world like this: footsteps, knocks on doors, buzzing phones, minds being blown apart. Ridley watches, his hand to his mouth.

"I don't understand," the cop says again, as he's said every time she watches the video, and the several times she watched it when she posted it to streaming sites. She was being thorough in case

some black hand might act quickly to take the video down. Within twenty minutes, the clip is on all the social media sites. Within twenty-five minutes, it is trending everywhere.

The body cam reveals her naked brother lying facedown on the pavement, dead beyond recall, gone forever. Ridley stutters out words only he can understand. He is heading down his own tunnel now, entering his own cavern at the end of it, feeling himself expand, and Laina will not interrupt.

Upstairs, someone makes a noise, muffled through layers of walls, and something crashes loudly. In the hall, footsteps quicken. Outside, a car screeches to a halt. The neighborhood is an egg cracking open.

What will come next? They will try to deny this video, discredit it. She can't control that. She has done her part.

"Who leaked it?" Ridley asks her. He is shaking, struggling to keep himself together.

She doesn't need to say it. Already, he is watching her face, reading the truth clearly written there.

"Babe, they'll come for you."

"Who will?" she asks.

Sweating, Ridley glances around the room as if people were hiding in the walls. This is the only answer he's capable of offering.

Don't worry, Laina wants to say. *I didn't use my personal accounts. No one knows who I am.* But even as she thinks the words, she knows that she could be terribly wrong. She has kicked something whose contours she can't begin to imagine. Perhaps she has miscalculated completely. Perhaps this is all a game happening above her head and *she* is the sacrifice.

"Pack some bags," she says.

As Ridley rushes to the bedroom, she listens to people yelling

outside. Now the noises are too much; she can't track it all. She hears Ridley pull a large suitcase down from the closet. Should they even be wasting time with suitcases and clothes? She pictures men in dark clothes approaching the apartment building. It might be too late already.

"Just keep watching the television," says the voice, this time right in her ear.

Breaking News flashes on the television, and then another video comes on, this one an aerial shot. A helicopter? No, too close to the ground. Maybe a drone? The video is very clear, crisp in a way hers is not. Something like relief fills her when she sees, with absolute clarity, a pack of large animals forming a line all the way across what Laina knows to be MA 28 North connecting to Interstate 93 South. Is it strange to feel relief at something that terrified her only hours before? But even with the shock of everything, Laina understands that this can only be good for her. It means she is not alone, that it will be much harder for anyone to discredit her brother's death. The line of animals, wolflike now that she can see clearly, stand a few feet apart. She counts seven in all, blocking traffic in both directions. Lincoln was not alone, either. He had family.

Ridley rolls out a large suitcase and stands next to Laina, saying nothing, all the noise of outside now inconsequential compared to the image before their eyes.

A wolf howls, and the rest join in, the sound sustained and ghostly like wind through hollowed bones. They all begin to rise on their hind legs, and even from this distance it is clear to Laina just how massive they are. As they stand, their bodies begin to shrink, their fur pulling in, heads compressing down into something more compact. Within a matter of moments, they've transformed, and now a line of seven naked men and women, of different hues and

body types, stand across the highway. Ridley makes a quiet, muffled sound, part groan, part sharp inhalation. But Laina keeps silent, her breath and body held tight.

The video cuts out in response to the sudden appearance of the naked men and women. But even though Laina has met Rebecca only once, she recognizes her immediately, standing at the center of the line, in a position of power, fierce eyes aimed straight at the camera.

Laina surprises herself by smiling.

EMERGENT SYSTEMS OF BEES

HAROLD SHINER
WATERTOWN, MASSACHUSETTS

FOUR MONTHS AFTER THE FRACTURE

Harry knocks only twice before the door opens.

The first thing he sees as he enters is a twin set of arched staircases, with a gold-and-crystal chandelier hanging above them like a swollen uvula. The butler doesn't lead Harry up either set of stairs, but between them, where a short hall extends deeper into the house. They walk some distance down the hall, then turn left and stop at a pair of red double doors.

Harry takes a step back. The butler, seeing his hesitation, smiles and says, "Oh, yes, the door. It belonged to a church Mr. Trapp went to as a child. The church burned down a decade ago, and Mr. Trapp helped rebuild it. They gave him the old door as a gift, and he restored it to its original color and put it here."

Harry nods. Sweat trickles down his rib cage, causing his whole body to twitch spasmodically. The butler doesn't seem to notice. He opens one of the doors, and the creak echoes off the high ceiling. Behind the door, a dimly lit flight of stairs spirals down, twisting

into darkness. The butler walks confidently into the black. With a gulp, Harry follows.

As they descend, the butler starts talking again. "It was important to Mr. Trapp to have a house that went as far underground as above. A lot of this was expanded when he bought the house. He planned to have these exclusive parties. He had often entertained in his earlier home and hated how it encroached on the rest of the house. People would go exploring places they shouldn't. He'd find strangers asleep in guest rooms, doing drugs in the bathrooms, having sex in hall closets—all sorts of odd things. Plus, the noise traveled. Late-night parties woke up Mr. Trapp's daughter when she was trying to sleep. She's all grown up now, but Mr. Trapp always thought he'd adopt another child in his later years. He hasn't yet."

Harry is sweating through his clothes. The stairway is cramped and hot, but there's also the lack of sound from below, which has begun to unnerve him. The butler's words bleed together, and all Harry can hear is *trap, trap, trap.*

At the bottom of the staircase, the butler stops—another door, of some dark wood color, like varnished mahogany. This door does not scream out in warning. Harry's most noticeable feeling at the moment is annoyance. How many more doors will he have to go through? Will there be another descending staircase below this one? Mixed in with the annoyance is the steady pulse of fear, same as before.

The butler pushes the door open. "Watch your step," he says.

13

Harry was married for ten years. He met Eleanor through Janet, a professor of philosophy he'd known since their tenure-seeking days. Janet invited him out to a bar after his late class, and when he arrived, Eleanor was there. Eleanor saw him first, and somehow knew who he was even though they'd never met. She waved him over, and as he came closer she brushed a strand of golden hair behind her ear.

Janet and Eleanor were sitting side by side in a booth, so Harry sat across from them, sliding all the way in against the wall. Janet made the introduction, and Eleanor stuck out her hand. Harry took it and shook vigorously, his palm a sweaty mess. Eleanor was all smiles. She had an intense yet playful look in her eyes.

Over the next couple of hours, Harry drank way too much and rambled on about the complex behavior of honeybee colonies.

"Let me give an example. Honeybees form these swarm clusters on tree branches when they're ready to start a new colony. The wind

will shake these tree branches, and the bees will actually change the shape of the cluster to keep the structure stable. Just imagine, thousands of bees adjusting their configuration as a unit. They will ventilate their nest sites the same way, using these emergent wing-fanning configurations that respond to the environment."

Harry went on to explain what he meant by emergent wing-fanning configurations.

"Is it intelligence?" Eleanor asked when he was finished. Harry could see that the question wasn't feigned interest, but actual curiosity.

Buzzing from excitement and intoxication, he searched his brain for the right words. "A sort of intelligence, sure. Evolution and physics working together on the collective level. But the bees don't think. Not like we do."

Eleanor, for her part, talked about modal realism.

"Oh, no, I take it literally," she said. Harry was at the end of a tall glass of a dark beer whose name he'd forgotten the second he ordered it. "The worlds we imagine really exist. They are beyond some veil we can't cross. We glimpse them through our literature, our movies, our music. They exist, but we can never visit them, can never confirm their existence." Eleanor wore glasses, and as she said this the light from the lamp overhead obscured her green eyes.

"Like a cat in a box—both dead and alive," Harry said. He was in love already. "Your idea requires a certain amount of faith. Do you believe in God?"

"No."

"But you believe our thoughts make universes. Isn't that an act of God?"

Janet looked from Eleanor to Harry and smiled. She sensed it too, he could tell: a kindling. "Can't back out now," Janet said to Eleanor. "You said you believed this literally."

NO GODS, NO MONSTERS 59

Harry could feel the heat on his cheeks. He ordered another beer, letting the question hang in the air between them. The waiter said the name of the beer again to make sure he got the right order. Harry nodded and promptly forgot the name again.

Eleanor laughed, a little chuckle of realization. "Maybe I do believe in God. A little."

They got married a year later. It was an easy year, filled with quiet movie nights and long walks with sporadic conversation. They didn't talk a lot, Eleanor disappearing into her own mind, Harry perfectly content to let her. She was quicker to smile than he, and she marveled at things in a way he never could muster. She drew joy out of him, a peaceful sort of joy that slipped into everything, the way a pleasant scent can linger in clothes. He loved her, but more than that, he loved the ease. She demanded little, and so he didn't give much. At the time, he didn't realize what a gift that was, how she made him light by not adding weight. He managed the same early on, but he didn't have her talent for it. As time went on, he demanded more, wanting her to fill roles in his life. Work was stressful, so he got angry when he came home to find her eating a sandwich. "Couldn't you have at least ordered something for both of us?" When he had to grade papers at the end of term, he became belligerent when she didn't pick up any slack. "Couldn't you clean up the living room?"

It didn't matter that he had made the mess. It didn't matter that she, too, had papers to grade. She worked at a private high school, teaching literature to spoiled rich kids. She didn't bring her stress home, though Harry later reasoned that she must have experienced it. Eleanor didn't yell. She didn't even cry, really. During their marriage, she had lost her father, and when he came home, he found her at the kitchen table, writing in her journal. "Dad's

dead," she said. When he asked how she felt, she smiled and said she was processing. Her eyes were a little red—whether from weariness or tears, he couldn't tell.

One time when he complained about her not ordering food, she turned to him with a stony expression and said, "When was the last time you ordered food?"

Surely, he must have, though he couldn't think of a specific time. When he didn't answer, she flicked on the TV and stared at it expressionless, ignoring him the rest of the night.

Eleanor still challenged him intellectually just as in the beginning, but over time that gentle flirtation he once detected had withered into something cold, distant, and vaguely frustrated. He couldn't tell for sure, and when he asked, she denied it.

Then one Sunday morning, she called out his name, a sunbeam lighting half her face. "I think we've reached the end," she said.

Just like that. She pulled a silver strand of hair away from her face and tucked it behind her ear, like punctuating a very long quote: their marriage.

Later, when he wouldn't stop calling, she sent him an email.

I did love you. But I think we left each other alone for too long. We weren't very good at our marriage. But you were worse.

She didn't explain further, but he felt the truth of the words. He smashed all their pictures. He sent a few bitter voicemails. She was kind enough not to respond.

After Eleanor left, Harry began digging through message boards. He couldn't remember how he'd found the forum. On the site, they discussed different sects of Gnostic Christianity and some of the secret religious orders of the past few centuries. Harry's particular interest was the late nineteenth-century Hermetic Order of the Golden Dawn, which he discussed at length with a few of the other anonymous academics. The Order had first piqued his interest because he loved the name. But he eventually got swept up in its belief system—particularly the idea that "Secret Chiefs," a group of supernatural beings that governed the cosmos, made up the third and innermost engine of their magical cosmology. Of course, only a special few could actually communicate with those beings. Harry loved how these societies encircled themselves like tree rings, hiding their secrets within layers of unverifiable statements.

His friend 6Alfred9 liked to discuss the Order's vast web of influence: "It's connected to a lot of big stuff!" he would jabber

excitedly. "Even something like Scientology—you trace it back far enough, and there's the Hermetic Order. People don't know that!"

The worst thing you could do was ask him how, which Harry did. Then 6Alfred9 would recount the whole history: how one of the founders, Samuel Liddell MacGregor Mathers, was great friends with the occultist writer Aleister Crowley, who had founded the Thelema religion; how Jack Parsons, a rocket propulsion researcher at the California Institute of Technology, was a secret Thelemite and friends with L. Ron Hubbard. The two would go on to conduct a series of religious ceremonies called the "Babalon Working," to bring into the world an incarnation of the Thelemite goddess Babalon—who, coincidentally, turned out to be Parsons's wife, Marjorie Cameron Parsons. "She was a poet and artist of the Beat generation," 6Alfred9 said. "She was also a Thelemite, and her belief in the occult added to her work. Anyway, Hubbard went on to form the Church of Scientology."

Harry found 6Alfred9's trail of connections amusing but good for little else. The Golden Dawn inspired myriad occultist groups and had offshoots of its own extending into the present day. These sorts of connections could be drawn all over the place, to any group imaginable. The Order's connection to Scientology was more an occult game of degrees of separation. But Harry knew 6Alfred9's real motivation. He wanted to talk about Cameron, who had become his true obsession. No one shared his interest, so he found ways to bring her into the discussion. "She knew everyone," he'd say. "She did everything." Harry suspected that his friend was a bit unstable, but he admired the guy's passion, his breadth of knowledge, the random tidbits of information he interjected into conversations.

Harry didn't understand how close they all were to the slippery precipice. They made jokes about this stuff. It was just an

intellectual fascination. Harry did it to keep his mind busy, to quiet the arguments that followed him into his dreams. He had left things alone too long. He'd lightened his marriage to nothing at all. It was his fault really.

Then werewolves showed up on the news, and after that, strange things started to happen.

The initial news footage had captured werewolves turning back into humans—Harry had seen it happen—but subsequent videos had those last few seconds edited out. People claimed that their own recordings had been shortened as well. No one had video of the change. It had been cut from existence.

This scared a lot of people into silence. They found it easier to doubt their own memories than to believe that the change had been pulled from everyone's computers, phones, and cameras. Mainstream news stopped airing the videos of the protest and the police shooting. Suddenly, experts were "verifying their authenticity." The person who leaked the shooting had never surfaced.

Social media was filled with people discussing the events—*#monsters* was always trending—but a lot of people were ignoring it too. Of those talking about it, many had written the whole thing off as a hoax. It was like those videos of Bigfoot or big-eyed humanoid aliens. Or someone spliced some footage together. They're dogs. They're bears. They're just regular wolves. With the available video footage, it was impossible to win a debate.

But again and again, the signs were beginning to reveal a brewing hysteria. In Austin, Texas, a Latino man was pulled from his home, doused with gasoline, and set ablaze. A video surfaced of the man running around screaming until he collapsed, his horrified family watching it all through the front window.

In Orlando, Florida, an Indian woman carrying groceries was

hit over the head, her oranges spilling into the street. Unsatisfied, the man standing over her brought down the bat several more times. By the time they pulled him off, the woman was dead.

On a lonely stretch of highway in rural Alabama, a Black teenage boy was found, his throat cut. His shoes had been taken and a Bible placed on his chest.

These things had happened before, had always happened, but now the reasons for them had changed. In Madison, Wisconsin, a house was set on fire. The old Black woman who lived there had no family, no meaningful relationships with any neighbors. Sometimes, people heard yowling from the house late at night. In the charred ruins, they found the burnt body of the old woman, three blackened cages containing bird carcasses, and several cats. An anonymous note was sent to a local newspaper. The first line: *Mildred Cather was a witch and deserved to die.*

Harry noticed changes on the forum, too. Members had never studied lycanthropy before, but now almost every other post was about some bit of werewolf lore connected with the occult.

SURGEON_NEMESIS615: Accounts of theurgy have been recorded throughout the history of god-working practice: humans could take on the qualities of animals, transform into them, communicate with them. Wolves have lived alongside men since the birth of civilization.

SHAMAN&DEVIL: Occultist Austen Osman Spare believed in "atavistic resurgence," where one could draw on previous phases of evolution, including various animal forms, and magickally (that's how Spare spelled it) take on those characteristics.

HERMETIC_HARRY: The Hermetic Order of the Golden Dawn had many transformational rituals. Not saying they could pull off such a thing, but academically speaking, it is an interesting idea.

6Alfred9 stopped talking altogether, preferring to post Cameron paintings: intoxicating portraits of messy-haired humans with wings, and women with serpent tongues and whip-thin tails dancing, embracing, or making love.

Harry could tell from the posts that something was happening to everyone. People who were normally on the site only once or twice a week were present all day, making or responding to posts, sending each other down rabbit holes of research and then returning with answers. Were these werewolves magicians? Were they members of secret orders? Had they simply succumbed to the malady? A post about the history of Afro-Caribbean voodoo and obeah practices. Another post about occultist experiments on marginalized groups in the early eighteenth century. They all lingered on the message board, sharing thoughts on old things, knowing that it was really a discussion about the new. No one posted or talked about the monster videos directly, but it was in the air, so to speak—the unwritten subtext of all their conversations.

Harry started sleeping with the lights on. He checked the door to his apartment several times a night. He would play music until sunrise, which helped for a while, until he started hearing, instead of drums, footsteps coming down the hall. Voices behind the singing. Odd whisperings.

6Alfred9 posted a Cameron self-portrait to the message board: *The Black Egg*. It depicted a thin white-robed Cameron, a lion's mane of reddish hair fanning out unnaturally around her, and a

black egg cradled to her chest in her long, delicate fingers. None of this particularly alarmed Harry—not even Cameron's wire-thin appearance. Rather, it was her large eyes, which were drawn as empty sockets, black as the egg in her hand. The portrait had been placed at the center of an altar during her memorial service—something Harry found equally disturbing: those black not-eyes staring out from death at a living world.

And then Harry's friend disappeared right after posting the picture. It had been weeks since 6Alfred9 wrote any actual words, but now there was nothing at all. Harry had no way to contact him. Between giving his biology lectures, Harry would go on the message board to look for his friend. Months passed that way, Harry religiously searching the message board for signs of 6Alfred9. He went to other forums. No sign of anyone with a similar name or interests.

Harry was about to give up hope when a photo surfaced on the message board: a newspaper clipping posted by 6Alfred9. Under the clipping was the word *zoom*, the first word 6Alfred9 had posted since the world half-learned of monsters.

Harry was compelled to obey.

15

There is another door at the end of another hall, but through that double door the space opens up into a high-ceilinged banquet hall filled with people. The center of the room is empty, but the walls are lined with a series of long tables. People are seated at the outer edge of the tables, facing the room's empty center. On a raised platform in front of the room, another long table stretches almost to either wall. Men and women in formal attire sit eating and talking. Soft piano music plays over speakers Harry cannot locate. Gaudy chandeliers hang from the high ceiling but give off only a muted glow more befitting a working-class tavern. Harry looks around the room. No one seems to be acknowledging his entrance, occupied as they are with the conversations at their tables. He counts maybe sixty people in the large hall.

"You were a little late," says the butler. "The feast has already started." He leads Harry to a table that has space for one more person. Harry takes his seat between a man and a woman. Both greet him with a smile.

"Welcome, friend," the man says. He is big, both heavyset and tall, with a broad nose that suits his face, and generous eyes. He's in formal dress, but the shirt is slightly wrinkled and has no tie, and the gray dinner jacket looks a bit worn.

Seeing the man, Harry relaxes. "Thank you," he says.

"You look like an academic," the man says. "I'm pretty good at recognizing fellow travelers."

Harry nods, takes a sip from the glass of water in front of him. "I'm Harold Shiner," he says.

The man looks at Harry as if he's been slapped in the face. "John Norell, professor of psychology," he gushes, and then, "Hey, you're not Hermetic Harry by chance?" Seeing Harry's sudden blush, he laughs and points to himself. "I'm ShaMan&Devil."

Harry doesn't really like ShaMan&Devil, but he is happy to find someone familiar, and the actual guy in person has a charm missing in his more confrontational online persona.

Harry asks him, "Have you met anyone else from the message board?"

John shakes his head in understanding. "Just you so far. I've also been looking for 6Alfred9. No luck."

A man comes over to the table and hands Harry a menu. "We have a roasted duck that's been popular with the other attendees. And a seared tuna with lemon sauce if you want something lighter. We also have vegetarian options."

Harry nods and spends a moment looking over the salads before requesting a Caesar and handing the menu back. The waiter smiles and drifts away.

"It really is good, you know," John says. "The duck."

"I can't handle anything like that right now." Harry lowers his voice: "Do you know what this is about?"

"No," John says. "But so far, so good. No red flags."

"Not even that red door upstairs? The dark staircase? Mr. Trapp?"

John laughs. "I found that funny too."

"But you're not worried?"

"Why would I be?"

Harry stares at John, wordless.

The woman on John's other side finally speaks. "You all were brought here by following clues, right? My most optimistic bet is that this is an induction ceremony."

"Exactly," John says.

The woman smiles in a reassuring way. "I'm Karuna Flood."

Harry smiles back. He knows this woman—recognizes the name, anyway. "I'm a fan of your work," he says. Then, feeling self-conscious, he asks, "What kind of induction ceremony?"

"For a secret society," she says, not missing a beat. No follow-up about his love of her work. "I imagine hundreds of these will be springing up all at once—secret alliances against what's coming."

"And what's coming?" Harry asks, feeling a jitter of concern.

Karuna shrugs. "We now know there are shadows deep enough to hide in, to keep things hidden. And now they are coming out. Not unreasonable to think there's more to this."

"So, you believe in monsters?" Harry asks.

"Yes," Karuna says without a hint of self-consciousness. Harry is surprised to feel relief wash over him. He hasn't realized this was what he needed: to be in a room with someone who isn't afraid to admit an uncomfortable belief.

"I don't see why you'd create more societies," John says. "This is proof that secrets cannot last." He seems to have no knowledge of Karuna and no interest in acquiring any.

Karuna smiles minutely. "Not proof. The emergence of monsters could be by accident or design. The smarter bet is on design. Monsters pushed out of the shadows wouldn't even have to know why. What we don't know is who pushed them. It makes sense that those with enough forethought would try to muster counterpowers against those still hidden."

By her looks alone, Karuna is younger than John or Harry, but she seems much older, like a person long settled into herself, completely and without equivocation. She is of Asian descent, dark freckles dotting her almond cheeks, her hair cut close to the scalp, which, Harry imagines, is for ease and comfort over style. She almost sounds American, but a certain lilt points to some European origin, perhaps in the British Isles. And then those eyes. Karuna's eyes are *awake*. Harry tries to find a better way to describe them, but all other words fall short.

"What else could this be?" Harry asks. "You said an induction ceremony was your optimistic bet. What is your less optimistic theory of why we're here?"

Karuna smiles at him, and in that gesture, Harry finds the tiniest glimpse of Eleanor, the way she used to smile in that understated way. He also gets the sudden image of Cameron cradling the black egg in her delicate fingers, staring at him through empty sockets. Both impressions are gone in an instant.

"A coin is in the air," Karuna says. "This society could be new or old. We are at a disadvantage not knowing, because if it is new, we might find friends here. But if it is old—"

"Your salad, sir," says the waiter, placing it on the table. Harry glimpses a tiny crescent scar on the waiter's hand—pink and smooth as if a piece of flesh had been cored from the spot. Harry looks up at the waiter's face and catches the tiniest glimmer of something,

though the expression is so strange, he can't read it. The waiter floats off to another table.

Harry looks back at Karuna, and she is watching him, staring into him. She continues. "If it is old, the hierarchies are long established and so are the methods of recruiting new members. The method that brought us here was too simple, so my least optimistic bet is that it was a lure."

Harry tries to take a bite of his salad but has to put down the fork and place his shaking hands in his lap.

"An interesting thought," says John, whose earlier silence Harry notices only now that he is speaking again. "I guess we will know soon enough." He motions to the front of the room, where a pale man has just stood up on the platform.

The pale man clinks his glass with a fork and, in a voice that resonates through unseen speakers, says, "I think it is about time we begin the ceremony."

16

How honeybees ventilate their nests is an emergent system.

Over time, the air in a nest can get really warm, which, if not managed, can cause significant harm to the developing brood. Honeybees are constantly going in and out of the nest opening. They fly off, gather resources, and bring them back. Guard bees linger at the entrance, looking for predators and defending the nest. If the temperature somewhere along the nest entrance rises above some threshold specific to the bee there, the bee will point its abdomen away from the nest and flap its wings.

One would think that flapping its wings would lower the air temperature, but that's not true. The bee is drawing air out of the nest and this warm, stale air from inside the nest actually warms the neighboring air. This is very important. Other bees will feel that heat and begin to flap their wings, not likely because they're paying attention to what the other bees are doing but because their

temperature threshold is being triggered by local warming. One bee becomes five bees. Five become fifty.

Elsewhere, cool, fresh air will enter the nest, filling the vacuum. The bees at that entrance are less likely to flap their wings. Positive feedback where the bees are fanning. Negative feedback where there are fewer fanning bees. Spatial patterns emerge where certain regions have bees that are more effective at drawing out air. Over time, this process creates larger and larger clusters of bees that are fanning their wings until there's just one dominant group.

It is a trick: a marriage of evolution, emergence, and the physics of airflow.

The intermediary between an orchestrated event and chaos is manipulation. Bees are manipulators. They don't even have to know why they do what they're doing. No single actor has the whole picture of how everything works.

And that's the thing. No one can completely control the outcome of events. But any organism can learn a few tricks. Positive feedback where a trick works. Negative feedback where it doesn't.

Harry is too serious a researcher to consciously admit how deeply connected his interest in emergent patterns is with his interest in secret societies. He hates bee analogies. He hates even more the idea that his interests are anything more than academic. But no one's interests are ever strictly academic.

Here's the real point: Paranoia has a physics to it, and even with something as insubstantial as paranoia, over time it gains substance, has weight. Secret societies are a *result* of paranoia, not the cause. *Someone else somewhere knows what's going on*, anyone might think. *I should too.* Conspiracies are also a result, a sensing of heat. There is no way of knowing how many world-changing

events were precipitated by the phantom cause of paranoia, but the number is sure to be vast.

Anything with substance can be manipulated.

One becomes ten, then a hundred. And pretty soon, the whole world flaps its wings.

Harry did not find the clues all at once, because they weren't all given at once. Over weeks, 6Alfred9 sent newspaper clippings, each time with the instruction *zoom* written below. Harry quickly found what he was looking for: the initials *O.Z.* in the margins of the clipping next to some word, letter, or number. He got seven clues this way before he started getting impatient and did some digging of his own. He found some of the corresponding articles online. It didn't take him long to find the pattern: all major US newspapers—though never the same one back to back—each clue dated only days from the one before, starting not long after the werewolf protest.

Harry started buying the newspapers himself. The clues were found only in print and only at certain venues. Harry would buy five of the same issue from several places across Boston and was never certain whether he missed a clue, until 6Alfred9 confirmed his work. He missed a lot of clues. It was hard to imagine how his friend didn't. Did he have allies? Did he buy newspapers from everywhere in his

own city or town? He couldn't; that would be a full-time job. Harry began marking where he found his clues, and found no pattern. Was it all random? No, not possible. There had to be a pattern.

He found his answer when he tracked the times of his purchases. Early mornings, he realized. That was the key. Someone was printing these clues on the earliest copies to be sold, which required a level of planning and inside access he couldn't imagine. The other option was magic, which Harry found himself unwilling to consider, since that was firmly outside his comprehension.

He collected the clues dutifully, until he was sure of the complete message.

There was a date: *March 27, 2023.*

And a location: *6567 Aldridge Road, Watertown, MA.*

And a warning: *Tell no one. We will know.*

Harry wondered how they would know he told someone. He quickly settled on the two equally terrifying possible answers he had come to before: a massive conspiracy, or magic. Either way, he'd better not test it if he did decide to show up.

6Alfred9 went silent again after the last clue. Harry's efforts to prompt a response from him got nowhere. Harry had suspected from the very beginning that the person sending these clues as 6Alfred9 may not be the man named John whom he considered a friend. If that was the case, he knew he wouldn't have the power to save 6Alfred9. Whatever this turned out to be, it would be above his head. Yet he stared at the date. It was only a month away.

The night before the date, Harry watched an interview on NBC—Richard Wallace discussing his new book. Wallace was an anthropologist and historian and a writer of popular books. He was the sort of academic Harry wasn't. Suit-and-tie type. A

seeker of relevance. In the interview, Wallace's gray hair was gelled back, his face shaven, a look about him reminiscent of the actor Ted Danson.

The Fracture Effect was the short book's title—it had to be short to hit the presses so quickly. This was also the name Wallace had coined for the split in the collective consciousness of humanity after the events of November 5.

"We've had stories about these creatures since the beginning of recorded history," he said, imbuing each word with a sheen of ordinariness, like his hair and his suit and his tie. "But our modern minds are incredibly secular. Even among the religious, there has been a fracture. Some of us simply can't believe monsters could exist without our knowing. Of course, there are reasons we might not have known."

He went on to list a few.

"One is the technological barrier. Stories could have been contained before. They can't now, not in the era of viral videos. The other reason has to do with authority. Any random individual can have a story, but such stories can be dismissed. So can personal images and videos. There have been documented sightings of aliens and sea serpents and upright ape-men for centuries, but all those accounts have been dismissed as inconclusive.

"Official narratives are harder to ignore. But even an official account can be obscured by new or contradictory evidence or by a greater authority. A dismissal by an expert carries a lot of weight in our popular conception of what is factual.

"Not everyone saw those early broadcasts of unaltered video. It was early morning. People were asleep, driving, on flights, at work. People were on vacation, walking the dog, or off the grid, unplugged from superfast news for reasons of resources or intention.

"And then the videos were altered from their original airing, which brought the events into question, even for people who saw the original footage."

The reporter, Janet Evans, looked uncomfortable. Wallace was excited, his voice pitched higher, a sort of wide-eyed reverence crossing his face. Evans didn't stop him, but she did lean in ever so slightly.

Wallace picked up on this. Harry saw the moment when Wallace remembered that respectable people didn't mention altered original footage. "When it comes to the question of altered footage, researchers and public officials have floated the idea of mass delusion," he said, his voice milky smooth again. "And reasonable people have incorporated this into their own narratives. 'I was mistaken. I got carried away.'"

"And what do *you* think?" the reporter asked.

"The book isn't about that. It's about the phenomenon itself. A sober look at how different people have constructed their worldview since the event. *The Fracture Effect* is about the breaking down of individuals and communities. Social organizations have noted a downturn in engagement. Depression and suicides have increased since the event. Hate crimes have skyrocketed, especially among already marginalized groups. The book makes a correlation between those facts and the events of November fifth."

"Yes," Evans said. She was also very put together, not a hair out of place. "But what do you think? Are monsters real?"

It was rude to ask this question in polite company, and unsurprisingly, Wallace looked taken aback by the question. He wanted to remain impartial, but he couldn't say "I don't know." Not here. He stuttered out something, but the words were too low and jumbled for anyone to pick up. She asked again.

"I'm agnostic," he said. A cop-out.

She could have let him go but didn't. "What does your gut say?"

It was hard to tell, but, yes, Wallace was sweating. "My gut says that for a moment, we all believed. And then we had to decide which version of the world we could live with."

"So those animals on the freeway. Were they just dogs? Or werewolves?"

"I don't know," he finally said, and then he remembered who he was, and stumbled through an explanation from his book, about strange animal behavior, predators hunting humans in cities, dogs catching buses and subways. That sort of thing. Not exactly normal, but not abnormal either. Not supernatural.

Harry flicked off the television.

He went to his room and put some music on like always. It played through the night, stitched itself to his dreams. He woke several times, only to lie in bed staring up at the ceiling fan as it spun slow and steady. The night-light in his room and the light from the bathroom kept most of the shadows around him in their nonthreatening corners. He could see whatever came for him.

Harry had been alone for over a decade. He had become a very timid man, always quiet now, what little voice he possessed slowly leached out of him by time and a growing self-consciousness he couldn't control. He had nothing in his life. His mother was in a nursing home and couldn't remember him most days. His father had been dead for decades. No brothers or sisters. His relationships with extended family had atrophied beyond his desire to remedy. His work, a sinking ship he'd been bailing the water out of for a long time. And Eleanor—a distant memory thinning by the day, a wisp of something once real. Janet had lost touch with Eleanor too, and so Eleanor had made a clean break. He'd been severed like an unwanted appendage.

Harry's interest in secret societies had become an answer to his loneliness, something to fill the vacuum Eleanor left. 6Alfred9 was an extension of this answer, a friend to share his secret fascinations with, someone Harry could accept in all his eccentricities because 6Alfred9 had accepted him. He didn't feel good about the realization. It seemed that this was all he could manage: a relationship with letters and numbers, companionship in ones and zeros.

That's what made him finally decide. Because he had nothing, he had this. He would throw himself against this mystery and see what he found there, what it would make of him.

The CD player skipped and then went silent. Harry got up and saw the error message on the display. He considered putting in another disk, but instead he went out and shut off the bathroom light and returned to his room, pulling the night-light from the wall.

When he collapsed back into bed, the apartment was without noise or light, the sounds outside muted by closed windows. Harry did not dream the rest of that night or else could not remember his dream. It was the same either way: a long, gentle descent into the black.

18

The pale man clears his throat before speaking again. "I'm Twenty-Nine, as some of you know," he says. "Apologies for Seventeen's absence, but I will be handling proceedings tonight."

Harry takes a good look at the man, who reminds him of portraits of Andrew Jackson. All the features are there: the long face, the pronounced widow's peak, the pointed nose. Small eyes stare out from under thick brows. He is very pale, but that, too, can likely be said of his famous spitting image. In truth, "Twenty-Nine," as he calls himself, even sounds the way Harry thinks Old Hickory would—an old-fashioned quality to his very formal English.

"We have a dozen new guests with us, sitting at that row of tables over there"—he nods in Harry's direction—"and as members of the Order of the Zsouvox, I'd like us all to extend our welcome."

The room raises glasses in unison, and a few give audible affirmations. Harry smiles and gives a quick nod of acknowledgment. In the corners of the room, he notices that some of the waitstaff are

still standing around, hands clasped behind them. In one corner, a woman stands with a large book in her hand. Her hands are straining under the weight of it, and she is muttering softly to herself. Harry looks in Karuna's direction and sees that she has her eyes on the woman as well.

Twenty-Nine continues: "The Order of the Zsouvox is an old one, existing for many centuries. Our mission remains the same: to come to understand the Beast-under-the-World and bend it to our will."

Harry's attention shifts back to the platform.

"What did he just say?" John asks out loud, though perhaps not addressing anyone in particular.

"As part of the Ritual of Knowing," Twenty-Nine says, "we will be sacrificing our valued guests so that we may someday fulfill this task. Valued guests, we are grateful for your offering."

Someone down the line of tables drops their fork. The black egg cracks, spilling.

"Come to the center," Twenty-Nine orders.

Altogether, the twenty newcomers, including Harry, stand up. They all try to resist, but their bodies no longer answer to them. Their voices, however, remain their own. A woman screams. So does John. "What is happening here?" he asks the room.

Harry is moving his chair aside, stepping out, pushing the chair back under the table until the polished wood of the chair's back touches the white tablecloth. All this he is doing robotically, his mind detached from his body. He follows everyone, shuffling out from a gap between the tables. All the guests are merging into one straight line and walking slowly to the center of the room. Harry and Karuna and John join the procession. Some people are screaming, pleading, crying. It is all around Harry, a mix of shrieking

voices reverberating off the high walls. Please stop. Please help. I didn't know. Oh God, please let me go. I'm an important man. Don't you know how important I am? My husband is expecting me. I have a daughter. Oh God. Stop this. Stop this now.

Harry is the last in the line, so he gets to see the moment John faints, his head lolling off to one side. The rest of his body moves all the same, like the dead reanimated. Harry isn't screaming or crying or pleading. He is in shock. He doesn't notice that Karuna is also silent, though he gets glimpses of her as John's head sways unnaturally. The urge to be close to her fills him. He wants so desperately to be close. He wants to be safe.

The line stops, and so does Harry. They all turn at once to face the platform ahead.

"Kneel," Twenty-Nine says, and they do. "Put out your arms," he orders, and not a single one hesitates. The pungent smell of urine catches in Harry's throat.

Then Twenty-Nine lifts his hand and a side door creaks open, right where the woman is standing with the large book. She steps aside, and behind her, a young child with a shaved head appears in the doorway. The child stands there for a second, looking down, and then a disembodied hand nudges the child forward, the hand floating in the doorway for just a moment before turning to smoke. Harry doesn't try to understand what he is seeing. He can't think. His body burns with the need to reach Karuna, but his voice is trapped at the bottom of a great well. He can't call out to her, can't do anything but watch the events before him creep forward to some unknown end.

The child comes to Harry first, walking from the corner doorway to reach him. The child looks at him, the androgynous face seeming apologetic. The child has dark eyes, the skin brown with a tinge of . . . *green*? Or is that a trick of the light?

What are you going to do? Harry wants to ask but can't.

As if in answer to the secret question, the child gently lifts Harry's left hand, straightens the fingers, and puts the fingers in his open mouth. The child bites down gently, holding the fingers in place.

"Please," Harry finally says. He doesn't know why he says it; the word just floats up from the well.

The child looks at him. With Harry on his knees, they are face-to-face.

"Begin the ritual," orders Twenty-Nine.

A single tear falls down Harry's face, and his lip quivers. "Don't," he says. He doesn't know what he is asking not to happen. He sees another version of himself, lying in bed, music playing loudly from his old speakers. He pictures himself safe, and Karuna with him, sitting at the foot of the bed, her fingers clutching a black egg. It is cracking open, bleeding light, but the light is warm and comforting and he feels wrapped up in it, protected by it.

The pain pulls him back. It is sharp and instant, shooting through his arm. He shouts in surprise, looking at the child, finding that the air around the child's mouth and his arm is rippling like water. Plumes of fire flow out from the sides of the child's mouth and around Harry's hand, licking the air like many tongues. The heat of it burns his face, but the pain in his arm is much worse, as if he had placed his hand inside the sun. He watches in horror as his hand begins to turn black and large blisters spread up the entire length of his forearm, bursting open as the black follows behind, turning everything the color of burnt wood. Harry screams as this happens, his own anguished squeals finding company amid the wailing of the other sacrifices. The child's eyes turn full black, but in the center is a small dot of red like a drop of fresh blood, the

little pupil darting around in a frenzy in the child's bulging eyes. The green hue of the child's skin intensifies—there is no mistaking it now—and the soft flesh turns hard with platelike scales. Harry doesn't marvel at the change or feel any additional terror from it; the pain takes up all the space in him, filling him up until there is nothing but the screaming want for it all to end. His body shudders all over, and his vocal cords tear themselves apart.

When the child starts chewing, Harry loses consciousness.

THE FRACTAL SEA

DRAGON
WATERTOWN, MASSACHUSETTS

FOUR MONTHS AFTER THE FRACTURE

For the next day and night, the child crawls to the toilet that juts out from the wall of his cell to spew charred skin and bits of bone into the waiting water. He flushes quickly, not wanting to see the evidence of his crimes, and slips back to his cot, only to return to the toilet minutes later. He completes the ritual again and again: the crawl, the spew, the flush, the sinking feeling of shame that he only half understands. The walls around him are the same in the dark, but lights dance before his eyes every time he lifts his head from the toilet. He doesn't know what these are, doesn't know the words to ask about them. So many things he doesn't know and probably never will.

Tomorrow, Smoke will come with a tray of real food. The child has requested pancakes and eggs—no bacon, because the smell will turn his stomach—and for lunch, he will have fresh bread and lentil soup and a chocolate milkshake. For dinner, he will have a black-bean burger, the bun toasted, a slice of cheese melting on top of the patty, everything smothered in spicy ketchup. The child

dreams of this food when he crawls back to his cot on the floor. He closes his eyes and imagines how it will taste, the texture of it in his mouth, the feeling of being full after, full without shame.

Before the ritual, Smoke underfed the child for several days so he would feel something like hunger when he performed his duty. The child was ordered to chew and swallow what he burned— that was part of the ritual, he was told—and he started to feel sick only when he reached the third person in the line. By the sixth person, the child lost his will, and then the witch compelled him to complete the final three.

The child thought he had done well, but Smoke was disappointed. "You couldn't finish," Smoke said when the child returned to his cell. "You've lost three of your meals." In the end, the child would still receive six special meals, one for each hand he had devoured. Special meals were limited to milestones and birthdays. The child got his last special meal after Smoke ordered him to set a man on fire. The child didn't know the man and didn't know why he was being punished, but this was the way it had always been: doing horrible things and not knowing why.

"Pancakes," the child whispers, practicing the word. He doesn't know why they are called that. He sees only the pancakes, not how they are made. Making noise in the cell is punished with beatings, so when he whispers the word again, it is softer and more careful. It was Smoke who taught him the word *pancake*. Smoke taught him all the words he knows, including the name the child should call himself: Dragon, the first and the only.

"Dragon. Are you sleeping?"

Dragon doesn't flinch when he suddenly sees Smoke leaning against the cell bars, because Dragon knows Smoke can be wherever he wants at any time.

"No, Smoke, sir," Dragon says, and sits up to face Smoke out of respect and fear and love. "Am I needed?"

"You've done your duty as best you can. I'm just checking on you."

Dragon smiles a little at that.

"Are you in pain? You've been vomiting."

Dragon's heart leaps at the question. "I feel much better, Smoke, sir."

"Good," Smoke says. "I can give you the meal early if you want."

Dragon thinks hard on the offer. He is still sick, and good food might unsettle his stomach more. "I can wait," he says.

Smoke nods. "Get some sleep if you can. I will give you your first meal early in the morning."

"Yes, Smoke, sir." Dragon lies back and closes his eyes. He doesn't listen for footsteps. Smoke seldom bothers to use his feet to get anywhere.

Dragon doesn't fall asleep. He stays awake behind his closed lids, thinking of his morning meal. Minutes pass, and then an hour, and Dragon still isn't sleeping. His stomach bites at him and he thinks soon he may have to crawl to the toilet again.

He is so caught up in his own thoughts, he doesn't hear the clomping of little feet. And since his eyes are closed, he doesn't see the ants crawling on the wall, their abdomens glowing a faint red. While he lies there in the dark, the ants connect, head to abdomen, so that they are a single entity, and then they form a circle.

Seconds later, an ant crawls onto Dragon's face. Instinctively he bats it away. Two more replace it. Only then does Dragon open his eyes and see the ring of ants on his wall.

He doesn't do anything, only sits up, watching with interest. He

adds glowing ants to his catalog of things in the world he doesn't know. He is watching them when their abdomens flare bright three times, and witnesses the very moment the area of wall inside the circle shimmers and disappears.

Dragon jumps up from his cot. He makes too much noise when he does this, and so he stands completely still for a moment, listening for footsteps or the light rustling that signals the arrival of Smoke. When nothing happens, he takes a few steps toward the circle and the hole in the wall, peering into the opening.

Dragon fails to steady his breath. What he sees isn't the neighboring cell, as he would have expected, but rolling shadowed hills peppered with distant lights. These hills descend into a body of shimmering water, the water reflecting those distant dots of light as long, pale illuminations. The water continues to the thin line that separates it from the black sky. Above the water, grayish clouds migrate across the sky.

None of this makes sense to Dragon, of course. He has never seen rolling hills, or distant artificial light, or a body of water larger than his toilet bowl. He doesn't have the word for clouds and hasn't seen many animals other than insects and humans. Thus, what Dragon is seeing and what he can understand of what he is seeing don't overlap much. He can't really put together what he is looking at. What Dragon can tell, in the way any person can when witnessing something that transcends language, is that this image before his eyes is beautiful.

Dragon also notices more comprehensible objects in the foreground. He sees wooden bars extending half his body length above the ground, topped with long wood planks that, taken together, look almost like the bars of his cell but that someone else would recognize immediately as a porch railing. Beyond the porch, trees sway

in a weak breeze. Dragon has seen trees before, but only through windows. Smoke told him what they were and what they did.

"Trees are the lungs of the earth," Sir Smoke had said, and then Dragon learned what lungs were. Since then, he has imagined the ground under his feet as one giant living thing.

The opening smell has the faint scent of salt water. Cool breeze brushes across Dragon's skin. He is also close enough to see one of the ants crawl over his brethren and disappear on the other side of the opening. Dragon reaches out his hand and feels the cool breeze again, this time on his fingertips. He hears the rustle of the trees and the low chirping of invisible insects.

"If you want to escape, step through," says a voice pitched to a whisper. Dragon realizes that it is coming from the ants. "Come on," they say. "We don't have a lot of time."

Dragon places talking ants into the category of things in the world that he now knows exist. He considers his breakfast on one hand, and freedom on the other. "Will there be food?" Dragon asks.

"All the food you'd want," the ants say.

On the other side of the opening, a cool breeze again caresses his fingers. It doesn't seem dangerous, though Dragon considers Smoke and what he will do if he finds out. Smoke can go anywhere. And Dragon has seen what happens to others who try to escape. He has never considered escaping, even on the worst days, when he wants to curl up and die. He doesn't know if the world outside is a place worth escaping to. Even now this is a concern. Talking ants and calm, glittering nights seem like a kind bit of magic. But all things look kind from a distance. Dragon remembers the surprise on the faces of the sacrificed when he started to cleanse them with fire, how they didn't believe the threat until it was happening. Dragon feels the shame rise again and must fight the urge to

vomit. What a horrible thing he did. What a horrible thing he was made to do. Not Dragon's choice. Someone else's. If he stayed, this would always be true.

It is inaccurate to say Dragon thought these things. They existed not in words but in emotion, a sudden sense of wrongness that could only be approximated. The words were inadequate to the feeling.

"Will you protect me?" Dragon asks the ants.

"Yes," the ants say.

And with that bit of reassurance, Dragon steps through.

20

The closest Dragon has ever gotten to the outside was the room Smoke brought him to for sunlight. In that room with its large glass ceiling, the sun peers down on Dragon like an eye of fire. Dragon likes the sun. He imagines other dragons up there, keeping it lit. Three days a week, he is brought up into that sunroom for an hour or two. Dragon looks forward to those days, marks them in his mind while he waits. Most of his time he has spent down below in his cell, the only home he has known for as long as he's had a mind to know things.

The hole he entered has disappeared, replaced with the solid wall of a house. The ants have dispersed, and so Dragon is on the porch, surrounded by swaying dark trees and hillsides of flickering lights. Up in the sky, he sees a small glowing sphere. Dragon knows about the night sky but has never seen it. The cells are too far underground to catch anything but artificial light. The sphere has a bone-white glow, and he thinks this is what happens when

dragon flame runs out. Dragon finds the thought of the nighttime sun comforting.

Because he is looking up, he notices a red light streaking across the sky.

It is small at first—a blood-colored teardrop against the migrating clouds. As it travels, it grows and changes course, heading for the spot where Dragon stands. He considers running but stays still. The flaming ball is slowing down. Several feet above the ground, it stops and extinguishes itself completely. Then Dragon hears something solid land beside him on the porch, though he can't see it.

"Hello, child," says a voice from nowhere and everywhere. A strange woman's voice, soft and very close, with a singsong quality that Dragon has not heard before.

"Hello?" Dragon says.

"Come inside. Let me introduce you to the rest of us."

Dragon stutters out a yes and then follows the light footsteps to a closed door. As he follows, he can feel the wind whip around the unseen thing in front of him. When he reaches the door, he watches the knob turn on its own and the door swing open.

"Close that after yourself," the voice says, and light footsteps go into the dark interior, echoing softly off the walls.

Dragon obeys, but the reverberating thump of the door makes him lose track of the footsteps for a second, and then afterward he cannot hear a thing. A moment passes before, somewhere deep in the dark house, another door opens and light spreads out across the space, dimly illuminating the path in front of Dragon: a room with a couch and a couple of chairs, a kitchen just beyond with a small dining table against the wall, and beyond that a sharp corner where the source of the light emanates. Dragon follows the light, rounding the corner and walking down a hallway that ends at an

open door. He comes close enough to the source of the light to hear three distinct voices talking softly. Dragon hesitates at the doorway.

"Come in," someone says, and Dragon recognizes the voice as that of the ants that freed him from his cell. Again, he obeys. Inside the well-lit room is a desk with three chairs in front. A thin-faced person with a large mane of kinky hair sits behind the desk, the hair forming a sort of shroud. The person's sharp eyes turn to Dragon as he enters, a subtle smile accompanying the steady gaze. Two of the chairs are empty. Another person is sitting in the chair nearest the wall, where a bookshelf rises almost to the ceiling, its many shelves crammed with thick-spined books. The woman sitting near the shelves looks to Dragon and smiles. An empty chair creaks, and it is the most terrifying thing of all the things Dragon does not know.

In total, three others are in the room: the smiling woman, the person behind the desk, and the invisible woman.

"Please," the person behind the desk says. "Join us."

It is the voice of the talking ants again. Dragon steps forward and goes to the empty chair that has not creaked. He checks it before sitting. After sitting, he watches the person behind the desk, observing the high cheekbones and wide-set eyes.

"My name is Melku, and I'm a monster, like you."

Dragon frowns. "I am not a monster. I'm a dragon."

"That's great," Melku says with an amused smile. "On your left is Sondra, and she is a monster."

Dragon turns and observes the woman. She gives a curt nod of her head. He mirrors the gesture.

"On your right is Sonya. She, too, is a monster."

"Nice to meet you," says the voice.

"Another monster lives here too," Melku says. "You'll meet her another time."

Dragon blinks.

"What's your name?" Melku asks.

"Dragon."

"Of course. It is a fitting name." Melku smiles again at Dragon, and it feels warm and genuine. "Should I tell you why you're here, Dragon?"

Dragon nods.

"You don't know us, but we are the Order of Asha, and we help people like you. Special people. We have larger plans too, which you play a very important part in. The world has changed, you see. A few months ago, most people wouldn't have known you exist, or that any of us exist. But now they know. They are looking for us, and they are starting to find us. And we need to respond. Are you following?"

Dragon shakes his head.

"You're going too fast," Sondra says.

"Melku knows what they're doing," Sonya says.

"I wasn't talking to you. Why don't you come back when you're actually willing to be here."

"Traveling like this is faster," Sonya counters.

Sondra makes a face. "Traveling like this is faster," she mocks.

"Okay, both of you," Melku says.

Dragon finally smiles. Something about the exchange reminds him of conversations with Smoke, though Dragon has never talked back to Smoke like this.

"Let me try this another way," Melku says. "We help special people like you. We helped you in hopes that you'd help us help others like you. Would you be willing to help us?"

Dragon stares. He doesn't like the question. He thought he would be free here; he assumed he would be. But now he is learning

that the feeling of freedom doesn't last long, breaks easily, is as delicate as a moth's wing.

"Melku," Sondra says. "Maybe this is all too fast. He's—"

"Can I say no?" Dragon asks hesitantly. "What if I say no?"

"Then we will find you a home with some kind people we can trust. They'll give you food and shelter and clothing. Everything you need."

"What will happen to the other people if I don't help? The people like me."

Melku looks sad at this, more concerned than disappointed. "Some bad things will happen, but it will be a long time from now. Nothing to worry about."

Dragon nods, trying to understand. Melku is worried, though they're doing their best to hide that fact.

Melku adds, "I know we are asking a lot. But it is truly your choice. We won't force you."

Of all the things Dragon has imagined, he has never considered himself special beyond his part in the ritual. He has known himself as a thing to be used, not a person to be needed.

"How do you know bad things will happen?" Dragon asks.

Melku looks to the others and then back at Dragon, staring at him a long time. "There's a monster whose gift is to know what will happen, and sometimes we are lucky enough to know what she knows."

Dragon blinks, not understanding at all.

Melku smiles. "Okay, that's enough for today. We'll talk again tomorrow." They look to Sondra. "Can you get everything arranged for Dragon to sleep?"

Sondra's face changes to annoyance. Dragon has seen the expression many times before because Smoke looks at him that way when he's disappointed in something Dragon has or hasn't done.

"If you wanted me to leave, you could have just asked," Sondra says, standing up. "Come," she tells Dragon, and he obeys.

When they're out of the room, she stops and turns her head just a bit and asks, "So you're a dragon, huh? Can you fly?"

Dragon frowns.

Sondra laughs. "Okay, okay. Sorry I asked. You're cute. Anyone ever tell you that?"

Dragon blushes, shakes his head. He doesn't know what it means to be "cute," but he likes the way Sondra says it.

"Well, you are. I'll get you some clothes to sleep in, all right? Follow me."

As Dragon follows along behind the woman, he feels himself warm to her again. He likes Sondra. He likes her very much.

The house Dragon spent his whole life in was endless. He had never actually seen the limits of it. By comparison, this house isn't very big: a small kitchen, a dining room, a living room and three bedrooms down a narrow hall, a bathroom between the second and third bedrooms. But as they walk back toward the front of the house, Dragon's eyes wander everywhere. He is overcome by the sheer newness of the place. They pass the bathroom, and Dragon looks inside. It is far better than the toilet in the corner of his cell: tiled floors, a sink, and a toilet bowl so clean that it practically glows. The floral shower curtain at the far end confuses Dragon for a moment. He does not know what "floral shower curtains" are, but he remembers the plain plastic draped over the bathhouse showers, and he can see the similarities. They pass the closed door of the second bedroom. Dragon senses someone behind the door, and it gives him a sudden chill. They stop at the first bedroom, the one closest to the kitchen, and Sondra opens the door, flicks on the light, and nudges him in. She enters behind him and closes the door.

From the hallway, Dragon's and Sondra's voices pick up in muffled conversation as she gets him settled. Theirs are the only sounds in the house. The conversation carries on for a moment before Sondra opens the door again. Light escapes into the hallway.

Sondra tells Dragon good night and then shuts the door behind her. She heads back to Melku's room and pokes her head in to say that the boy is set up for the night and she is going home. A few parting words, and she is gone.

All this happens in a matter of minutes.

Back inside the room, Melku waits. The house is completely quiet now, with Dragon behind a closed door all the way down the hall. Melku listens for another minute before touching something on their desk. Three things happen. The door slowly swings shut, a light goes on above the door, and the room buzzes with some unknown energy, all the walls singing at a low frequency.

Melku nods at the empty chair that isn't empty.

On cue, Sonya starts talking. "The Order is in civil war, and the rogue faction is winning. They've killed Seventeen, and Twenty-Nine replaced her. Some of Seventeen's inner circle have allied themselves with Twenty-Nine, but most have gone into hiding.

"The rogue faction have taken to calling themselves the Cult of the Zsouvox. I think they have the Zsouvox, but I haven't been able to confirm. Smoke disappears for hours at a time and returns to the Trapp compound, but I can't follow him when he goes—his power doesn't allow me to track him."

"That's fine," Melku says. "Anything else?"

"Seventeen's inner circle had no idea what the rogue faction was doing. They didn't know anything about that werewolf pack, or any of the other recently turned monsters. And the Cult made sure Seventeen wouldn't give us a heads-up either. Twenty-Nine

openly opposed the clean-up after the fifth, which tipped his hand to Seventeen's inner circle. Twenty-Nine knew he'd been burned. That's what started the coup. No one knows about our involvement in the leak."

Melku sits with this information for a moment. "What about relations with the Order?"

"Twenty-Nine wants to pretend like it's business as usual. They'll honor the truce."

Melku smiles. "Good. That's all good news. It means we have time." A silence descends that is expressive enough to chase the triumph from Melku's face. "What is it?"

"Smoke loves the boy. He hasn't said anything, and I can't explain it in words, but his love is obvious whenever he's around the child. He'll come looking, for sure." Another pause, equally expressive. "I think you should talk to Cassandra about it."

Melku sighs. "She's been quiet as death lately. Won't tell me anything I want to know. Only the things I *don't* want to know."

The silence that follows is longer than the others, and it causes Melku to shift uncomfortably in their seat.

Sonya's voice cracks a little when she speaks again. "I recommend you ask anyway."

Melku looks both relieved and distressed. "Okay, I will."

"End of report. I'll go now."

"Wait," Melku says.

The chair doesn't move.

Melku hesitates.

The chair shifts minutely.

"Okay, okay. Don't be mad, but I just want to know how long it has been since you've worn your skin."

"I don't know," Sonya answers quickly.

"You know what will happen if—"

"I don't need reminding of the risks. I am fine. I am getting what I need. Don't worry."

Melku frowns a little and quickly brings their face back to neutrality. "I'm sorry."

"It's fine," the voice says, and then, "I'm going back to work, okay?"

Melku only nods.

The chair where Sonya is sitting slides backward across the floor just a bit, then eases back into its original position. Melku releases the lock on the door and it swings open. Soft footsteps fade from the room, and moments later the front door creaks open and closed.

Alone, Melku sits back in their chair, lets out a long, deep sigh, and drifts off in something like thought, except that their mind is completely and strangely absent of activity. Minutes pass this way—Melku's calm breathing, their eyes gazing at the ceiling— before Melku's eyes somehow settle on mine. They smile, and it is conspiratorial, as if we're both in on some joke. They say, "Don't be rude. Introduce yourself."

Terrified, I push myself out into the fractal sea.

HOME

Right before a plane lands at Cyril E. King Airport on St. Thomas, there is a span of seconds when you can stare out the window and see only ocean below. For those seconds, it looks as though you'll land right in the water. And then, right as murmurs in the cabin give way to held breath, the runway appears at almost the last possible moment, and the plane lands.

This is always my favorite part of coming home: the way the water comes up to meet you and then you've arrived. If you get the right crowd, the first-timers will actually applaud, and there's this sense of pride, as if you'd performed a trick for them yourself, even though you had nothing to do with it. It's like saying, "I almost had you, didn't I? Welcome to my home."

No matter how long you're gone, it still feels like this. Like home.

I am shaken awake. "We're here," says the flight attendant. "You're a deep sleeper."

I look around at the empty cabin. "I'm sorry," I say.

"It's no problem at all. We just landed. Please, enjoy your stay."

I grab my carry-on from the overhead bin. As I leave the plane, the sun is so bright I'm dazzled blind for a moment. A wave of sticky heat hits me, and with each step down from the plane I feel heavy, as if I have ankle weights on.

Cyril E. King is a small airport by most standards, but for most of my young life it was the norm I compared other airports to. As I walk to baggage claim, it feels as if both experiences had merged: the young man and this older one, belonging and not belonging. When I arrive at the claim belt, I see that it has already stopped and my suitcase is waiting on the side for me to pick up. Brian is standing near enough to it that it seems to be his.

As I approach, he says, "I figured this was yours. What you want to do?"

"Get a drink," I say without hesitation.

For the occasion, we drive up Northside to Sibs and sit at the bar, where I order a passion-fruit Cruzan rum and cranberry.

Brian gets an Angry Orchard. "Rum gives me a headache," he says.

"Everything gives me a headache now," I say.

Music is playing from the speakers, an old-school hip-hop song: Big Pun's "Still Not a Player." Sibs is frequented by expats, but a few locals are in the bar. The bartender passes me my drink and I take a sip. It's okay; I got the drink more for the experience anyway, being at home and wanting something local. A few sips in, the stuck-in-molasses feeling I've been having begins to dissipate.

The light in Sibs is dim. I have always found it intimate and cozy, but when I look down at the floor and notice some of the grime, I realize there are other reasons for keeping the lights low.

Sibs is as old as they come. It has existed in its current form for as long as I can remember. The quintessential Northside bar,

it is the meeting place at the center of three roads that eventually will take you anywhere you need to go on island. An organ in the body of St. Thomas—a place for things to pass through before they arrive at their destination.

I wanted to come here because it's out of the way. Though an organ, it is a minor one.

"You know what you'll do for work?" Brian asks.

"Teach, if they'll let me."

"Charlotte?"

I laugh. "God, no. They won't even let me in the gate."

Brian places a hand on my shoulder, familiar and compassionate. "A lot of people saw through that tough-guy act you played in high school. You might find a warmer welcome than you think."

I smile, but all I can feel is the shame of that version of myself.

Brian is watching me, and it is clear he knows where my mind has gone. "Drink's on me. Don't worry about it."

We've drifted over the years, but Brian was there through all of it. He can probably quote back to me the words I'd said in that hospital bed, angry and bruised, while Cory watched over me. No matter what, I couldn't escape it. There were witnesses.

"I was thinking UVI," I say. "Maybe just a class to start. Get my foot in."

"I know someone up there. You do too. You remember Greg? He teaches history or something. Want me to reach out?"

"If it's not too much trouble."

Someone taps me on the shoulder, and I turn.

Rob has some gray in his beard and is rounder in the face, but it is the same dude from high school.

I stand up. "What going on?"

"Me'n see you in the longest," he says as our hands make

contact. He brings me in for a quick half hug, our clasped hands still between us. He does the same with Brian. "You, I can't get rid of," he says to Brian. Then back to me: "Where you been?"

"Around. Went off to school and things. You know."

"Yeah, a lot of a'you does run off stateside," he says, swaying a little. "What bring you back?"

"Just miss home."

"Ain't no place like it," he says. A few beats pass, and I see that his eyes are full-on glazed. "So, where my boy Cory? Me'n see him in a minute either."

I can't find words, so I simply gape at him.

Brian watches Rob as if he had just sprouted wings from his neck. "Rob, come on."

For a brief moment, he looks confused; then he puts his hand to his mouth. "Oh, shit, man. I'm sorry. I remember hearing about something, but shit, man. I had a few drinks. I don't know where my head was at."

"It's okay. Happened a long time ago," I say.

He nods and then stands there looking horrified. "Sometimes I think about Omari and it takes me a minute to realize he gone too. I mean, how do you even process that shit, you know? Dread. Look at me here, still running my mouth."

I hadn't realized Omari was dead, but the news doesn't surprise me. Omari got into a lot of trouble in high school. I think about Cory, how many people felt the same way about him. How many people heard about him and weren't surprised?

"Really," I say. "Everything safe. It good seeing you."

"Yeah, me too." He pats me on the shoulder. "Take care of yourself."

He can't get out of there fast enough.

That night, I borrow Brian's Honda Civic and go to see Gina. When Keren answers the door, she stands there for a while just staring at me. "It been a long time," she says.

"I've been hearing that a lot."

She smiles a little.

"Sorry for just showing up."

We stand there a moment longer, looking each other over. Then Keren remembers herself. "Well," she says, taking a breath, "come on in." She opens the door wide, and I step through. "Sorry about the mess. Gina in her room. Gina!"

"You have a good place here," I say. It is true. The apartment is small—a public housing unit—but Keren keeps it nice.

"We manage," she says. "Gina, come out here for a second!"

A door opens in the back, and light spills into the hall. "What, Mommy," she's saying as she stomps into the living room. "I trying do my homework." She stops when she sees me.

"This your uncle," Keren says.

"I know who he is," Gina says.

Keren looks surprised at this but doesn't ask any questions. "Well, don't be rude. Come over here and say hello."

Gina comes closer. "Hello," she says, keeping her eyes on mine the whole time.

I smile at her, and unconsciously I put my hands in my pockets. "I just thought I should stop by. Tell you I was on island."

"I already knew," Gina says.

Keren looks to Gina and says, "But how did you know that?"

"I have my ways," Gina says, and then, when her mother's expression turns sharp, she quickly adds, "Social media." She turns to leave and throws back a final word: "Welcome home. Thanks for dropping by."

"Gina," her mother calls.

"It all right," I say, and in that moment, I realize that I've slipped completely into the local dialect. I lean in further. "I wanted to give a'you my number. So you could reach me, in case you need anything?"

Keren is still looking in the direction Gina went. "Okay," she says, and when her attention turns back on me, she wears regret so plainly on her face, I almost reach out to pat her shoulder. "She is a good kid," she says. "But she can be a little strange. Reminds me of Cory." This last part comes out shaky, and it is obviously hard for her to say the words.

"I can see it," I say.

We exchange numbers. I say I have to meet up with someone. It is entirely made up, but because of the hour it can be interpreted only one way. Keren smiles, a bit of amusement in her eyes.

"You'll give her the number?" I ask.

"Of course."

• • •

Later, I get a text:

> This is Gina. I lied when I said how I
> knew you were here. I knew you were
> here because Daddy told me.

And another text, right after that:

> Sometimes he visits me in my
> dreams.

23

"She's been spending a lot of time with you."

There isn't anything I can gather from the statement. Yes, Gina has been spending a lot of time with me. I liked her spending time with me. "Is that a problem?"

A short silence. "No, but I just want to make sure . . ." Keren trails off. The thread of her statement hangs there, the meaning in it a ghost yet to be born.

"I moved back," I say. "I'm not leaving."

I can hear her breathing; then she says, "You know my history. Bad men. Followed by worse ones."

"I know."

"It didn't get better after Cory."

"I figured," I say, and regret saying it.

"She's been through them all. Even the ones she says she doesn't remember, she does."

"I just want to be in her life."

"You were gone a long time. No, don't say anything. I know. But Gina didn't do anything wrong. She came into this world; that's it."

I get a sick feeling in the pit of my stomach. "I was wrong to stay away. I want to do better."

"For her sake, I hope that's a promise."

Gina is looking at me. She's gathered up the conversation from what I've said, and her eyes are taking it all in the way Cory used to, those same searching eyes. "It is a promise," I say.

Keren's breathing keeps time for a few moments more. The sick feeling in my stomach stirs, and I feel a bout of nausea.

"All right, then. Bring her home later," she says. "I cooking."

Keren hangs up and then I put down the phone.

"She miss me, don't she?" Gina says, more statement than question.

I want to ask if her mother will be okay if we hang out at their place more, but I know the answer to that question as soon as I think to ask it. Keren can never be my friend, not really. "She says you need to come home for dinner," I say.

Gina nods. "You coming over too?"

"I don't think—"

"It's fine. Don't worry about it." She looks away from me.

Over the past week, I started picking Gina up from school. I rented a car to get around since I couldn't keep borrowing Brian's. There isn't any ride-sharing on the island, and taxis are a terrible amount of money. It is getting to the point where I'll have to put some money down on a car of my own. But for a week it is okay, maybe even for a week more.

After school, we go to the movies or out for food, or just hang out at Brian's house watching TV, which is what we are doing now.

We talk about a lot of things, but mostly she has questions about Cory. Keren doesn't talk much about him, and Gina has made her cry too many times forcing the conversations out of her. I didn't start with the intention of inserting myself. They are painful for me too, these conversations, but they bring me closer to Gina, help me get under her defenses. And I find that I like being close. She's just started high school, but she is already too cool for anyone above the age of twenty. But I've somehow gotten past all that, slipped through without suspicion.

The other reason I have these conversations: at moments, talking to her feels like talking to a version of my brother.

"When I told you I see him in my dreams, I didn't expect you to believe me," she says.

"I've seen him in my dreams too. What's not to believe?"

She shakes her head. "Not like no silly dream. He's real. Flesh and blood. I remember all our conversations. I know things about him nobody has told me."

"Like what?" I ask.

"Like his favorite band was Rush."

I turn to look at her. "Keren told you that?"

She chupses her teeth and shakes her head. "Only thing he won't tell me is how he died." She looks pointedly at me.

It takes my brain a few seconds to catch up. "You mean, your mother didn't tell you?"

"She told me a version of it, but I don't know if it is true."

"What did she say?" I ask.

She stares at me. "I'm not giving you the chance to lie to me."

"And this dream Cory—he won't tell you?"

"He says to ask you." At my hesitation, she adds, "I know more than you think I do, so just be honest with me."

Well, fuck. A perfect trap. I won't be able to dodge this without losing ground with her. Again, she reminds me of him. It is strange to see pieces of him in her, as if she'd captured bits of his soul. Even this, the way she's thought of everything ahead of time, reminds me of her father. He used to set traps just like this one, and I used to fall into them every time.

I sigh. "Give me a second," I say. I go to my room and reach under my bed to pull out a large box. Written on the outside of the box is the word *files*, though the contents are so much more than that. The innocuous description is the point, really. I take a breath before opening it. I have to pull out quite a few folders before I find the one I'm looking for. It is labeled "Version017." Spread around me are other folders: Version003, Version1123, Version067 through Version081, all in a row. I have an external hard drive with all these "versions" as well, and another collection buried in my documents folder on my laptop. I'd sent the hard copies through the mail, paying extra to make sure they didn't get lost. I've been paranoid for years about someone finding these and reading them. I've never shared a single one with anyone. My little big secret.

The folder itself is over a decade old at this point, but except for crinkled edges, it's still in good condition. I pick it up and return to the living room. I sit down beside her on the couch. The folder is heavy in my hands. I set it on the cushion between us. "You found this in my things," I say. "I did not give it to you."

Gina picks the folder up, and I pretend not to notice. She looks at it a moment and then opens the folder. She glances over the page before looking back up at me. "What's this?"

"The story of how your father died," I say, but it is so much more than that. It's also the story of how I survived.

AFTER THE CHANGE

24

REBECCA VÁZQUEZ

Rebecca grew up in Norwell, Massachusetts, down a narrow winding road that turned to gravel before hitting right up against their house. Despite the out-of-the-way location, the house wasn't big—just one floor and three bedrooms. She and her brother shared one bedroom until Rebecca got big enough to get her own. Even then she had to carve out space in her room, pushing her mother's collection of things to the corners, where they trapped dust and dead insects and sometimes little field mice. Her father was loud, and Rebecca supposed she got her fire from him. They had intense shouting matches when she was a teenager, his voice quaking, hers reaching a tight shriek. Her mother and brother looked on like the trapped children of a loveless marriage.

Her father hit her only once.

That day, he had come home from work and switched the channel on the television to watch one of his car shows: *American Trucks*. Her father was a short-haul truck driver and loved these

stupid shows. Rebecca snatched up the remote and changed the channel back to *Buffy the Vampire Slayer.* "For all the shows about cars you watch, and all the driving you do, you're still a terrible driver," she said.

Rebecca had no clue why that set him off. She didn't see his hand coming. She tilted forward and her vision went cloudy. Her head felt like an hourglass that had been flipped, the dull throb in the back of her head spreading down her face and settling there. Her bruised nose bled once she lifted her face from the carpet.

Through her blurred vision, she saw her father, his mouth open, mirroring her own astonishment.

She never let that go, always found ways to remind him of it. She left the knife in and twisted it whenever she felt the need. He didn't want her going out late. *Twist.* He didn't like her friends. *Twist.* He would rage at her, but the shame was there too. It worked every time. She could see him holding back furious tears. She would have felt guilty about it, but he'd hardly apologized. "You know I didn't mean it," he had said. That was it. Those words hung between them right up until she left for college.

On that last night before she was off to campus life, Rebecca found her father sitting in the dark, in the recliner near the door. She was going to sneak out to spend one more mediocre night with her friends, but she stopped cold when she saw him there. He didn't speak right away. She considered the possibility that he might be sleeping, but something about the way his body was set put her on edge.

"Dad," she called out.

He took a short breath and shifted in the recliner. "You going out?"

"Yes," she said. No use trying to cover it up now.

"Okay," he said.

Rebecca blinked, wondering whether the person sitting there was really her father. "I'll be out late."

"Be safe," he said.

Rebecca didn't move, her body aching with anticipation.

He took another breath, long and labored, a soft groan tagging in for the finish. "I never meant to hurt you. That day, I almost hit a teenager. He ran across the street and I was so tired," he said.

Rebecca stood there listening to her father, the way the whole story rolled out of his mouth as if he'd been holding it just behind his lips the past few years.

"I work hard, Rebecca, to take care of things around here. Your mother is smoking herself into an early grave. And you children, you don't understand how hard it is to live in this country. I have to take risks so we can survive."

Something in his tone turned Rebecca against him. He almost had her, right up until the end. "You want me to give you a pass for hitting me because you work hard?" she asked, her voice cutting like a well-honed knife.

"You are such an ungrateful child," he said without his usual passion.

"If you are going to apologize, just do it. Don't make excuses."

"I won't always be here for you to abuse, Becca."

"So, I'm abusing *you* now? Well, I'll be out of here tomorrow, so I guess we'll both catch a break," she said before storming out the house and letting the screen door slam behind her. She stood in the dirt in front of her house, listening to her father as he got up from the couch and locked the door. The rest of the night, she sulked around with her friends, complaining about her life, how happy she was to get out of that damn house.

Her friend Dina punched her in the arm. "You got it good, Becca," she said. "You don't know how good you got it."

"He hit me," Rebecca said.

"Once."

"Just because you're used to that shit doesn't mean it's okay." Rebecca was a wildfire, burning everything in her path, and Dina had put herself there.

Dina stared at her, the smoke in the car fogging up everything. Rebecca could see that she was holding back tears. "You think you're so wronged," Dina said. "You don't see how you are."

Rebecca was upset for the rest of the evening. She blamed her dad for that too. And the next day, as he drove her to UMass, she told him as much, clearly still high and not caring that he knew it.

"I hope you learn some things about life while you're away," he said, shaking his head.

"Like you?" she barked back. Her mother was in the front passenger seat, quiet as always, her little brother asleep beside her, treating the argument like a lullaby.

"Not like me," he said.

She must have said something else to him, but he stopped responding after that. She'd burned the fight out of him. When they arrived at school, everyone helped get her stuff to her dorm, and then, one by one, they hugged her goodbye. Her father was last. "I'm going to miss you, Becca," he said.

She didn't respond, her anger still boiling, threatening to foam over as white fury. At the time, she thought it was enough that she didn't use the moment to turn the knife again. Later, she would wish she had just said it back. What would it have hurt, to give him one moment of reciprocated love?

When she told Laina about that day, Laina grabbed her

by the shoulders and said, "There's no excuse for what he did. Ever."

Rebecca nodded, but the words didn't balance the scales in her heart. Sure, she agreed with Laina. That had never changed. But later, she found out that beatings were the way older Puerto Ricans disciplined their children—even some of her parents' friends. Her father and mother had made the decision never to do that. There was room there, maybe not for forgiveness, but for understanding. Her parents had shown incredible restraint with her and her brother, had buried a lifetime of cultural conditioning for her and her brother's sake. Her father had failed to do this once. Rebecca had lived a life of many mistakes she couldn't take back. At the very least, she knew what that felt like.

But it really wasn't about the thing itself. Rebecca was mourning all the other things that mistake stole from them. She and her father had both paid a price in lost time—a bitter, ugly, deep hole they could never fill.

25

EIGHT MONTHS AFTER THE FRACTURE

Rebecca wakes to clanging kitchenware. This is one thing she hasn't adjusted to after the change. Every damn thing wakes her up, from the refrigerator to people walking outside, to the soft shivering of nighttime trees. It is Sarah, she knows. Eating. She picks up her phone and sees the time: 5:02 a.m. Why is Sarah eating at this hour? Only the Devil is up at five in the morning.

Next to her, Laina is fast asleep, looking as beautiful as ever, her chest rising and falling, steady and slow. Her mouth is slightly parted, where the tiniest whistle of air escapes. Her face looks serene in that way only sleeping faces can be, the world outside shut out from the world within. Rebecca slips out of bed, careful not to wake her. She puts on her house slippers and creeps to the door, opening it slowly.

She finds Sarah in the kitchen, pouring milk into a large bowl of cereal. Sarah looks up and nods at her. "You want a bowl?" she asks.

Rebecca just glares.

"The wolf is anxious," she says in explanation. "Did I wake you?"

Rebecca sighs. "Give me a bowl."

Sarah pulls a bowl down from the cabinet, this time careful, almost as if she was capable of it the whole time. She grabs the box of cereal next to her bowl and shakes some out. She passes the bowl and milk to Rebecca. "Pour the milk yourself. Don't want you chewing me out like last time."

Sarah is a stout girl with a pronounced Boston accent. Pale with long dirty-blond hair. But by the way she talks and the way she moves, you know she grew up around kids who didn't look like her. She's relaxed, which relaxes everyone around her.

Rebecca pours a lot of milk in her bowl. She likes it that way, the cereal drowning in milk to get the crunch out. It is worse now. She hates the sound of loud chewing, and now all chewing is loud. "Has your wolf been anxious a lot lately?"

Sarah nods. "Fucker won't let me sleep through the night."

Rebecca uses her spoon to submerge the little toasted O's. "With me, it's the sounds. Everything bothers the shit out of me now."

"The smells," Sarah says.

Rebecca nods. "I know too much about everyone."

Sarah laughs and says, "Connor said his wolf liked trash."

Rebecca almost spits her cereal out. She coughs, swallows. "What kind of trash?"

"Smellier the better."

"He never mentioned it."

"He's embarrassed. I mean, I'd be embarrassed too. Jesus."

They both snicker and look over at his closed door, but then they remember that Connor isn't there anymore. "We need to get a new roommate," Rebecca says, then lifts her hand dismissively before Sarah can say anything. "No one is going to know."

"Except the world already knows. They just don't know they know, until our faces remind them."

They spend the next few minutes eating quietly.

Rebecca gets most of the crunch out of her cereal, so she can eat it in relative peace. Of course, she starts thinking of Lincoln again, of his body lying in the street. She feels that old itch again.

"We okay on rent?" she asks, trying to rub the itch away.

"We're in on time," Sarah says, and watches Rebecca with her too-perceptive eyes. "Don't worry."

Rebecca lifts a spoonful to her mouth, then stops. "Utilities?"

"You're hopeless."

They've been trying out income sharing, something Ridley enthusiastically told them about a few months ago. Everyone puts their rent-and-utilities money in a shared account, along with some money for food and group recreation. It's been working so far, worked even better when Connor was still contributing to the pot, but even with just the two of them, the income sharing has decreased a lot of the anxiety they have about the future. It probably wouldn't have worked if their pack weren't so close, but some bit of the magic that changed them also bonded them, Rebecca thinks. They trust each other despite their histories.

Still, if they're going to keep this going, they'll soon need a roommate, preferably someone open to income sharing as well. Someone who will trust them and whom they can trust with their secrets.

"She's up," Sarah says.

"Who?" Rebecca asks, and then she hears it too, the bed creaking from behind her bedroom door, faint but certain. "Hey, how much can you hear from out here?" she asks.

Sarah just smiles. "You should finish up. She seems to be in a rush."

Just then, the door flies open and a disheveled Laina steps out of the room, still buttoning her pants. When she sees Sarah, she stops and smiles, part bashful, part playful. Rebecca's cheeks warm. She loves that smile.

"Sorry, I thought only you were out here," Laina says. "It's so early."

"Couldn't sleep," Sarah says. "Want some cereal?"

Laina smiles again, and this time Rebecca warms all over. God, that smile. "Sorry . . ." Laina starts to say.

"You have to go?" Sarah finishes. "I can tell."

Laina walks over and plants a soft kiss on Rebecca's lips. "See you later at the bookstore?"

Another thing that has changed for Rebecca. Her desire only simmered before. Now it burns like a furnace. "I'll be there," she says. Her eyes linger on Laina's lips.

Laina must have noticed, because she kisses her again, laughs, and dashes to the door.

"Need me to give you a ride?" Rebecca asks, or tries to, but Laina has already slipped on her boots and is heading out the door.

"She's wonderful," Sarah says after the door closes. "Don't fuck it up."

Rebecca tries to read Sarah's face and, of course, isn't surprised by what she discovers. Sarah is smiling, this half-grin thing, but around the eyes and furrow of her brow is a deep, inescapable pain that makes the curl of her lips seem devastating. "Don't let that one go," is what Sarah is actually saying. "Don't let go or you'll regret it."

Rebecca thinks of words to say. Nothing feels powerful enough to turn such a hope into promise. She doesn't have complete control

of Laina or herself, and worse, she doesn't have any control of the world. It seems foolish to say anything, so she just takes it all in without comment.

Sarah seems satisfied. She turns away from Rebecca and starts washing her bowl in the kitchen sink. At one point, she puts her forearm up to her face and wipes away something. The room isn't hot. It can be nothing else. Sarah continues washing other dishes in the sink. The movement of her shoulders obscures any sign of distress. "I can get that bowl when you're done," she says, her voice a forced calm.

Rebecca considers bringing up the conversation again, but she knows that Sarah will put off talking to Laina until she is ready. Eventually, she'll do what is needed. Rebecca just has to stay out of the way. She looks down at her half-eaten bowl of cereal and accepts defeat. She brings the bowl over to Sarah. As she puts it in the sink, she bends forward a little more than she needs to, hoping to get a good look at Sarah.

Sarah watches her and says, "You ain't slick." She is wearing her best smile, a convincing approximation of okay-ness. She looks at the bowl. "You need to stop wasting cereal," she says, and dumps the milk and cereal out, washes the bowl quickly, places it on the drying rack. "You don't have work until later, right? I was wondering if you'd take me out to the woods. Let this wolf run off whatever is bothering her."

"Sure," Rebecca says.

26

By the time her father died, Rebecca was already using. Cocaine was her drug of choice, carried around in a little tube of lip gloss in her bag. In college, she stayed up on weekends, partying until sunrise. She crashed on Sundays, sometimes Mondays if she couldn't make it out of bed. Her grades tanked. She was prickly before, but she became paranoid, and with the paranoia came cruelty. She and Dina fell out almost immediately once she left for college, and before long only her party friends could stand being around her. Her relationships with these friends were punctuated with fights and fallings-out, melodrama spilling into every part of her life.

At a party right before Christmas break, Rebecca punched her friend Kathy in the face. The next day, she couldn't remember what happened, but some blond kid from her World Mythology class filled her in. The guy had been nursing a crush on her for a long time—she knew but pretended otherwise—and when she came into class, he asked her if she was okay. She must have seemed

confused, because he smirked and said, "Yeah, you busted her lip pretty good. You were yelling something about her not paying you back for tickets, and I couldn't understand the rest of it. Something about lip gloss? You both were fucked up."

This could have been a wake-up call, but Rebecca was mostly annoyed at making a spectacle, and a bit unnerved at how fast the guy had realized that she didn't remember. What else had she done and forgotten? She laughed off the whole thing and spent the rest of class paying too much attention to the lesson, watching the way her professor's mouth moved as she talked, trying to catch every moment the woman's lower teeth peeked out from her thin, slightly cracked lower lip.

The day would have disappeared in obscurity if not for the text after class.

Come home, it said. *Your father is in the hospital.*

She did come home, and when she saw him lying there in the hospital bed, she knew that whatever he had wasn't going to get better. How had she not known? She went over the past year in her mind and saw the signs: her mother repeatedly asking her to come visit, her father unusually quiet when she called them to cancel her trip back on Christmas, her brother telling her she was a selfish brat and hanging up on her, and, once, her mother actually saying the words "your father is sick," which Rebecca mistook for something trivial because she was high enough to down an airplane. She had no memory of her response, but it must have been bad, because her mother pretty much stopped calling after that.

In the hospital, her father watched her from sunken eyes, wordless.

She couldn't stay. She ran out of the room and disappeared down a stairwell. *I could break my neck*, she remembered thinking

as she flew down the stairs, her heart thumping in her chest like a wild animal attacking its cage. She remembered wanting to so badly, relishing every moment that her foot landed on the nosing of each step, the worn soles of her shoes sliding dangerously across the knife's edge of each miniature cliff. She could break her neck and she wouldn't have to burn this horror out of her. She wouldn't have to be a good daughter. She wouldn't have to be anything at all. She could be cracked stone and fine soil. She could be a bed of weeds.

Outside in the cold winter air, she struggled to find her breath, and then when she couldn't she pulled back into a corner of her mind, watching like a hunkered gargoyle as her body collapsed on the sidewalk and she lost consciousness.

She woke up in her very own hospital bed, a nurse staring down at her. "You fainted," she said, stating the obvious. Then Rebecca remembered her father, and again she struggled to breathe. The nurse put a hand on her shoulder. "It's okay," she said. "Everything's okay. Try to relax."

Her words shouldn't have worked. If Rebecca were in full control of her body, she would have rolled her eyes at the woman. But in her desperation, she took hold of those words and pulled herself out from her panic, the effort so exhausting that she drifted back off to sleep.

Rebecca wasn't sentimental. She wasn't prone to fainting at any slight hardship. She considered herself sturdy, pragmatic, even if she sometimes let her passion show. So, the shame of that first response to her father in the hospital bed stuck with her through his illness, caused her to shut all her pain and fear away. This did nothing for anyone, least of all her. Through her mother's and brother's grief, she was as impenetrable as if she weren't there at all. She could see

that her father wanted more as well, but she couldn't give it without risking herself. Even as he went through the final stages of his illness, she didn't give him the daughter she knew he wanted. She wouldn't show him her tears. She wouldn't show him how terrified she was of a world where she couldn't yell at him or pretend he wasn't there, a world where he really wouldn't be.

The last day of his life, he told her to take care of everyone, that she should be the one with the responsibility. Not her brother. Not even her mother. "You have my heart," he said.

At the time, she didn't understand what he meant. The words sounded unlike her father, too romantic. But she realized it later that night as her thoughts kept her awake. She was like him. Her heart was like his. She wanted to argue with him—*I'm not like you at all.* But she knew the truth of it, hated him for cutting so close to the bone. Those were his last words. The bastard went out with the last word.

She wished she could say she stopped using then, but it would be years off still, after she was at her lowest point, after she was tweaking in a park, wrapped up in layers, a bottle in one gloved hand, looking out into the darkness at a set of red eyes; after the thing rushed at her and sank its curved teeth into her arm and she struggled free and ran into an intersection, almost being sideswiped by a van; after the next four nights in a hospital, her body shivering with withdrawal and the change; and further still, once her arm was healed and her mind was clear and she found she didn't want to burn her horror out of her. Not just yet—maybe someday soon, but not now. That was when she finally went to rehab and asked for help, feeling the magic in her rumbling awake, and her father's heart beating in tune with it, and a new desire to be what she'd been fighting against for so

long: someone who could turn the blade of her heart against the things that deserved it and not on herself or the ones she loved. Only then did she stop using. After that, she came close only a few times. And over time, she found other people she could help, and through that she found Lincoln and the others, a warrior family she could nurture and help grow.

It's an hour's drive out of Boston to Norwell, Massachusetts. They drive out to their favorite spot along a small tucked-away road, a short walk from a meadow. Sarah gets out of the car and strips down immediately. In seconds, she's changed, and the wolf is there, standing on all fours with her ears pointed to the sky. Sarah's change is faster than most, which is good. Rebecca is out of the car and leaning against it, watching as Sarah's gray-black wolf disappears into the waiting tree line.

How to describe the change? Rebecca has tried explaining it many times to herself. It is something like a rubber band coiled taut around a solid thing, only you're the rubber band *and* the solid thing, and the rubber band isn't really rubber but a bundle of nerves straining against the solid thing, which isn't solid but actually a mesh of bone, blood, and tissue rearranging themselves with no attention to physics, breaking and tearing and turning momentarily to soup—like the inside of a fleshy cocoon, the chrysalis oozing

out of its shell of nerves as hair and eyeballs and teeth—all this too fast to track, only the pain and the fire burning everywhere at once and you can't scream, because your vocal cords are soup and you are at the edges of yourself, existing as pure mind where time stretches and collapses like a fever dream. Once the change is done, you can barely remember it, because the memory will use you as fuel and there will be nothing to return to, which is to say, any explanation fails, because the memory is incomplete and the event incomprehensible.

Right before the change, however, there's this sort of anticipation, a sliver of recollection, the vague awareness of an approaching hellish rapture. Rebecca likes this part. Not the change itself. Lincoln did like the change. He said it felt like being destroyed and reborn. She supposes that could have been attractive to someone like Lincoln. Sarah too, probably, though she never actually volunteered her opinion on the matter.

Rebecca can still hear Sarah mixed in with everything: small animals (squirrels mostly) scampering through trees and surrounding brush, a few deer grazing quietly a few miles out, and cars speeding along on the main road—not too far off, but far enough not to interrupt the sounds of nature. She likes being out here because she doesn't have to dull her senses the same way she must in the city. Whatever magic created the wolf makes life difficult in the city. Too many sounds and smells. Here, the magic spreads out, and it feels good—almost like getting high, though Rebecca feels uncomfortable admitting that. When Lincoln died, she thought about how it felt to let the magic take over, spread out, how it can sometimes trick you into forgetting where you are. A werewolf can get careless if it isn't careful. Lincoln wouldn't have done it on purpose. Addiction doesn't mix well with magic. It would have

been a slip, an expanding, and then, without realizing, he would have been on fire. No stopping it then. It's a miracle that none of the others have lost themselves, a greater miracle that she hasn't.

Lincoln had made progress. He wasn't using. He was pulling his life back together. He even wanted to mend his relationship with Laina. But magic is a terrible thing. It makes itself *useful*. Nothing is more dangerous than something useful—for anyone, but especially for people like them.

Rebecca pauses. She can't hear Sarah anymore.

The panic is immediate, amplified by the thoughts she's already having. She stretches her hearing, and distant softer sounds sharpen in her ears. No Sarah. She takes in a breath to yell, *No, not here! Not again!* Then she hears it: a familiar predator pushing off from fallen leaves, and something smaller springing into movement. The predator lands, something squeals, and then quiet.

Her tension easing away, Rebecca keeps her attention tuned to the spot of the commotion and listens as soft steps come closer. Sarah enters the clearing. A rabbit hangs limply from her mouth. Sarah doesn't come all the way back but settles in the middle of the meadow, dropping to a crouch and placing the rabbit between her two large front paws. She starts eating.

Sarah is stout and powerful in human form, and that has carried over to her wolf: formidable hind legs, a thick neck, and solid shoulders. Nothing about Sarah's wolf seems unnatural, though. Seeing it makes Rebecca feel that werewolves are something true and central, a long-kept secret spoken in whispers through time.

Rebecca and her pack had thought life would be different after their protest. They had walked into it with both eyes open, prepared to be arrested or worse. But the cops who arrived on the scene simply let them gather up their clothes and escorted them off

the highway. Rebecca remembered the vacant look on those cops' faces. There and not there.

The pack left in peace, and cops visited each of them the next day. The cop who visited Rebecca was a tall, bone-thin man with the brightest blue eyes she'd ever seen. When she answered the door to her then apartment, he was standing there in full uniform. No words were exchanged between them; he just handed her a piece of paper and walked away. He had the glazed-over expression of someone drunk, but his movements were controlled. He was gone before she read the words on the paper. It was a list of names, in four even columns. Most of them she didn't recognize, but near the top were several she did. Friends and family. Some school acquaintances she hadn't seen since high school or earlier. There was no indication what the names meant. The threat was left unspoken. But those vacant eyes gave Rebecca a glimpse of a deeper story. They had done something truly dangerous, and the normal rules of engagement didn't apply here. Werewolves weren't the only things lurking in the dark.

They had already learned that when the last few seconds of the protest video were edited. And each of them had received that same slip of paper, the same vague threat, the same vacant eyes. Three of her pack members left right away, off to Colorado together. Connor stayed the longest, but eventually he left as well, saying that people were following him around and he was worried about his parents in Texas. Rebecca made no attempt to stop anyone from leaving. After that, it was her and Sarah. Rebecca took the warning to heart. She kept her head low. The quiet that followed was both relief and terror.

And now here they are, their resistance shattered, the evidence of their deed obscured. So it fucking goes.

In the meadow, Sarah looks up for a moment from her meal, then returns to eating. Rebecca leans back against the car and pulls her magic in, then expands it back out across her whole body. She imagines her body as a pulse beacon. She can almost feel the source of it, eyes like nebulae staring back at her, but as quickly as she feels the source it slips away again, as evasive as in those early years of life when memory and dream are indistinguishable, like the change itself. If only she could understand what is happening to her, why it is happening. But she can't risk stirring up whatever evil they almost awakened.

Fuck does she need a cigarette.

A minute later, Sarah traipses over and hunches down under the car. Her return to human form is equally fast. She rolls out, and there's no sign of distress, no apparent memory of the change.

Rebecca tosses Sarah her clothes.

28

Rebecca works afternoons and evenings at Anarres Books. She's a roaming worker. She has worked at the small café on the main floor, which is busy on weekday afternoons and on Saturday and Sunday mornings. She's also worked a number of unruly Anarres events: board game nights, murder-mystery role-plays, painting and wine nights, speed dating, speed-dating board game nights, queer speed-dating board game nights, and, of course, movie nights. Rebecca does author events, too, where she is required to do seating arrangements and attend to the author's needs. She has gotten many authors glasses of water. On the events calendars, author events are listed as the name of their book. Too often, Rebecca has puzzled over an event only to realize that it is just a book title. One event, *Murder Your Friends*, had her both confused and excited, only to find that it was a humor book—no friends actually killed during the making of.

Anarres Books sells a lot of science fiction and fantasy because

the original members are all genre nerds. SFF books are downstairs in the basement. On one side of the room is a teensy beer bar (they don't have a full liquor license) and a few tables for sitting; on the other side are rows and rows of shelves filled with genre books. The Le Guin shelf always has *The Dispossessed* displayed prominently, the name of the title's main planet being the store's namesake.

Rebecca enjoys stacking, loves wheeling the cart heavy with boxes of books down every row. She has just finished stacking the Le Guin shelf and is taking her time placing new books in their sections, organizing them among the other books, reading random pages, and taking home a copy or two to make her staff pick selections. Rebecca enjoys autobiographies the most—stories of people's actual lives told by the people themselves—but she is downstairs a lot and has developed a burgeoning interest in SFF. By now, she probably knows the basic plots of several hundred SFF books—she rarely reads the whole thing—many of which are contemporary fantasy novels in which the monsters somehow come out on top. This feels like a mockery of her actual life, where she is powerless. Here, there are no enemies to engage in epic battle, only secluded forests to run through and attention to avoid. She wants to live and be happy, but her story will likely end with her dead one day, as the villain. She will end up in someone's memoir or biography, already dead, all the monsters vanquished.

Rebecca opens one of the boxes on her cart and lifts out a hardcover book. She reads the title: *Dead Things.* The copy on the back cover reveals it as one of those mash-up books—a crime novel in a sci-fi novel. Monsters are created through genetic manipulation, and a murder sends the detective character down a convoluted path that leads him to a dangerous discovery. Rebecca turns the book over. It has a beautiful cover. She saw the advance reader copy when it came through a couple of months back. One of the booksellers

got it from a rep at a trade show. They voted to carry it, but Rebecca wasn't really paying attention to what it was about. She didn't have a vote yet anyway—another three months before her candidacy period is up and she can potentially become a worker-owner.

"Excuse me. Where's the bathroom?"

Rebecca looks up from her book. A man is standing there. He smells like one of those strongly scented soaps people get at hotels. A whiff of sweat carries underneath. She points to the bathroom, tucked behind a corner next to the stairs.

The man smiles, and his mustache obscures his upper lip. She notices something strange about the man's expression, but he doesn't linger. He turns and heads for the bathroom.

Rebecca surveys the room to anchor herself again. She's been stacking books more slowly than she realizes. They have talked to her about this. It is good to appear busy. The bar won't open for another two hours. Once it does, there will be more people, off from work, stopping in for a drink and looking through the shelves. It will be harder to get work done when that happens.

She doesn't see Laina approach, but she does smell her.

"I've been wanting to ask you something, and I don't know how."

"Just ask," Rebecca says, and places the copy of *Dead Things* on the shelf. She reaches in the box for another book and repeats the action.

"I don't know," Laina says.

The same man from before has returned from the bathroom. Rebecca smiles, trying to be pleasant. She watches the man disappear behind a bookshelf. "What is it?"

Laina still hesitates.

"You get a free token to ask whatever you want. Nothing off-limits."

"Would you ever turn someone?"

Rebecca turns and really takes in how nervous Laina looks. She considers lying, closing this door and locking it before they go further. She looks around. No one is paying attention to them. Her voice is even softer now. "Maybe, under the right circumstances."

"What are the right circumstances?"

Rebecca smells the cloyingly sweet scent of soap, but no one is in view. "Sick or dying," she says. Rebecca puts up a finger and listens. The man is standing in the row of shelves behind theirs. He is close, the shelving acting as a thin separation.

Rebecca points in the direction where she knows the man is standing.

Laina gives her an incredulous look.

"Sir," Rebecca says, "are you listening to our conversation?"

No response, but they both hear the footsteps. Moments later, a man bolts to the stairs.

Rebecca looks at Laina's worried face. "It happens sometimes. Nothing I can't handle."

Laina doesn't seem convinced. Rebecca isn't, either. It is just the kind of thing she has to say.

A few months before, Rebecca worked a night shift downstairs. That night, a customer came over to her and said a man was standing by the bookshelves. "He was looking at you," she said. Rebecca had not noticed, and the words had bothered her for days. She was now wondering whether it was this man.

Sometimes, people did recognize her despite everything. Rebecca grew her hair out and bleached it. She wore glasses. She quit her old job, moved out of her apartment building. She abandoned social media. This worked to some degree. Her name appeared on only a few conspiracy sites. Most established news

sources kept her out of print. And still, people recognized her. An odd look on the subway. The occasional horror-struck expression from a stranger on the street.

Rebecca remembers Laina's question. "Why are you asking me this, anyway?" But she knows why Laina is asking, guesses why Laina in particular would ask. "It isn't glamorous to be what we are," Rebecca says.

"I know that." Laina looks around. Apparently, she's caught Rebecca's paranoia. "But I want to understand what happened."

"*I* don't even understand what happened," Rebecca says, but then she looks again and sees that Laina has missed the point entirely.

Sometimes, guilt and loss push a person into becoming more than singular. They split in two to resurrect what they've lost or live in service to what was lost. A lover will take up the mission of the dead partner. A mother might take up a dead daughter's hobby to feel close to her. A sister might flirt with the notion of becoming a monster, to fill in the parts of her brother she doesn't know. *To understand what happened.* Those words are bigger than a single event. They're a question to the universe itself.

Rebecca decides something difficult then. "Come with me tonight," she says. "I want you to meet someone."

29

Rebecca has a recurring dream about her father's hands. She's standing over his coffin and looking at them. They're thin and cracked, with a sheen to them, like varnish. She's wondering how they get his hands to look that way, lifelike but divorced from anything alive. Manufactured. Formed. As if inspired by the thought, the wall behind her father opens up and she sees little people in the back room. They're constructing her father from flour, water, and yeast. She watches her father rise, his dough fingers plumping with air. Then the little people etch the ridges of her father's knuckles with little knives and set him to bake. They pull him out all golden brown and coat him with egg. They use tiny brushes to make their way across his steaming not-flesh. Rebecca reaches down and pulls off one of her father's fingers and finds it spongy inside. "It is okay," the little people say in unison from the kitchen. Rebecca puts the finger in her mouth and chews. Her father's finger crumples softly as her teeth crack the thin crust of skin. It is still warm, the sudden

escape of yeast sticky and rising to the roof of her mouth, the soft, stringy fibers and pockets of air delightfully complex. This isn't her father, she thinks as she eats. This is nothing. The stone on her chest rolls off, and finally she can breathe.

She wakes up from this dream feeling relieved, and this terrifies her more than the dream itself.

These dreams started happening after the change. Rebecca first interpreted them as an animal urge, but she soon shifts to another interpretation, a dangerous thought.

In that chrysalis that turns a person to wolf and back again, the body must heal itself. Rebecca's bad knee doesn't hurt anymore. Her teeth are healthier. Her skin, though it holds on to scars from childhood, heals from new wounds without even a blemish.

Magic is useful, and useful things beg to be used.

When she first gets the thought, it is faint, like the line between water and sky on an overcast day. She smiles at it, looks away. But then it returns again and again and again until there is nothing else.

You can save everyone, is the thought.

No one ever has to die.

30

Rebecca's mother takes a long time to answer the door.

"Mom, this is Laina." Rebecca's face is hot. She puts her hands to her face, and her palms are clammy on her cheeks. "Laina, this is Mom."

"It is good to meet you," Laina says, smiling her very best smile.

Rebecca's mother smiles back, but it doesn't reach her eyes, and her nose wrinkles ever so slightly. Rebecca has never been so keenly aware of her mother's face: the minute actions, the rippling of it, a familiar landscape that turns with unfamiliar life. Strange she didn't know that her mom's nose wrinkled like that.

"Come in," her mother says, and leads them both to the living room.

The room is neat, but boxes have been pushed to the edges, stacked like large bricks forming inner walls within the actual walls of the house. The coffee table is layered with dust everywhere except for a square where something, maybe books, has been cleared away.

Rebecca and Laina sit on the couch together, and Rebecca keeps her eyes on her mother.

"You must be special," her mother says. "Becca doesn't bring anyone by."

"Guess I am." Laina looks at Rebecca and back to her mother. "I'm surprised she brought me here myself."

"Well, that makes both of us. I'll make you two some tea." Her mother presses down a bit of loose hair that has gotten free of her ponytail. Her hair is messy, and the action calls attention to it. She gets up, heads to the kitchen.

Laina leans in and whispers, "Why didn't you tell me we were going to meet your mom?"

"So tell me," Rebecca's mother yells from the kitchen, "how do you two know each other?"

"A common friend," Rebecca says.

When her mother returns a few minutes later, she sets down a tray with three cups, directly on the spot with no dust. "Who's this friend?" she asks, picking up her cup of tea. Rebecca and Laina follow.

"He died," Rebecca says.

"He was my brother," Laina adds, placing her hand on top of Rebecca's.

Mother sees this, and her smile falters slightly. "I'm sorry to hear that."

Nervous, Rebecca pushes her heels back and hits something under the chair. It rattles and clanks. Without thinking, she puts down her tea and slides the thing out. It is a plate filled with bones.

Rebecca quickly pushes it back under the couch. She looks to Laina first, right as Laina's eyes swing up to meet hers.

"I must have forgotten that there," her mother says. She slaps down the cup of tea, spilling some. The landscape of her face changes again—a smile, pulled taut. "I like those rotisserie chickens from the market, you know? Sometimes I'll eat a whole one while watching TV."

Rebecca's favorite thing to hunt is squirrels. They aren't easy to catch for a werewolf whose instincts are still developing, but there are so many of them. Like bobbing for apples, it can be frustrating, but patience and technique pay off.

Her mother has a thing for squirrel heads. It was quick, but she counted four.

Both Rebecca and Laina give her mother polite closed-mouth smiles. "I like rotisserie chickens too," Laina volunteers.

"I really shouldn't indulge so much," her mother says, but the words are empty of performance. She tries fixing her hair, and she's a little more successful this time. Her hair has some gray in it—the same proportion for two years now. "Does she know about what you are?" her mother asks.

It is all obvious now, no use pretending. "Yes," Rebecca says. "Laina knows."

"Why did you bring her here?"

"I wanted her to meet you," Rebecca says.

"I'm not a show pony you can trot out when you decide to," she says, her nose wrinkling again. A snarl, Rebecca recognizes now. Laina drinks some of her tea. The slurp is deafening.

"I should have called," Rebecca says.

"You shouldn't have come," her mother says, the words cool, like slow-acting poison.

"I'll go." Rebecca gets up, and her mother says nothing and makes no attempt to stop her.

Laina puts her half-empty cup back down next to Rebecca's full one. She gets up too. "Nice to meet you."

As they are heading out the door, her mother finally speaks. It is directed at Laina. "Be careful of that one," she says. "Becca does what she wants."

31

For Rebecca's whole life, she's had to fight the smell of tobacco smoke in her possessions. She sprayed her shoes with air freshener. She kept her clothes for the next day hung outside on the porch, waking more times than she could count to find them damp from dew and rain. She would pull out notebooks from her book bag and catch the faint whiff of cigarettes. She once smelled it on her glasses and then spent the rest of high school packing all her accessories in Ziploc bags.

She didn't like inviting her friends over. She could see it on their faces the moment they stepped into the house, sometimes even on the front porch. She tried not to look, tried not to see their expression change, the polite smile they affected for her benefit, but she couldn't help looking. Better to see, better to get it done with right away. Friends still came over anyway, and Dina never seemed to make a big deal about it. "Your house smells like a bar," she said once, and that was it. Rebecca relaxed about it over time,

the flinch of self-consciousness subsiding into a slightly pained ambivalence.

By her teenage years, Rebecca also noticed all the stuff her mother kept around the house. It grew steadily, into towers of dusty boxes and stacks of worn magazines. Rebecca's house was in a constant state of anti-entropy, a forever onslaught of ordered stuff popping into existence. It was a habit her mother had gotten from her own mother, who grew up during the great depression. Rebecca's mother was very organized with her hoarding, and so her father fussed about it, but he came to accept it as the price of their marriage. Early on, he might have tried throwing things away, but that fight had long been settled in some unknown past. Rebecca had also made noise about it, even tried throwing something away from time to time, but her mother had a sixth sense about her things. Once, she came into Rebecca's room and told her plainly, "If you touch my stuff, I will touch yours." Rebecca was going to call her bluff, but then her mother added, "I know where everything is in this house. Every hidden thing."

Rebecca's blood turned cold. She had weed stashed in several places in the house, and a phone she got from Dina with all her "fun" pictures of her doing stuff she wasn't supposed to be doing. And then there were her stacks of erotica. Some were actual books, but most were bound print paper, already showing her preference for steamy queer romance. She hadn't officially come out to anyone in her family, though all her close friends knew she liked girls. Rebecca had decided early on to save that particular fight for college.

Her father had as much finesse as a grenade launcher, but her mother was as precise as a poisoned dart to the heart. She was gifted at quashing Rebecca's will. Too many times, Rebecca would plan to

oppose her mother on something, only to realize that her mother had won that fight months ago with some stray comment. Her mother had trapped her at every holiday dinner by getting her to commit to them before she even had an opportunity to make plans, adding, "If you break your promise, I will hold it against you." If she tried to get out of her commitment, her mother wouldn't argue, just nod silently, and then Rebecca would discover the price much later. A party she couldn't make because she had to babysit her little brother. A friend who couldn't come over, because they had "something very important to discuss," which turned out to be a planned trip to see Dad's mother in Puerto Rico. No one could tell Rebecca this wasn't intentional, calculated steps to checkmate her at every turn. In her teenage mind, her mother was an evil genius.

Only later would she come to understand that her mother was locked in a deep personal struggle. All through Rebecca's childhood, her mother had tried to quit smoking, only to pick it back up in a matter of days. She would get up in the middle of the night to go through a box of stuff, only to throw out nothing. She wrote journals to herself about things she wanted to say to her husband, Rebecca's father, about affairs she suspected he was having. Rebecca's younger brother suffered from severe asthma attacks, and Rebecca had two ear infections when she was a kid. In her journals, her mother blamed her smoking habit for every illness in her household. She might have been right about a lot of it, but some of it bordered on paranoia. She blamed herself for every cold, every fever, even Rebecca's acne.

Rebecca knew this only because her mother left her journal out while she was planning Dad's funeral. In those pages, Rebecca found out a lot of things. She learned that her father had already been sick before she went off to college. She learned that he hadn't told

anyone. He was too worried about the cost of it on their substandard insurance. By the time Mom found out, it had progressed beyond treatment. Rebecca learned the specific illness too: cancer of the lung. Her mother wrote that over and over in her journal, the ink on those pages warped by what could only be tears.

Her mother must have noticed that the journal was missing, but she never asked about it. Rebecca eventually returned it to the living room where she found it. She waited for her mother to ask if someone had taken it, but the question never came. Eventually, she reasoned that this, too, was one of her mother's subtle actions, her mother's way of letting her know everything she carried inside. Rebecca honored that interpretation by never bringing up any of it.

The night after the funeral, after everyone had left their home, Rebecca went over to her mother and hugged her, kissing her on the forehead. "I was a terrible daughter," she confessed. She'd meant to both her parents, but specifically to her mother.

She gave Rebecca a sad smile. "This is life. Don't go rewriting the past out of pain."

Rebecca wanted to tell her mother to take her own advice, but of course, her mother was giving it in hope that it could do them both some good—a spell against the treacherous parts of themselves. It came a little late to do its proper magic, though. The incantation floated like a ghost up into the air, where it stayed, of use to neither, their futures already written in bitter regret.

"Don't get sick," Rebecca said, and when her mother gave her another sad smile, she knew what was coming. If it hadn't arrived, it was on its way.

32

On the long drive home, Rebecca has to break the silence. "Do you still want to be changed?" she asks. "Because if you really want this, you can't hate me if it doesn't turn out the way you wanted."

"I need to think it over."

Rebecca can feel the unspoken hovering between them. "Please just say what you need to say."

The words spill out immediately. "Did you even ask her if this was what she wanted?"

Rebecca shifts into the middle lane and gets stuck behind a slow-moving minivan. "Did I ask my mother if she wanted to become a monster? No, because I didn't want to frighten her."

"It's more than that, and you know it."

"I thought you'd understand better than anyone. If you could have saved Lincoln, even if it was against his will, wouldn't you?"

Laina makes herself small against the passenger-side door. "Your

mother is still here to hate you for your choices, so just acknowledge what you did and stop being righteous about it."

A few years ago, Rebecca would have resented Laina for being right. But at this moment, she chooses to recognize where the words are coming from, the pain at the center of them. Rebecca reaches out again and finds Laina's hand. "I'm not letting go," she says. "I'm sorry but I'm not letting go."

Laina doesn't say anything. She sits there, terribly still.

"I'm going to talk to her," Rebecca says. "Really. I promise."

"Good," Laina says.

Rebecca squeezes Laina's hand. "It isn't selfish to protect yourself from abusive people."

"It is selfish. But it's the kind that looks good on paper."

"You have the right to protect yourself."

Laina doesn't offer another reply.

Rebecca puts her free hand back on the wheel. "Hey. I love you."

Laina wipes away tears and laughs at the same time, a trembling laugh that could just as easily go either way: turn dark or lead to the light. This time, the incantation works. "Yeah, yeah, I love you too," Laina says.

BIRD OF HAPPINESS

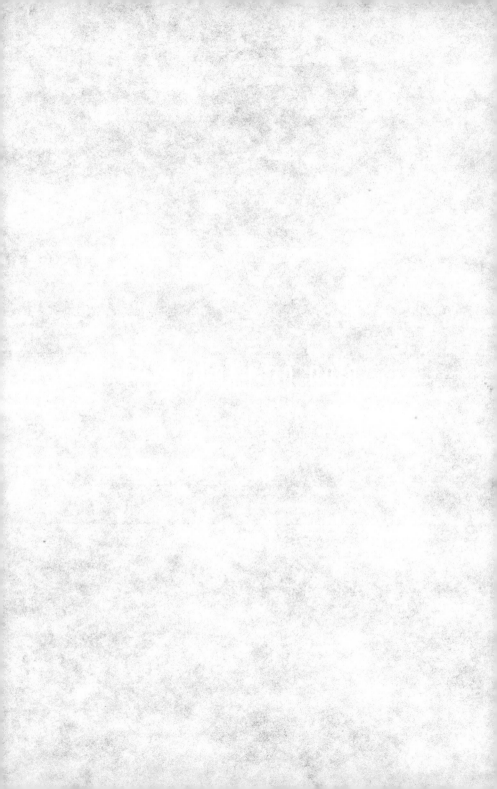

33

RIDLEY GIBSON
INTERSTATE 81

EIGHT MONTHS AFTER THE FRACTURE

Ridley is taking the road down from Boston to Harrisonburg, Virginia. The drive takes him through the Blue Ridge Mountains. Fall is the best time to pass through. The beautiful rolling hills are ablaze with reds, oranges, and every hue of gold, in that liminality between life and death. It is a long drive and a peaceful one, which Ridley passes relistening to podcasts he's already heard. One in particular, a series on the disappearance of the now-famous sociologist Karuna Flood. He lets his thoughts weave through the water of human conversation unencumbered. Airplanes never allow for this sort of expansion; the little anxieties of that passive travel mode create too much static. Flights also force Ridley to limit his preparedness. In his car, he can carry things he only thinks he'll need, like his bag of wood and his carving tools.

When Ridley was a kid, the city was half the size it is now. Over the past couple of decades, Harrisonburg has grown from a smallish Southern burg to a city of about 50,000, in part due to

the influx of immigrants brought to the area by the chicken farming industry. Ridley went to college locally, but his politics led him up north when a friend of his wanted to open a cooperative bookstore. Ridley, seeing it as seizing the means of production, put in a bit of his own money and moved to Somerville, Massachusetts.

He started driving at five in the morning, so it is late afternoon before he gets into the city. The first thing he does is head to Flex Barbershop.

When he walks in, a Black man notices him first. "Did you need something, or you just hanging out?" he asks.

"I was trying to get a haircut," Ridley says.

The other man in the barbershop is stooped over a customer. His back is turned away from the door, but there's no version of Ridley that wouldn't recognize him.

"Regina got a salon down the street," the first man says. "I can give you directions if you need—"

"That you, Riddle?" Marcus still hasn't turned, but Ridley can hear the smile on his face. "I got you. Just let me finish up here."

The man puts up his hands in defeat. "My bad," he says.

"Yes, it was," Marcus says. He stops his work and finally turns his head.

"Been a minute," Ridley says.

"You don't have to tell me." The man in Marcus's chair has his eyes closed in that intimate, completely off-guard way you see only at barbershops. He is so relaxed, he could be asleep.

Ridley takes a seat in one of the chairs near the door. The other barber is sweeping up around his station but continues to glance up at Ridley. He's used to this. Ridley won't give him the satisfaction, instead busying himself by looking around the shop. On one of the white walls is a black frame painting of Muhammad Ali standing

over Sonny Liston, Ali's muscles bulging and his teeth bared. A large knitted rug hangs behind the suspended TV—a portrait of Bob Marley. His dreadlocks are thick black tree roots falling to his chest. Ridley thinks he notices that the canines look a little sharp. On another wall is a black-and-white painting of all the Mafia men: Tony Soprano to the right, a glass of wine in one hand and a lit cigar in the other, the smoke curling like talons. In the center, Scarface points a submachine gun in the air. To Tony Soprano's left, Jimmy Conway sits smirking. To Scarface's left, not one but two Vito Corleones, arranged in different poses. Two small banana plants sit in the storefront window, growing from Chinese vases. Another black-and-white photo, this of the fictional Rocky Balboa in his iconic stair-climbing scene, leans against the storefront wall. Stacks of magazines rise precariously toward the television: *National Geographic*, *Sports Illustrated*, *Maxim*.

"I'm heading out," the other barber says.

"All right," Marcus says.

The man spares one more look at Ridley. Ridley stares back and keeps watching him until he is out of the shop.

Ridley hears the slap of the barber's bib and turns as the man in Marcus's chair is getting up. Marcus whips the bib again to get all the hair off.

The man passes Marcus a twenty. "Okay, now, y'all have a good one." As he leaves, he nods at Ridley.

Ridley smiles. "Enjoy your evening."

The doorbell chimes goodbye.

"Sorry about dude. He's an asshole," Marcus says, walking over to the door. He flips over the open sign and locks up. "You ready?"

In answer, Ridley gets up and sits in Marcus's chair.

Marcus turns on the music system, and "Two Weeks" from

FKA Twigs swells up around them. Marcus drapes the barber's cape over Ridley, wraps a piece of Sanek strip around Ridley's neck, and fastens the cape's collar over the thin paper. Marcus nudges him, and Ridley leans forward for him to tuck the cape between Ridley and the chair back.

"What you want?" Marcus asks.

"Bald fade."

Marcus looks at Ridley's head. "High or low?"

"Low."

Marcus pulls one of the combs out of his Barbicide jar, wipes it off with a towel, and begins combing through Ridley's hair. Ridley watches flakes of scalp fall to the black barber cape. Marcus flicks on the clippers and makes a guide line along Ridley's head, the blade cutting all the way down to his scalp in a thin, even curve from one side of Ridley's head to the back and then to the other side. Ridley closes his eyes when Marcus starts removing the hair below the line.

Kanye West's "All Falls Down" starts playing from the speakers; the base thumps; the sample loops.

Ridley opens his mouth to say something.

"I don't want to hear it. This is classic Kanye."

Ridley laughs. "I was just going to say—"

"Shut up, Riddle." Marcus gets another clipper, this one not as sharp, and holds Ridley's head steady to start blending the fade. "How's Laina?"

"She's good. We got married."

"Congratulations," he says. Marcus continues to blend Ridley's hair into the fade, but he doesn't speak again. He applies force to the side of Ridley's head, moving it in the desired direction, but it isn't enough. Marcus applies more force, and Ridley lets

his neck go slack, eases into the force to let it carry him. This is apparently enough. Marcus moves the blade of the buzzer along Ridley's hairline, and it feels like being stabbed repeatedly with a sharp needle. Marcus keeps going over the same spot, perfecting his line. Ridley winces.

"It was a small thing," Ridley says into the silence. "We got the license at the courthouse. Then we had a little reception in our friend's backyard."

"Sounds lovely. Wish I could've been there." Marcus sprawls his fingers over the entirety of Ridley's head, as if holding a basketball, and twists. Ridley goes slack again to minimize resistance. His neck craned at an awkward angle, he tries to hide his discomfort. He feels the razor again, the sharp sting along his hairline. Marcus uses a soft brush to clear away hair, but his movements are hard, quick. Ridley can see flakes of his own dry scalp falling like snow. He feels suddenly self-conscious.

"What do you wash your hair with?" Marcus asks.

Ridley thinks for a moment. "Whatever cheap shampoo I can get."

Marcus kisses his teeth. "You can't do that. It's not good for your scalp."

He goes over the top of Ridley's head with two strokes of the razor, then three strokes of the brush, evening out the hair on the top of his head. More dry scalp falls, collecting on the black bib. Another four long strokes of the razor and two quick flicks of the brush, scalp raining down before Ridley's eyes.

"Your scalp wasn't this bad before," Marcus says.

"Yeah, I know. I haven't been taking care of it like I should."

"You want to grab a bite after?" Marcus offers.

The subject change catches Ridley by surprise. "I'm sorry. I haven't gone home yet."

"Oh, I'm glad I was your first stop."

Marcus's phone cycles through a few songs, mostly hip-hop, and Ridley listens, letting the moments go by, a heavy silence resting under the thumping base and looping samples. When Marcus is done, he rubs alcohol along Ridley's hairline and releases him from the chair.

"It's on me," Marcus says. "Welcome back, brother."

"Thank you so much."

"I got some things to do before I lock up," Marcus says. "See you around?"

"Yeah," Ridley says. "I'll be seeing you."

Ridley is home in time for dinner. His parents are around the table when he walks into the foyer.

"Just leave your stuff and come grab a plate," his father yells from the dining room.

Ridley gets his plate and joins them at the table.

"Your hair is so short," his mother comments. She reconsiders. "But it's nice, clean-looking. I'm happy to see you've been taking care of yourself."

Ridley doesn't respond to his mother with words, only nods slowly. The gesture reminds him of his father, and he stops mid nod.

"How's the business?" his father asks, as if he's noticed Ridley's attention drifting to him, even with no outward indication.

Ridley tenses at the question. This is what he'd hoped to avoid—the little knives he can't dodge because they seem so innocent. "Good," he says, hoping that will end it.

"You hired any more people?" he asks.

"We voted in another worker-owner a couple months ago. He's a hard worker. Smart."

"How many employees is that now? Seven?"

"Six worker-owners. And a few new people over the last year still on their way to full ownership." Ridley again dares hope that this is the end of it. He looks down at his plate, slices off a bit of chicken breast, and stabs through it with his fork, picking up some of the creamy scalloped potatoes and pulling the mix of savory flavors into his mouth.

"So the business isn't growing, then?"

Ridley chews slowly, looks over at his mother. She is paying careful attention to her peas. "We're growing just fine," he says. "We're investing a lot of our earnings back into the business, buying more books, expanding our community events, pulling in bigger-name authors. We earned enough to give ourselves a two-thousand-dollar raise last year." That last part is a slight embellishment.

"Oh? How much are you making now?"

"Sixty thousand," Ridley says flatly.

His father forks a piece of broccoli into his mouth. It is subtle, like all his father's expressions, but Ridley sees the tiny smirk come and go.

His mother must have seen it too. "Your father and I just want to make sure you're okay. All that's been happening. Maybe you want to make some changes?"

Ridley raises an eyebrow. Changes? Has he secretly begun a life of crime? "I co-own a business. I'm doing something I'm good at. I have a steady relationship. I'm making a difference in my community. What changes are you talking about?"

"Son, we're just looking out for you." His father again. "Times are hard right now and you're so far away. Lots of crazies running around these days."

This is what they do. His father attacks, his mother reframes the entire argument, and then his father picks up the reframed argument as if it were his idea all along. "Just say what you really want to say."

His father puts his hands up as if he's been assaulted. "All I'm saying is, we're worried. Your wife telling us that her brother was a werewolf certainly didn't inspire our confidence."

Ridley gets up. "I work where I want to work. I marry who I choose to marry. And I'm not coming back here to be under your thumb. I have a life. It is mine and I am happy. Goddamn you and your confidences." Partly in anger and partly in shame, he leaves the room.

Upstairs, Ridley falls onto his childhood bed. They've kept his room as it was when he left, and by the feel and smell of his old comforter, they haven't washed it in some time. Ridley is too tired to bother getting a new one. He looks up at a blown-up poster of *The Lathe of Heaven* he printed as a teenager. He can't remember why he didn't take it with him.

Growing up, Ridley didn't like his hometown. He was asexual and trans, with a white mother and a Black father—both upper-middle-class doctors in a town that vaguely resented them and outright resented him. His parents didn't handle any of it well. In order to be "well-rounded," he'd been made to learn line dancing, wood carving, horse riding, pottery, and the piano, which—obvious to him but not to his parents—didn't help ingratiate him with his peers. The wood carving had stuck, but Ridley had excised the rest from his life. As a teenager, he spent most of his extra-extracurricular time in his room reading Emma Goldman and Rudolph Rocker and Mikhail Bakunin, at first so that he could argue with his father at the dinner table, but eventually

because he had learned enough about the world to know that he was an anarchist.

When he was thirteen, he told his parents that he wanted to change his name from Rachel to Ridley. His mother took it hard at first, but eventually adjusted, though she still occasionally forgot when discussing hair and clothes. His father adjusted immediately, which surprised Ridley at first, until he realized that like everything else with his father, it was a calculation. Ridley's father hated his radical leftism, but he was a secular man and presented himself as openly tolerant. Despite her mistakes, his mother had real love behind her acceptance. Ridley suspected that his father was simply trying to win an argument. His father's father, gods rest his soul, was devout and intolerant to the point of cruelty. Ridley's father hated being compared to him, even though they were actually a lot alike.

Neither of his parents was supportive of Ridley's chosen profession. They had always thought he would go into science, and when he changed his major to humanities in his sophomore year, his father stopped talking to him for three months. His mother came around to it but never said as much in front of his father.

And then there was Laina, whom they both had disliked from the very beginning. A nice girl but seems to have very little aspirations. A nice girl but doesn't have a good relationship with her family. Oh, no, we're not saying she's bad for you, of course not, but we'd always hoped you'd find someone who would push you a little. You've always needed a little pushing.

When Laina's brother died and the video came out and was eventually edited to remove her brother's body, Ridley's parents were the first to pretend there had been no final seconds of the police video. They also conveniently misremembered the final seconds of the highway video. Animals behaving strangely, they

said. Rabid dogs. A normal problem, not worth their attention. Laina, of course, was angry at this. So she called them up, told them everything she knew.

Now it was, nice girl, but don't you think she should talk to someone?

Ridley looks back up at the *Lathe of Heaven* poster. It was the first novel by Le Guin he ever read, about a man whose dreams could alter reality itself—a power that eventually passes for a time to the man's therapist, through a device called the Augmentor. Strange how time changes one's relationship to a work. Back then Ridley saw the story as distant from the reality he lived in. Now he sees all the ways reality can be written and unwritten before his very eyes. True reality is scary, and so we've fashioned a pretty substitute, agreed to it. To live within it, people have augmented themselves.

Ridley yawns, turns off the lamp, sets his alarm to five. His parents won't be up until six at the earliest. He can slip out before breakfast. This time, he'll take the poster with him.

35

The series is called *Karuna Flood*, named after the woman herself, and this is fitting since the podcast is only tangentially interested in her disappearance. Little is known about it, anyway. What the podcast focuses on is her life, which is equal parts mundane and strange. The accounts were taken from people who knew the scholar and eccentric at different parts of her life. Classmates, colleagues, friends (or the closest thing Karuna managed to friendship), and neighbors. One neighbor in particular, who, as a boy, had a crush on Karuna. A close friend of the parents. And a lot of material lifted right out of Karuna's blog, where she was at times very intimate.

Ridley knew of Karuna Flood before the podcast. He read some of her work on cooperatives, particularly on solidarity commonwealths—the idea that co-ops could form co-ops of co-ops. Networks of federated cooperatives leading all the way up to national or international co-op cooperatives, and all the way down to a neighborhood co-op grocery store, bike repair shop, or

bookstore. A system of descending and ascending ladders of cooperation, representatives on each rung rooted in some community somewhere.

The idea of a co-op, of people co-owning and -running companies and organizations, apartment buildings and homes and even neighborhoods, was still quite exotic within the popular culture, despite the idea's being anywhere from over a century old to ancient, depending on who you asked. There were over four thousand worker-owned businesses in the United States alone, but people knew very little about how they worked. Few even cared, thinking the idea of cooperative ownership was a lot of magical nonsense, right up there with Communism or Esperanto.

Flood treated the topic like something utterly mundane and logical, which appealed to Ridley because it fit his own experience of co-ops. Her academic papers were as dusty and dull as any other scholar's, but her popular essays were sharp and persuasive. "Imagine a world made of bottom-up networks of cooperation, where power resides in the hands of everyday people," she had written in her essay on the solidarity commonwealth. "No reason to believe it couldn't function just as well as our top-down hierarchies. Or better."

Ridley read only her stuff on co-ops. Her interest in other areas of social organization, the subfield of sociology she was a part of, didn't generate the same fascination—until now, of course, and only because they, too, seem more relevant to his experience.

Some things he learned about Karuna Flood since beginning the podcast:

Karuna was born in Kathmandu, Nepal, on March 7, 1985, and was adopted by an Irish couple. By her seventh month, she was relocated to a small village in Ireland's countryside: Monageer

in County Wexford, population 200. The nearest house was half a
mile away. Her school class had twelve people in it.

Karuna's biological parentage is unknown. On her blog, she
joked that she was descended "from the gods themselves" while
they were vacationing in the Himalayas. What is known is that
her adopted parents were both farmers and that her mother was
the one who had decided not only on adoption but on the place
(Nepal) as well, and on Karuna in particular. "My father went
along with all of it, but he has always been the warmer of my
parents. I've never doubted his love for me. I have always doubted
my mother's love."

In this, Ridley found a mirror.

Her classmates from her school in Monageer referred to Karuna
as "very strange," but said she was also too quietly confident in
her strangeness for it to cause a fuss. Her classmates gave up either
bullying her or trying to befriend her. Bullying would have back-
fired anyway. It wasn't that she had a thick skin. It was more of
a solid, impenetrable wall, letting nothing in. No one could tell
what Karuna was thinking, and that terrified the other children.
She got into a fight once, slammed a boy's head into a desk. It was
the only time and happened only because the boy had touched
her without permission. That was enough. Everyone understood,
Karuna was not to be touched.

She was what people might have called boyish, which meant
only that she did things mostly expected of boys for cultural reasons.
On her own terms, Karuna described herself as a staunch individu-
alist and believed in culture only from the perspective of injustice.
Either way, she explored and played outside a lot and did most
things by herself, even at a young age. Sometimes, she even fell
asleep outside, in meadows, against tree trunks, slumped in the

crook of sturdy branches. "King's chairs," she called them on her blog. Her family had three dogs, and they would come with her, then leave her behind when it was time for dinner. She'd wake up in the middle of the night to stargaze. Karuna's dad had an amateur's knowledge of the zodiac, and he taught her the constellations and the stories behind them and marked off meteor showers on the calendar so they could watch them together.

Her father did worry when she was out there on her own, but her mother never did. "I always know where she is," her mother was known to say in her toneless voice that Judith knew well enough to impersonate in the podcast.

Judith was their daughter by birth. Two years older than Karuna. The podcast producers never found a reason why the parents sought to adopt their second child. They both died a couple of years before Karuna's disappearance.

Judith was the only child who could enter Karuna's circle, and only through being invited in. Karuna was kind to her older sister in that she allowed Judith to love her and hold her and give her kisses "without complaint," recounted Egan, the neighbor boy with the big crush. "Judith was her polar opposite: warm, quick to laughter or tears. Quite a pair, those two."

When Karuna was thirteen, for no reason that was ever made clear to her, they all moved to Baltimore, where Karuna and Judith finished high school. Karuna attended a local university and then Trinity College back in Ireland for her graduate studies. There she studied what would become her life focus: social organization.

From the start, Karuna had a deep suspicion about the world. From her blog: "I always thought it was strange that people went about their day as if any of this made sense. There were huge gaps in the story of it. This world. I wanted to find those gaps. Fill

them." Karuna used her study of social organization to do just that: unearth the "engine of the human world."

At Trinity College, she fell in love with a boy. Alfred was from her hometown, but she did not immediately recognize him. Until he spoke.

"I've thought about you almost every day since I was eight," he said, and touched the scar on his forehead. "I'm so sorry I did that to you."

He must have meant touching her, to which Karuna simply said, "We're even."

He laughed so honestly, Karuna started paying attention. Alfred was handsome enough. Like most things, love first came as a decision: I'm going to look harder at this one.

She finished her degree and came back to the United States with Alfred. They got married, had a daughter. And then Alfred died in a traffic accident, which by all appearances was truly an accident. A driver asleep at the wheel rammed him from behind and he crashed into a barrier.

So it fucking goes.

Karuna didn't date after that. She raised her daughter by herself for a couple of years and continued her teaching, her research, her papers to scholarly journals, and the ramblings on her blog. Many of her blog posts were quite personal, but they didn't gain much of a readership until close to the time of her disappearance. Her academic papers on secret organizations were never sensationalist, so only the most obsessed fans read them. She referenced the known quantities, cited other researchers in the field, made unremarkable claims within her area of study. It was her blog posts that drew attention. She was magnetic in her direct and frank discussion of the subject.

One theory caught the interest of monster enthusiasts. Karuna believed in a shadow society; the emergence of monsters was proof of it. Networks of secret societies, dark organizations, private interests. Maybe even conflicts between secret groups with different agendas for the world. Most of the crazies thought that a single group was responsible for the leaked footage and the suppression afterward. It was Karuna who suggested that it could actually be multiple organizations acting independently. "Perhaps it was the terms of a truce," she wrote in her blog. "A cover-up that served multiple factions."

It was these ideas that eventually got her fired from UMass Amherst a month before her disappearance. And then, on the day before she was never seen again, she dropped her daughter, Alice, off at Judith's house. "I'm going on a work trip," she told her sister. An interview for a new position. Two days passed, and when Judith couldn't reach her, she notified the police.

Most sane people thought she had orchestrated her own disappearance or, at the very least, decided to abandon her life. She was eccentric, and this could be believed. The conspiracy theorists thought she was in a dungeon somewhere for unearthing the truth. Or dead. The podcast treated either theory as a matter of speculation, and like many respectable investigations post–monster emergence, it left out the discussion of whether monsters are real.

Ridley is on his third hearing of the podcast. He read articles about the disappearance. He also followed the investigation, but not religiously. The podcast itself has a small cult following. The true die-hard Karunites hate it. Ridley isn't part of either community. He is interested in Karuna the woman. He wants to find some ethereal connection in her to himself.

As Ridley gets dressed at five a.m., he listens to the podcast.

He is on the tenth and final episode. He continues listening on the forty-minute drive to Elm Tree Intentional Community. He arrives too early for the day's events, so he waits a little way down the stretch of road leading to the farm and finishes episode one. By fifteen minutes to eight, he's on episode four again. He shuts it off and drives the rest of the way down to the farm.

Elm Tree Intentional Community has a four-hundred-acre peanut farm. Several large buildings on the property overlook the peanut field, which stretches on in even lines of green. As he heads down the stretch of road, he sees a digger already out in the field, pulling up peanut plants. A few years ago, on Ridley's first visit to the farm, he was surprised at how close to the ground the plants grew. Wiley, one of the worker-owners, explained that peanut pods develop underground, through a rare process of plant reproduction called geocarpy: "A single plant can grow forty or more peanut pods in the soil. Love those little mud-babies."

The community makes and sells peanut butter through its worker cooperative Peanut Life. They also sell their peanuts at a local farmers' market. Nearly a hundred people live on the farm, run the business, raise families, and share resources. When Ridley first developed his interest in cooperatives, he had no clue there was such a large functioning agricultural co-op forty minutes from his family home. He learned about it only when Wiley joined the collective.

When he pulls up, Wiley is out on the front porch of their main building, talking to an older man. She stands as Ridley gets out of his car. "About time you showed up," she says, and takes him around back to a barn they've converted into a meeting hall. The SEN Collective members are sitting at one long table, eating toast and drinking tea and coffee. The ceiling of the barn looms

like a cathedral vault high above everyone. A large kitchen, long tables, and a lounging area far in the back cut the large open space into thirds.

The SEN Retreat started the night before, but they never do anything on the first night, so Ridley took the opportunity to visit his parents. And Marcus.

"Look who I found wandering around outside," Wiley says, to which the room responds with a chorus of good-mornings.

"We got a certified vegan breakfast going," Nick says with playful affectation. "Come join us."

Ridley sidles up to the group and makes himself a peanut butter and banana sandwich. Seven of the eleven central collective members are in attendance.

"How was the drive?" Melku asks.

"Beautiful," Ridley says.

36

The meeting starts at nine. They sit around the same long table, their computers open, and begin check-ins.

Venda, from Washington, DC, has volunteered as facilitator and starts her check-in first. She has given birth to her second son. Her newborn has this strange tendency to stare at things with a sort of intrigued skepticism. The child has only one true expression: a wrinkling of the brow, which signals either an imminent bout of crying, or reluctant acquiescence. When he is awake, she has to keep him constantly moving or he'll remember his overall discomfort with the world and begin crying. She needed the break and is happy to have it. Her husband will carry on just fine until her return. "Check," she says at the end of her update, and the floor passes to Frankie.

Frankie has just moved out of her father's apartment and into a cohousing complex in rural Connecticut. She likes her neighbors but misses being close to Hartford. She's also taken up painting, which has helped with the adjustment. Check.

Minnesota Mitch has been sick. The flu—nothing serious, but it has meant time off work, which means he is behind on everything and feeling the strain. His worker co-op provides open-sourced web management alternatives to small and midsize companies. There are only three other members, and they've taken on a few clients at once. Not a problem usually, but Mitch has to kick work over to Thomas, whose plate is full, so of course Thomas isn't happy even though he agreed to do it. Check.

Wiley, Elm Trees' very own, has started writing again for the community's blog and is very happy about it. The farm is good. The business is steady. Her two partners are considering having a child together. Check.

Nick, from Rhode Island, has nothing much to report. Things are fine. He is thinking of starting a bookkeeping co-op with another person, but nothing has gelled yet. Check.

Ridley also has little to report, so he mainly talks about the bookstore. They aren't making a lot of money, but they aren't struggling, either. They've taken on a couple of new hires. Books have been weird. More monster-themed books, which are selling like crazy, even though people aren't connecting them to reality. Monster conspiracy books have also been selling well, though most of those have been mail-outs, which is no surprise. Check.

Melku, from St. Thomas, is the last to check in. A lot has happened lately. They've broken up with their partner. It was hard, but they're still working together. Started a new project together, in fact, which has a component that they want to share with the collective. They will explain when it is their turn on the agenda. Check.

"Sorry about the breakup," Ridley says.

"She says there were too many things between us. I suppose she was right."

"So *she* ended it?" Venda asks.

"We both did. For the best."

A nod travels around the table. Ridley has never met Melku's partner and can't remember a name.

At these retreats, after check-ins they always talk about budget, and so, unsurprisingly, they talk about their budget. They have four thousand dollars left after website maintenance and paying Frankie part-time for managing the site, editing, publishing articles and the occasional podcast, and keeping up with social media. They'll be getting grant funding from their two regular organizations, DECS and Virginia Solidarity—two thousand from the former and fifteen thousand from the latter, which should hold them over for the following year. Again they discuss a strong fundraising campaign and recommit to trying it. This year's attempt has produced a thousand dollars and change—not much, but more than they would have otherwise. It will come in handy for reimbursing travel expenses to and from last year's Worker Cooperative Conference in Ashland, Oregon. This year, they want to raise four thousand but figure they'll get half that. They spend some more time going over their list of donors from last year. Most of the big donors—"big" meaning one or two hundred dollars—are long-time subscribers going back years if not decades, when SEN was a quarterly newsletter of articles on solidarity economics. They discuss how they would change that, draw in more donations from younger subscribers. More podcasts, they think. More opportunities to interact with readers. Should they set up a few live streams? Should they do more interviews?

These ideas float in the air as possibilities. Fleshing out their potential will happen over the coming months, with some moving into the "we're serious" pile, which will give them a better chance at

getting done. They are mostly volunteer-run, so these conversations amount to a slow conjuring of power. Someone will eventually do something, and another person will do something else, the progression slow and cobbled together, with some objectives falling away. This is the process: one brain, slowly churning toward small actions.

"We should try to recruit more people," Nick says.

They all nod. They *should* try to recruit more people. Ridley guesses this statement will lead to maybe two recruits. One might stick around for the long haul. That is better than nothing.

Hours pass as they move from budget to fundraising, already behind on their agenda but not minding much. The break for lunch is a half hour late. As they eat peanut-butter sandwiches and cheese and crackers and half-ripe bananas, someone—Ridley doesn't catch who—brings up publishing another book of essays, and Ridley eventually gets pulled in and has to state facts: a print run is out of the question unless they are sure of a strong audience; it will still be better if they try an e-book first, to be safe. "Our last e-book had abysmal sales, though, so we'd really need to market this one."

Venda: "We need to remind people of our other books."

Ridley: "Absolutely. That's marketing. Our budget for that right now is nonexistent, but we should do a fundraiser specifically for promoting our books."

Nick: "Should we get blurbs from some names in the movement? Do new editions?"

Ridley (to both questions): "Sure."

Ridley knows these tasks would be difficult to pull off, but he doesn't say it. Let the difficult fall away in time. Also, he's curious what might come of this particular idea. If Ridley can find the time, several books could use updates. If he could get a grant, he could actually pay some writers to contribute to a new book of essays on

cooperativism. He always wanted to do a submission call for a solidarity fiction anthology. He could print it through the cooperative press they use. As he considers the options, his excitement grows.

Ridley: "Actually, I've been thinking about fiction. Maybe it could work."

Nick: "Maybe. I'm also interested in this project of yours, Melku. Please tell me it could help us get some more subscribers."

Melku: "After dinner."

Nick makes a face only Nick can decipher, and bites into his cheese-and-hummus sandwich. Ridley's attention lingers on Melku. Ridley always feels as though something more is going on with Melku; he just can't tell what.

Random conversation carries them into the afternoon agenda. Logistics for their next conference, still several months out, take them to dinner break. They order food from a Mexican place in town, and Wiley goes to pick it up. More random conversation. In the middle of dinner, Melku gets up and walks out of the barn, no word of where they are going. More talk about books. Ridley starts a draft of a grant proposal. Momentum achieved.

Then it is after dinner and time for Melku's secret discussion. Melku hasn't returned, but no one seems worried. Ridley feels a vague sense of uneasiness he can't shake. As they empty their scraps in the compost bin and divide the take-out containers between the recycling and trash, Ridley keeps glancing at the opening to the barn, waiting for Melku to emerge. Around him, the conversation continues.

Venda talks a bit more about her son. "He takes forever to settle," she says. "And he refuses to sleep through the night."

It sounds like normal baby stuff to Ridley, but he smiles along.

Melku returns fifteen minutes into their scheduled chat, with

someone new in tow. They both stroll up to the table and sit together.

"Sorry I'm late," Melku says. "This is Cassie. She needs to be here for this."

Cassie nods, tries on a courteous smile that doesn't sit right on her face. "Pleasure," she says.

Ridley blinks. Usually, guests are announced before the retreat. This is unusual. Other members are trading uneasy glances.

"I've been keeping this quiet because I didn't want to talk about it online," Melku says. "I wanted to be in front of you. See your faces."

Cassie is not smiling anymore. Her expression can best be described as a sort of vacant sharpness, focused but unsurprised. Somehow, this expression feels more natural. Ridley does not know what to make of this.

Everyone else is quiet, the discomfort palpable.

"I'm sorry to do it this way, but I had to be safe," Melku explains. "I won't waste any more time. Our collective's mission is to support the solidarity movement. Often, that has meant supporting marginalized people. Some of you are people of color, and some of you are part of the queer and trans community, like me. Many of the most vulnerable monsters are also a part of these communities, which is why redefining solidarity to include them is so important. In that spirit, I think we should extend our support to monsters since it is likely that they're already in the movement but have chosen to remain silent."

Ridley feels the reflexive terror move through the room.

Nick and Venda actually twitch.

Mitch and Wiley appear calm, but their eyes go to Cassie.

Cassie's expression doesn't change.

Ridley and Frankie's response is to look to everyone else.

Nick speaks first. "When you say 'monsters,' who do you mean?"

Melku: "Vulnerable ones."

Nick: "And what does that mean?"

Frankie, glancing at Cassie: "Do you know any monsters? I've never met one. I'm not sure they actually exist."

Melku: "Yes. I am a monster. So is Cassie."

Frankie, turning red: "Oh."

Nick makes a face anyone can recognize, somewhere between shock and rage. He opens his mouth to speak, but Venda stops him, reasserting her role as facilitator. "Raise your hand and I'll add you to the stack."

Nick huffs.

This, too, feels like a coping response to the moment at hand. Venda is still finding her way to a response of her own, so she's protecting herself against Nick's with an appeal to rules of order.

Ridley doesn't know what he feels. When Melku said they were a monster, they looked right at him. Ridley doesn't know what he feels about that, either.

Melku: "It has always been dangerous to be a monster, but it is more dangerous now. We need allies."

Nick: "Stack."

Venda: "Are you finished, Melku?"

Melku: "Yes."

Venda: "Okay. Nick, then me."

Nick: "This is fucking crazy. *You're* crazy. Check."

Venda, ignoring Nick: "What would solidarity look like?"

Melku, also ignoring Nick: "Offering help to those who need it. A place to stay. Support through our networks. Protest. Protection."

Nick: "Fuck me."

Ridley raises his hand: "How do we protect monsters if we don't know who or where they are. If they don't know who we are? Check."

Melku: "Word of mouth. Showing up in solidarity. There's a series of protests—"

Frankie, raising her hand: "What kind of monster are you? What kind of monster is she?"

Melku: "Hard to explain. We're not well known."

Nick: "Well, we need to know, so try! Check."

Melku: "I'm a tech mage. I make and manipulate technology through magic. Cassie is a sight mage."

Nick: "A what?"

Melku: "A seer. She divines the future."

Nick, standing up and looking around the room: "What the actual fuck? Are you all hearing this shit?"

Everyone: Silence.

Nick puts up his hands in frustration. "Okay, I'm done. I'll be outside getting a smoke."

Nick pulls a flattened pack of smokes from his hip pocket, and a lighter from his front pocket, then strides off in unhurried steps toward the barn's entrance. They all watch him go, no one breaking the heavy silence. He stops at the entrance as if to say something, but he doesn't turn. Ridley figures by the hunch of his shoulders that he is just lighting his cigarette. He disappears from the doorway after that.

Frankie breaks the silence. "How many kinds of monsters are there? I thought those werewolf people were the only ones."

"*Shifters* are more different than you realize. Different magics." Melku gives "shifters" some emphasis. "And the others," they

continue, "are too many to count or name, though many have already died off." Melku is now being very forthright, a quality that surprises Ridley, since only moments before, no one knew they were a monster at all. Their eyes gleam in the artificial light, and Ridley has to consciously restrain himself from launching up out of his chair in fear.

Of course, Melku's answer only encourages more questions, though no one is quick to ask them. It is like being in a house full of locked doors, things breathing behind each one—no telling which is harmless and which is a creature ready to rend flesh from bone.

"You want to know what happened to the ones no longer with us," Melku says. Not a question. "My point exactly. The world was already dangerous when some people knew of us. It is even more dangerous now that everyone knows we are here."

Another question no one wants to ask: Who knew before?

Melku doesn't answer that one. "Some of us, like Cassie and me, have no other form. We don't appear monstrous at all. It is a title we claim out of solidarity. If we don't scare you, the others shouldn't, either, no matter their form."

Now, that part feels calculated. Is this why Melku brought Cassie, because she doesn't look dangerous? Ridley saw the unedited footage of Lincoln in his werewolf form. He'd never seen anything more terrifying. And Ridley isn't sure he's not afraid of Melku, either, and Ridley is sympathetic, having met others like them. It is presumptuous to think this can go well. Doing it this way would only force people to take sides, revealing at best intimate sympathies, at worst their own monster identities or the monster identities of friends and family. A confession—in person, no less—makes all of them dangerous, puts all of them in danger.

Mitch: "This is a lot to take in."

Venda: "A lot to ask."

Melku, nodding: "I know."

Wiley, who has been quiet this whole time, looks panicked. She did not invite monsters, had not known monsters would be in her barn discussing alliance.

Melku, looking at Wiley: "I am sorry I did this. I wouldn't have if I had better choices."

At that moment, Cassie flinches. It is only a little bit, but Ridley catches it, unconsciously at first; then it rises to the surface like a breaching whale. Even now she seems unaffected by the matters at hand, but something has caught her attention. Ridley sees no other indication except that small flinch beginning and ending in her shoulders.

Ridley looks around. No one else has noticed. Melku doesn't catch it, either, or pretends not to.

The conversation continues.

Venda: "We could post something on the site. Vague but specific."

Melku: "That would be a start. Hard to do more if most monsters decide to remain hidden. And we shouldn't announce what we are willing to do, either."

A conversation has begun, tense and halting. No one is saying they will do any of these things—only that they could if they decide it is worth doing.

Ridley offers no thoughts of his own. He is still focused on Cassie. That flinch—it had a familiar aspect, a specificity that Ridley is trying to pin down.

"We shouldn't discuss anything we would do to help, unless we have a secure channel."

"I can provide that."

There it is. Ridley feels it in himself now that he can name it. That was a flinch of anticipation, not of something happening, but of something that will happen—waiting for the jump scare, the shrill note, the known unknown.

"This is dangerous stuff, guys. We should make sure everyone is on board."

"Nick's not on board. That's for sure."

"I'm not sure I am, either."

No, not unknown at all. This has a fixed point of arrival, after a series of events already known. A horror of causality, the space between the bang of an aimed gun and the inevitable impact. Something has happened. Something is happening still. A horror already caused, the effect a speeding bullet.

Ridley watches the seer's eye dart to the entrance of the barn. "What is it?" he asks. Even as he says this, he knows that the answer will come before she can answer.

A man has appeared at the entrance. *Appeared* is the best Ridley can describe it. One minute, no one is there, and the next, a figure materializes, a cloud of dust forming flesh.

"You're not an easy person to find, friend," the man says. His smile is friendly enough, but the room chills under it, a detectable drop of temperature. No one answers him, but his eyes are sharp on Melku. "You have something that belongs to me."

"I don't think I do, *friend*," Melku says, mirroring the man's easy tone. A not-quite smile presses their lips tight, and then, "Either way, better to settle it just the two of us, no?" Melku's accent is thick now, richer than Ridley has ever heard.

The man chuckles, amused. "Yeah? Just the two of us, eh? You must be playing me for a fool."

Melku's smile is gone. "These people—"

"Are the reason you gon give me what I want." The man's smile slips into something predatory. Frankie gasps audibly.

Melku gets up and steps away from the long table into an open space. "Everyone," they say, "come over here and stand next to me." When no one moves, they yell, "Get over here now!"

The members of the SEN Collective quickly huddle around Melku. "What is going on?" Wiley asks.

The man, amused: "I'm faster than your toys, Melku."

Melku, whispering to Cassie: "How do we get out of here?"

Cassie, her voice flat: "I have never answered that question."

Frankie: "Where's Nick?"

The man: "On the moon." Nothing in his tone indicates that this is a joke. "Oh, there's still a bit left of him."

The man tosses something toward them. It lands in front of Frankie with a wettish thump. A moment passes before Ridley can make his brain understand what his eyes are seeing: an arm cut cleanly at the elbow, the index and middle finger still curved around a phantom cigarette. Blood pours weakly from the open end of the arm.

Frankie screams. So do Mitch and Venda. Wiley falls to her knees. Ridley's mouth hangs open stupidly.

Melku: "Will there be an opening?"

Cassie: "In ten seconds."

The calm of her voice is so incongruous, it startles Ridley into something like attention. The world around him drags as if they've all been caught in pine sap.

The man, smirking: "More than enough time to kill everyone here."

Too many things happen at once.

Melku tosses something into the air.

Ridley's eyes follow it until it stops a few feet above them, hovering: a gleaming metal hoop the size of a wrist bracelet. Immediately, it starts expanding, growing large enough to encircle their whole group. The man darts forward, and Ridley registers him right as he bursts into specks of black dust. He reappears above them, grabbing the expanding metal as he starts to fall, an insane grin on his face.

Melku tosses another metal hoop, which attaches to a wall. Ridley doesn't see this, but he sees the effect: the hoop morphing into a miniature cannon and sending a hyperfocused blast of energy at the man as he falls. The beam hits the man before he can react, and sends him flying, hitting the opposite wall with a loud crack. The sound he makes is more of anger than of pain, and Ridley feels his own body seize in panic. He knows what will come next. He can actually feel it, the man readying his next attack, the tangible drawing in of energy.

But then the man stops and looks up, and so does everyone else, a single expression on every face—a collective gaping.

I am the last to look. I am the last to shatter.

For a moment, I completely shut down; my mind flicks right out, my link with Ridley severed at its root. A short eternity passes when I can't tell where or even what I am. I've been cracked open. I've been pulled underwater.

I don't know how or when, but I return to myself. My sight returns first, then my brain, the machinery grinding and whirring back to life.

What I see is what they all see: the universe itself, stalking across the barn on two legs.

The thing, the colossus, isn't made of anything, though it manifests as the silhouette of a human body, amplified, its head in the eaves. Inside the silhouette is negative space, a hole in the world

that opens into starlight and distant galaxies, with two swirling nebulae where the eyes should be.

I feel myself through the nebulae, my flesh and meat and many cells revealed to me as distinct parts, my atoms turning their seven trillion trillion eyes to those two massive orbs.

Even though the earth is shaking with each step, the footfalls of the colossus are eerily soundless. The ground burns under its feet, scorched black. The thing approaches and then goes *through* us, its attention never leaving the scattered group below it. As it passes, I feel cold electric numbness surge through me, a buzzing settling in the roof of my mouth.

"Now," someone says, and it takes me a moment to match the flat, unsurprised voice to its owner.

With effort, I use my powers to tie myself back to Ridley, just as a string of lights pulls his attention to the floor of the barn. There, he sees, and I see, a solid circle of ants bound head to tail, their hindquarters glowing red. There is a pop, a sudden rush of air, and we're falling through the earth. We don't fall far. Ridley's legs buckle when he lands, sending him sprawling on his back. Pain shoots up his spine. (There is no risk of injury for me when I land, but I feel his pain through the link.) Lying there on his back, Ridley looks up as the pocket in space that we've fallen through flickers away, the singed ceiling of the barn replaced with darkness and echo.

Shallow breaths and screams transform the new environment into a gibbering cacophony.

37

Ridley has lost track of the time. It's the shock, really. No one has moved. They're standing in place or sitting slumped on the floor. Frankie is sobbing. Mitch's panicked breaths have slowed, become steady, and picked up again at least twice since everyone arrived.

What is the right reaction to what they've just experienced? Screaming? Sobbing? Panicked silence? On Ridley's part, numbness. All these things feel reasonable.

A bit of light is coming in from the warehouse windows. The windows have been blacked out, but the material is badly applied and peeling. Moonlight or ambient streetlight enters through the tiny openings, giving the interior some visibility. Ridley recognizes the industrial look of the place, the stale air and smell of sawdust: a warehouse.

Something catches his attention: an object near Frankie's feet. He isn't sure what it is, and then he is completely sure. Nick's hand came through with them.

"I'm sorry. I've made a mess of this," Melku says.

"Not good enough. Tell us what the hell is going on." Venda's voice is shaking in anger, terror, or despair.

"I can't tell you what's going on. Not entirely."

"Why the fuck not? Goddamn it, Melku. You better tell us what is going on, right now."

Frankie screams out, kicking with her legs. Nick's hand budges a little, rolling over in a sticky, heavy way that chills Ridley's bones. Her screams sink into violent sobs.

"This isn't something you can sweep under the rug. He saw our faces. He knew where we were. What's to stop him from coming back to the farm? We have children at the farm, Melku."

Wiley. Ridley had forgotten what her voice sounded like. It has a tinny quality now, as if stretched through phone wires.

"He won't hurt any of you, I promise."

"What the hell do your promises matter? Nick's dead."

Venda again. He can almost see them all, but the blotches in his eyes obscure all their faces. No one has mentioned the thing, the cosmos walking on two legs. Is that normal?

Melku sighs. "My most useful power is information. It is what protects me and everyone I care about. Except when it doesn't. But when my power fails, the last thing I should do is be careless with information. That's when I need it most. Letting you know what I know won't protect you. But letting the right person know what I know, emphasizing the depth of my knowledge, will. You'll be able to go back to your lives because of what I know and you don't. The second part is important. Your ignorance buys your safety. Look, I fucked up. I know that. But if I tell you anything right now, you'll never make it out of this. Believe me."

"I don't," Venda growls. "You were going to have us help

monsters without telling us about the danger, and now you want us to *believe* you? I have a family, a husband and two sons. I don't give a fuck about your powers. That doesn't give you the right. Nothing does. Tell us what the fuck is going on, or leave this collective."

Ridley turns to the spot where Cassie sits silently. "What was that thing?"

The room holds its breath.

Cassie shifts subtly, the black mass of her body shifting toward Ridley. "A lesser god. Or a great one, depending on your frame of reference. Timeless, and occasionally curious. We were . . . *curious*."

"Why?" Ridley asks.

"I have never answered that question."

There it is again, that odd declaration. She said exactly the same thing to Melku in the barn, right before that thing showed up. Not that she can't answer or won't answer. *She has never answered.* What a strange construction: a statement in the present perfect tense, yet oddly deterministic.

"Will I see it again?" Ridley asks as a test.

"I have never answered that question."

Ridley thinks he understands now. Some answers are *blocked*. If he wants answers, he'll have to ask the right questions. He clears his throat, tries again. "Will we ever find Nick's body?"

"No."

Silence lingers then, the revelation sinking in for everyone.

Ridley chooses his next question carefully. "How many other things like that are there?" Of course, he wants to know what a lesser god is or what "god" means, but he has a feeling those are blocked answers.

Cassie answers this one too. "Hard to say, really. Some gods can't be counted in human terms. But broadly speaking, not many."

"Where are they?"

"I have never answered that question," she says.

Ridley can't say how, but he feels Cassie's attention on him magnify. She is amused. He has somehow caught her interest.

"You're very clever," she says.

Melku cuts in. "I'll leave the collective. At this point, I think it is safest for everyone. But promise me you all will stay quiet about this. I can't protect you if you don't."

Venda folds her arms. "I don't appreciate being threatened."

"Not a threat. Just the truth."

The room falls back into silence, but there is a tangible feeling of relief since the conversation has shifted to terrors that everyone can partly understand.

"Who'll tell Nick's family what happened?" Wiley asks after the short silence.

"I will," Melku says. "As much of it as I can. And don't worry about your intentional community. I will take care of that, first thing. But I'll need to send you back there so I can get to work."

"How will we get back?" Frankie asks. Her voice still has that rattled quality. Of them all, Ridley thinks she will be the least okay after this.

Melku seems to know this too. Their voice is quiet, gentle. "I'm sorry, but you'll have to leave the same way we came in."

38

Marcus opens the door, and his face changes immediately. "You okay, man?" he says, making room for Ridley to enter.

Ridley takes a moment to look around. Marcus has a sparse living room—neat but a bit bland, like the inside of his barbershop. He's had no time to prepare, so this must be the normal state of things. Riley tries to remember what Marcus's place looked like all those years earlier when they were trying to change the world. Ridley can't make this apartment fit with that blurred image of Marcus in his earlier years. Either his friend has changed, or he has.

Ridley sits on the couch, a white, pleathered thing that squats close to the floor on short, stubby legs. Marcus brings him a glass of water. Marcus doesn't say anything, doesn't ask what has happened. He only takes the seat next to Ridley. Marcus leans against the arm of the couch, watching him.

"I can't talk about it yet," Ridley says.

"We don't need to talk about it." Marcus leisurely picks the remote up off of the table and presses "play" on the movie he is watching. He gets up and returns with a bottle and two glasses, pouring blood-colored wine into each glass until it threatens to spill over. Ridley carefully lifts his glass to his lips, and so does Marcus. Watching him, Ridley's mind empties like an unplugged basin. He looks away.

On the screen, a bird has just changed back to human form. It is quick and boneless, like the worst kind of CGI. Ridley looks up and sees the Titan, her eyes whirling. Dizzy, he puts down his glass of wine.

"Have you ever met a shifter?" Ridley asks.

"Have I?" Marcus repeats, surprised at the question. "Is that what people call those animal people?" He shakes his head. "No. To be straight with you, I'm not even sure they exist."

"So, you're a monster denier, then?"

Marcus picks up his glass again, takes a small sip. Then he leans back, looking at Ridley, measuring something. "Okay. You know about flat-earthers, right? Don't get me wrong. I know the earth is round. But I can empathize with the desire to hold things firm in your own hands. I've seen monsters the same way I've seen pictures of space. It makes sense to leave some room for doubt, to be uncertain. I'm agnostic about almost everything, so yeah." He sips his wine, shrugs.

"You don't believe in space?"

"I do. That makes sense. That's science. But the world is asking me to believe in magic. That gives me mad whiplash."

Space has legs, Ridley thinks. Cold hands are around him and he's being brought up into the Titan, and then suddenly he is falling in the dark, his wet eyes turning to blood-burst crystal, his face

crackling and turning black with frostbite. Ridley does not have the luxury of disbelief.

"My wife's girlfriend is a shifter," he says.

"Wait. Your *what* is a *what*?"

Ridley doesn't say anything, only smiles.

"Shit. She know you know?"

Ridley nods. "We're open."

Marcus freezes in place as if he's lost power. Ridley knows where he's gone. Again they have hit up against their essential difference. Ridley's view of closeness and within-ness was never the same as Marcus's, and all those long, painful conversations from years ago were still wedged between them. Even back then, up close, Marcus couldn't understand Ridley's asexuality. And now, at a distance, he's getting it wrong again, assuming that it was Laina who had decided to have sex with other people because Ridley wasn't interested.

But the truth is much simpler. Laina and Ridley had found each other exactly as they were, and loved each other still.

"I saw something tonight that terrified me. Can I stay the night?" Ridley watches Marcus and sees a mix of emotions cross his face. Concern, of course, but something else too.

"You don't want to go back to your parents'?" Marcus asks.

Ridley shook his head.

"What is this?" Marcus asks. His gaze is direct.

"Just a night. I'm not asking you to do anything but let me be here."

Marcus makes a face Ridley remembers well, and it breaks his heart again as if no time at all had passed.

"I'm sorry."

"We good," Marcus says. He smiles and touches Ridley's

hand. A silent pact, then: to be a little of what they both want for the night.

Without hesitation, Ridley curls into Marcus's arms. As they hold each other, men, who are also birds, fly into a limitless sky.

39

When Ridley wakes in the morning, Marcus is lying shirtless next to him, his muscled back to Ridley's face. The light from the window shines on the scar there, right above the blade of Marcus's shoulder, the line smooth and gleaming like a fresh-minted penny. Ridley reaches out to touch it.

College protests and rallies bleed together in Ridley's mind, but the memory of that scar is distinct, vivid from any distance. The day he got the scar, Marcus had punched a fascist in the face and received his own gift. The blade of the man's hunting knife went deep. Blood bloomed like oil from rich sands.

By the time the ambulance arrived, Ridley was painted with his friend's blood. He'd confessed everything to Marcus for the first time that day. "I love you." "I want to be with you." "Please don't go."

Marcus lived, but none of it would come to pass. When they had the time to say what they wanted, they learned they wanted different things.

In bed, Marcus sighs and turns, but his eyes don't open. For minutes, Ridley watches the sleeping face and long, curving lashes. He is even more beautiful in sleep.

Ridley imagines the Titan walking across the room.

He quietly slips out of bed, goes out to his car, and returns with his woodworking bag. Sitting down in a chair in the living room, he lays out his mat to collect the shavings, then takes out his multitool pocketknife, his thumb guard, and a moist cube of white cedar. He begins his bird of happiness by rounding off the edges of the wings, in the Russian tradition. He starts on the inter-lock, using his knife to score the wood on each side, so the block looks as if two little mouths had bitten into it. Next, he carves the wood down to a thin point to create the hinge for the feathers. He'll need to do this again, getting it down to the thickness of a toothpick, but he still needs some leverage for carving the body of the bird. He turns the tips of the feathers toward him and begins riving them. Cutting along the wood is almost as easy as carving through butter, the fibers splitting apart as the knife goes deep into the block. Each feather looks like a cross between a wooden tasting spoon and a throwing knife.

Several years ago, Ridley went to a workshop in Plymouth, Massachusetts. A woman there had made the birds for many years, and she gave everyone a demonstration.

She was this quick, anxious old lady with arthritic hands that affected the way she worked. Ridley was used to seeing people make wood carvings with a standard set of cutting techniques, but the woman wasn't using any of them. She sat on a shave horse and worked the wood with both arms, using a drawknife. Ridley was struck by how crude her movements were because he knew the finished piece she was making. She didn't seem to be doing a

great job. She started pulling the feathers apart, and some of them would flake off in her hands. Then she pushed everything into place and held up the bird. Ridley actually gasped.

It took her ten minutes to make the bird, but the carving looked as if it had taken months. After practicing it himself, Ridley learned the trick and could work a similar magic. He still wasn't as fast as the old woman, though. If he starts out with a block he prepared in advance, it takes him at least twenty minutes. He likes bird carving because it isn't a finesse project. He doesn't have to think too hard. Once you know the trick, it is simple manipulation of the wood. All you have to do is execute the movements, like in a slow dance.

This bird's body is more impressionistic than Ridley likes. He brought only his pocketknife, so he is relying on crude movements. The bird has a nice round belly, and since the wood is good, he carves the beak to a point. A hummingbird, then. He doesn't know this going in; the wood makes the decision for him. He carves two holes for the bird's eyes.

"Good morning," Marcus says.

Ridley looks up, sees his friend leaning against the wall. "Hey."

"What are you doing?"

"Making a bird of happiness," he says. Ridley sees that Marcus isn't satisfied, so he tells him the story he's heard, how in northern Russia there was a long winter and a hunter's son fell ill. It looked as though he might die. The hunter asked his son what he wanted before death. "To see the sun," his son said. It was too far north, and the hunter knew that his son would die before he saw the sun. But seeing the embers glowing in the fireplace, the hunter had an idea. As his son slept, he toiled all night, working a piece of wood into a bird. He hung the bird over his son's bed. The bird began to spin on its string, brought to life by the heated air rising from the fireplace.

When the boy opened his eyes and saw the bird, the light from the fireplace shining on its wings, he started to cry with happiness. "Here's the sun," the hunter said, and in the days that followed, the son miraculously recovered. People had been making these birds ever since.

"That's beautiful," Marcus says.

"It's just a story, but yes, it is."

As Marcus watches, Ridley returns to the feathers and shaves the hinge down to a nice point. He makes a judgment, separating the tail from the wings, and then begins the alternating pattern of interlocking feathers: one to the right, then one to the left, and again and again until the bird looks as if it might take off from his hands and fly into the air. He does the tail the same way, only this time he interlocks feathers to the left and right of a central feather. He has rived the feathers nice and thin, so the spread of the tail and wings is gorgeously full despite being crudely cut. He loops a piece of string around the bird's back.

"You want it?" he asks Marcus.

"Absolutely," he says. "Thank you, Riddle."

Riddle. That nickname still works so well on him.

Marcus drops down on the couch. "Hey, you hungry? I was thinking we'd go to IHOP."

"IHOP," Ridley repeats.

"Don't start. I'm taking your bougie-ass to IHOP whether you like it or not."

• • •

Ridley doesn't make it back to his parents' place, but after he gives Marcus a lingering hug goodbye, he texts his parents to tell them he's heading back to Boston.

Your father and I thought we'd see
you before you left.

Ridley apologizes. Easy to seem genuine in a text.
His father texts back:

Be safe, son.

I will.

He could have said, "No one is safe, not really." He could have said there are things in this world that can pull you apart and turn your body to smoke. That the universe sometimes walks on two legs and peers at you through distant clouds of stardust. But that won't do either of them any good.

We love you.

His mother again.

I love you, too. Take care of
yourselves.

It is interesting, the reversal of roles. He means "take care" the way a parent might. He understands a danger they do not and is shielding them from it, keeping them in the dark so they stay in the light.

Or perhaps, Ridley means "take care" as a child might, in that precise moment when the child understands that he knows more

than his parents yet must pretend otherwise for their sake. If they don't know the darkness by now, a good son would know better than to lead them there.

Better to say, "Stay in the light. I'm going to wade in deeper now. It is different here from what you think. No, I can't explain. I'm closing the door behind me."

DEVOTION AND MADNESS

SONDRA REED
ST. THOMAS, USVI

NINE MONTHS AFTER THE FRACTURE

"Really," Senator Reed says. "You were excellent today."

Sondra has already finished an entire glass of water and is now sipping on her strawberry daiquiri, which has the kick of too much rum. Senator Reed has already finished his rum punch. They're at Hookline and Sinker, a restaurant in Frenchtown, right on the water, and it has been a while since they ordered. Somehow, they've managed to spend all their time so far talking about the session they both just escaped. Most of the conversation has been specifically about her.

This was what Reed wouldn't shut up about. At the day's Senate session, Sondra had interrogated WAPA's executive director. For almost two weeks, the Water and Power Authority workers had been on strike, so Sondra asked what she thought was a fairly obvious question: Had he gone out and talked to the workers? The executive director sweated and stuttered through a reply: No, he had not. "Don't you think you should?" Sondra asked in response. The

director was so flustered, he actually said, "Yes." He would not actually go out and talk to the workers, of course, but the session had been recorded, which meant his feet could now be held to the fire. It was a minor win after waiting half the day for her opportunity to question the man.

Sondra doesn't take compliments well, nor does she think this a big deal. This is the job, after all. She is already tired, and all that her efforts have earned her is this awkward dinner meeting with Senator Reed. It is the second time today she has doubted her choice of profession.

"I don't mean to be rude," she says, "but—"

"Get on with it?" he says, laughing at his own perceptiveness.

Sondra gives a polite smile. It is hardly clairvoyance if you set yourself up for it first.

"I think we could help each other on policy, Senator Paige." Despite his formal speech, Reed has all the markers of a St. Thomian born and raised, the long *a*'s and *o*'s, the dropping of certain consonants.

Sondra has these, too, though less noticeably after long effort. She sips her daiquiri. "Oh, that's what this is about?"

He laughs again, sounding nervous. Sondra replays the conversation in her mind. Has he been nervous this entire time? She isn't sure, though it would explain the bush they're beating around.

"Statehood," he says.

No wonder he is nervous. "Even if you drum up enough local support, it won't move that stone uphill."

"Why? Because we're Black?"

Sondra gives a little sigh. "We still need a constitution. You saw how that went the last time. And even then Congress doesn't have to do anything. They didn't let Puerto Rico have statehood, and

they actually *have* a constitution." She has a feeling that this is only half the problem. She figures territorial status has economic and political advantages for wealthy mainlanders as well: a place to stash money, hoard land, and influence local politics from a distance. Maybe territorial status also allows more freedoms when it comes to covert US operations in the Caribbean, past and present. The first thought, she might say if she had a couple more drinks in her; the second was something she would never say out loud. Ever. "It is not going to happen. Try something else."

"Maybe it won't happen now. But in a couple years, with the right leadership, who knows?"

Sondra laughs. Of course that's what this is. She looks down mournfully at her daiquiri. Done already. She'll have to order another before the food comes. The senator is staring at her, waiting. She'll have to give him something. No way around it. "How do you know I don't have my own plans for the governor's seat?"

"If we both run, it'll split the vote. We're too similar."

"Are we? I'm not the one wasting time on statehood."

"What would you waste your time on?"

Sondra stops smirking. She tries reading the man's face again. The nervousness she thought she read in him moments before is gone. "It depends on what you're running on. Care to share?" He looks nervous again. It could be an act, but she can't tell for certain, and it seems to ebb and flow like the tide, which makes her nervous, too.

"Okay," he says. "Territorywide universal health care, a basic income, and a job guarantee."

Why did she agree to come here? This man is clearly insane. "You can't get all those passed, Senator. You'll kill your bid."

"Well, what about you? What you got?"

He is a moron if he thinks she'll divulge her whole strategy. "A word of advice. Don't shout your idealist plans to the world. The idealists will hear you, but so will all your enemies. They'll rise up and attack you, and you'll spend half your energy fighting them. A subtle hand gets more done."

Senator Reed folds his arms. "So you're a pessimist."

"I'm smart," she counters.

"I don't play games. I tell people what I'm going to do. That's how you build trust."

"It's also how you shoot yourself in the foot."

The waiter finally arrives with their food.

"Just tell me one thing," Reed says, and something in how he says this makes Sondra look at him with sudden suspicion.

Perhaps, he knows more than he's letting on. He can't know about the monster legislation, can he? Who would talk? And he doesn't have a history of monstrosity in his family tree. That she knows of. Too early for allies—the pieces aren't in place yet. Maybe she can offer a glimpse of the other thing, the part of the plan that looks like harmless economics. If she does, she'll have to run, so he can't press her. At least, not right now.

"Okay," Sondra says. She turns to the waiter. "Can I get this to go?" The waiter stares at her—a bit of confusion and thinly veiled annoyance—but then retreats back to the kitchen. Senator Reed opens his mouth to protest, but Sondra cuts in. "I am going to develop a solidarity commonwealth here in the Virgin Islands. Be my lieutenant governor and I'll tell you how I'll do it." The waiter returns with her container, and she starts to dump her burger and fries inside.

"Wait a second. What the hell is a solidarity commonwealth?"

So he didn't know about that. What a waste. Sondra smiles,

stands. "Look it up. I'll reach out in a couple months to see if you're on board."

Senator Reed continues watching her as she leaves. Sondra adds him to her mental list. In those final seconds, she picked up something subtle worth investigating. There's a monster in his family tree. She'll need to root it out.

When Sondra gets home, she smells her sister before she even opens the door. She doesn't say anything, only enters, putting down her food on the bar table. She doesn't bother with the light. Even now, after all this time, Sondra prefers to speak to her phantom sibling in the dark. Flicking the light on will only make the experience stranger. A voice coming from the dark makes a certain sense, but with the light on, she can't trick her mind into accepting the impossible fact of something coming from nothing.

Sondra takes a pen out of her purse and hurls it at the couch where her sister always sits, but the pen hits the back cushion and falls onto the seat before rolling off to the floor. Okay, so not there, then. She sniffs the air again. Yes. She was sitting on the couch, but . . . why the hell is she in there? Sondra walks to her room, opens the door. Her sister's scent floods her nose. Curled up on the bed is a concentrated knot of her sister's strange magic.

"Sonya, get up," she says.

The bed creaks, the comforter shifting like the stirring of a stingray on the seafloor. "I'm sorry. I fell asleep."

Sondra sits on her bed where the comforter doesn't squirm. "What is it?"

"I found her," she says.

"Who?" Sonya is silent for a moment. Sondra hates when she does this. There is no telling what she's doing in that silence. "Come on, spit it out."

"You must have wondered. There were no bodies. Must've thought, *maybe, somewhere out there.*"

Sondra turns to the spot where her sister should be. The comforter ripples and settles. A flurry of thoughts struggle to escape all at once from the tiny window in her mind. She cracks under the strain, the dominant thought forcing itself out: "Where?"

"Medford, Massachusetts."

"How did they get there?"

"She," Sonya corrects. "Only Mom."

"Where's Dad?"

"I don't know."

Sondra tries to digest this bit of information. "This is serious. You better not be keeping anything from me." Sonya is silent too long. "Swear to me."

"I can take you there tomorrow night," Sonya says—a clear and obvious deflection. The invisible woman and her many secrets.

Sondra wants to ask, *why not now, why not tonight?* But she knows there's an answer waiting, or a nonanswer, and either way, it will still be tomorrow night, because in this her sister has all the power. Sondra holds the hatred down deep so it can't hurt either of them. "I'll be ready," she says.

Sondra was an only child until she was seven. Her parents doted on her, amused by her every action. She shone under their attention. Her mother and father both came from families strong with the gift, so they weren't surprised when Sondra started showing signs of a keen nose and sensitivity to magic.

"Our daughter," her father said to her mother when Sondra first picked up their scent. He was glowing with such pride.

One night, she woke up and caught the scent of strange magic in the air. She sat up in bed, stared into the darkness. Nothing was there, but Sondra felt the chill of warning slide through her.

She got up and turned on the light. Nothing still, but her door was slightly ajar. She kept her door closed. She walked over, closed the door, and turned off the light, then smelled it again on her way back to bed.

Sondra woke the next morning to her father watching her.

He was just standing there, his entire body tensed in anticipation. "Don't move," he said.

And then she smelled it again, that same touch of wild magic, only closer now, right in her nose, so ripe it burned. She slowly turned in the direction of the smell, and that's when she saw it. Something solid had been lying right next to her, was now lying next to her. The bedsheets squirmed, moved by something that appeared as nothing.

Her father growled.

"I'm sorry," came a small voice. "I didn't know. Please." It was a young girl's voice, and she was crying.

In her skin, the girl was an accumulation of disturbing parts: skinny arms and legs, distended stomach. Her face was a sunken thing, dark circles around protruding eyes. The girl reminded Sondra of an owl, hardly blinking in her quiet observance of the world. Sondra imagined the little girl in other people's houses, in their corners, watching them eat or sleep or use the bathroom. Those same owl eyes, seeing everything.

It made Sondra itch, that knowledge, and she couldn't help but imagine all the private things the girl might have glimpsed when Sondra didn't know she was there. "We would have noticed," her father said, flaring his nostrils, but Sondra found no comfort in that. She remembered that night, sleeping beside her and not knowing, those owl eyes on her as she dreamed.

They eventually named the girl Sonya. Her father sat Sondra down and said, "She is a soucouyant. Do you remember the stories I told you about them?"

Sondra squirmed in her seat. Yes, she remembered: creatures who could remove their skin and live off blood. It was old magic, like hers, but rarer. They were also supposed to be extinct.

"She has no one to care for her, no one to keep her safe."

Sondra knew the rest before he got there.

"We've decided to take her in. It's done."

Now Sondra and Sonya would share a room. Twin beds on opposite walls. Now the owl eyes would watch her sleep every night.

Sondra tried to protest. "She is your sister now. Be a good sister," her mother said.

Sondra had tears in her eyes. "I don't want a sister."

Sonya was sitting at the kitchen table with a bowl of Froot Loops, watching the whole argument play out in the living room.

Sondra's mother glared at her. "I won't accept this behavior." Sondra didn't dare say another word.

That first night was terrible. She twisted and turned, unable to sleep. Sonya wasn't a talker. She was used to running around at night, so she wasn't sleeping, either. Sonya just sat on her bed, so still, so quiet, her breath a whisper.

Sondra wouldn't speak, either. It was a war waged through silence. Weeks of it. No exchanges between them. As time passed, Sonya got healthier, her face filling out, arms and legs strengthening. She was beginning to look like something nearer to human. Sondra's parents doted on the wretched girl, making sure she was clean and fed. They were teaching her how to read and write. They were buying her clothes. Sonya liked to watch the news, so they watched it with her every night. Sondra spent a lot of time in her room, which was also now Sonya's.

Sondra extended her silences to her parents, rejected their shows of affection, ignored their apologies for spending so much time with Sonya, their calls for her to "make Sonya feel at home." It wasn't Sonya's home, and they weren't Sonya's parents. She was a monster they had to stop from removing its own skin at night.

Several times, they found the skin lying around the house and had to sniff her out or else wait for her to return for it. Sondra hated the sight of it: pink on the inside, rubbery and wet, the soft hairs sticking out from pores, the greasy smell like burnt oil and raisins.

She held her grudge for months, trying to wait them out, make them suffer so they'd get rid of the girl. Sondra could not imagine ever loving Sonya as a sister. Sondra was young and never considered time with her parents to be anything but infinite. They would eventually return to loving her and only her, she thought, and their lives would continue in uninterrupted love forever.

On all counts, she was wrong.

Uncle Luke's three-story eggshell-white house sits on the crest of a steep hill in Solberg. The main road passes behind the house, and in classic island fashion, the top floor is at street level and facing away from the house's coveted view of Charlotte Amalie Harbor. Not uncommon for a hillside home that must attach itself to the existing road system however it can. Her uncle lives on the bottom floor—his adult children occupy the other floors—so Sondra has to take a long flight of stairs down from the street to a landing that turns onto his front porch. As she reaches the bottom of the stairs, she can smell her uncle's magic, strong and familiar, rich and generations deep. The magic of her family.

Her uncle is on his porch, sitting in a lounge chair, one of those flimsily made things meant to resemble the sturdier variety one might see poolside or at a beach resort, but which clearly isn't. He's stirring a sweating glass of something pink, the ice cubes clanking. Likely grapefruit juice and raspberry rum—her uncle's favorite drink, God knows why.

On this side of the house, Charlotte Amalie Harbor is revealed in all its glory. Sondra's uncle only glances over to her for a moment before returning to the view. Since he retired from housebuilding, Uncle Luke spends all his time on his front porch. He built the house with his own hands, the construction lasting decades, so Sondra can't fault him for enjoying the fruit of his efforts every chance he gets. She leans on the porch railing and follows his gaze. Neither one speaks. From here, Sondra can see cars moving along Waterfront, and the cramped buildings of downtown Charlotte Amalie. Luxury boats idle near Yacht Haven Grande, and a cruise ship is on its way out of the harbor, moving slowly past the edge of Frenchman's Reef. Sondra watches the smoke rise from the ship's funnels, and the way the surface of the harbor glistens in the afternoon sun.

"Good riddance," Uncle Luke shouts to the broad back of the ship. Then, without looking at her, he says, "Must be something important for you to be gracing me with your presence." It has its usual humor in it, so Sondra just smiles, not bothering with a reply.

She leans on one of the sturdy concrete columns of his porch. "How's the leg?"

He grunts in his characteristic way—sharp, the sides of his mouth curved in a deep frown. "You know better than to ask."

Uncle Luke is at least in his seventies, though he has never given a straight answer about his precise age. He looks to be in his fifties— full head of hair, the white coming in nicely. Whatever damaged his leg must have happened a long time ago. The musk of dark magic and the fact that it hasn't healed point to a curse of some kind, but Sondra has never been able to get the truth out of him. The pain gets worse as he ages, and eventually—maybe in a decade or two— the curse will take his ability to walk. Their kind can live very long if

they do everything right. Not forever. Not like her sister or some of the other shifter variants. Her uncle will die someday, and so will she.

"So, what really brings my famous senator niece to my doorstep?" Her uncle puts his glass down and finally shifts his entire attention to her.

"You know anything about the Reed family?" she asks.

"A little, why? You found something out about the senator?"

"More like I intuited something. He didn't have the smell of magic, but I could almost—I don't know what . . . feel something."

"That might simply be attraction, dearie." Uncle Luke laughs.

"Don't start."

"He seems like a good man, is all I'm saying. Sometimes, the magic gets to talking if you're willing to listen. Your magic might be telling you something."

"He's a colleague."

"And that matters how, with all the mess a'you senators get up to? Don't play me for no fool. I hear everything. At least you're not married."

"Uncle," Sondra says. "Just answer my question, please."

He chuckles to himself, as he always did when he thought he'd figured out something she hadn't yet. "Okay, okay. I'll answer seriously. There's some obeah business in his background, from way back when. The strong ones are all dead. He may have a little sense magic—could feel a storm coming or sight a bit of misfortune heading his way, but nothing he'd be able to name."

Obeah, the term for the magics of the West Indies. There were strong Caribbean witches once. All gone or dragged into hiding. Maybe that, too, had something to do with the societies.

Uncle laughs again. "He'd be a good addition to the family line, though. Yessah!"

"Close your mouth, Uncle. You catching flies."

Her uncle chuffs a little. Then his eyes thin with suspicion. "Now, what did you really come here to ask me? Don't look at me that way. You might be able to fool them people with that guard you put up, but you forget, I raise up your mother all by myself. Where you think you got your good sense from?"

Something in Sondra's face snatches the rest of his good humor right out of him. "What is it?"

"Sonya says she's found her."

"Found who?" he asks, but Sondra knows the question is out of disbelief, not uncertainty. "Where? How?"

She shakes her head. "Who knows? She doesn't tell me anything anymore. Even about this. But she says she is up in Massachusetts."

"Tell your sister to come see me."

"You know she won't."

"Those people she be with are dangerous."

"Uncle. Focus."

He chupses his teeth but looks away from her, working his jaw as if he had food in his mouth. Sondra knows the expression. All those times as a teenager and as a young woman when she brought up her parents in conversation. She thought her uncle's strange response was anger and bitterness. Now she knows what it really is: defiant pride masking shame.

"You told me they were dead," Sondra says.

"I thought they were."

Sondra considers spinning him around but instead steps in front of him. His eyes still do not meet hers. "Now lie to me face," she says, her accent coming in strong. "Did you know they were dead?"

"We couldn't find them, couldn't even pick up their scent." He looks up, swallows, changes his approach. "You were having

nightmares." Sondra keeps up her glare. "No," he admits, "I didn't know they were dead."

"I believed you."

"I loved your mother. Your dad and I butted heads from time to time, but I loved him too. I loved you children more. I won't apologize for that."

Sondra leans against the porch railing and curses. "You lied."

"It wasn't a lie. I don't see it that way."

"Stubborn old man."

"Stubborn young woman."

Sondra lets a bit of the anger slide away for just a moment. "I'm going to bring her home. Will you help me?"

"No," he says without hesitation. "She didn't come back for a reason."

"Maybe she couldn't."

Her uncle nods. "Maybe."

"You said you loved her."

"I did," he says. "I do. But I don't know this woman you're going to save. I made peace with the sister I lost a long time ago." Uncle Luke sits up, levels his first look of concern at her. "Guard your heart, child. Whoever you meet there won't be your mother."

Sondra leans forward and growls her reply. "You might have given up on her, but I haven't."

"You misunderstand me," he says, a look of honest surprise on his face. "She'll always be your mother. I'm just saying—"

"I understand you just fine. Your sister is in trouble and I'm going to help her. I'll let you know how it goes." Sondra puts her hand on her uncle's shoulder. He is still gaping at her, some response frozen on his lips, as she leaves him there.

In 1995, Hurricane Marilyn hit the Virgin Islands. It was also the year Sondra underwent her first change. In the cover of darkness and storm, they all went out together: her father, her mother, Sondra, and Sonya without her skin. It was the first time Sondra had seen her parents in their animal form, and it took her breath away. Their coats were brown and spotted with black and white. They had large round ears and a thick bushy tail. Their lean, powerful muscles showed under their short fur. Their long teeth gleamed. Her mother was bigger, but they both were quite large. Breathtakingly beautiful.

Sondra initiated her change, and it was easy, like falling into water. Instinct kicked in after that. They ran down hillsides and through the bush. A few times, Sondra was hit by flying debris, but they were fast healers too. She didn't have to slow down. Sonya was even faster than they, somehow managing to avoid any low boughs, briars, or flying debris. She was also screaming the entire

time, which alarmed Sondra at first, but then she realized that Sonya was just happy. To her surprise, hearing Sonya's joy amplified her own. They ran and ran, Sonya sitting on top of Sondra occasionally, holding her ears as she cut between trees and hurdled logs and stones.

The wind was lifting everything up, and branches and leaves slapped against Sondra, but she couldn't feel them. It was wondrous. The sky was gray-black. She could see the storm raging, a living thing made of wind and rain and lightning. The rain splashed against Sonya, sticking to her in places, and sometimes Sondra could just make Sonya out in her skinless form—the suggestion of muscle fibers, tendons, the hinges of her joints. She was beautiful as she screamed and laughed, her face the shape of a young girl's but without flesh. Sondra watched her and wasn't afraid.

The storm lasted all night and well into the next day. They returned home before sunrise and all curled up in bed together as the hurricane raged outside. They felt strong with it, but they also knew that it would leave devastation in its wake. People and animals had died, the scent of them carrying on the wind.

Sonya and Sondra had fallen asleep before Mom and Dad, and they woke up before them. It was midday when they went into their own room together, still tired from their adventure.

Sonya had put her skin back on. She looked radiant, her skin giving off a faint glow. "Can I sleep with you?" she asked.

"Okay," Sondra said.

Sondra lay down first, and then Sonya joined her. Sonya got really close, and Sondra put her arm around her. She responded stiffly at first, but then she relaxed. Sondra calmed down too. Sonya smelled like dirt and rain, and Sondra wondered how since she had left her skin behind.

"My mother swam out into the sea and burned up," Sonya said. It was so soft, a secret.

"How?" Sondra asked.

Sonya didn't answer directly, and Sondra knew there was a secret she was too afraid to say. "It hurt a little when I was out today, but it wasn't so bad. The rain isn't so bad."

"Yes," Sondra said, not knowing what she meant by "it hurt" but not wanting to push her into a confession.

"She didn't know I was there," Sonya said. Back to her mother again. Somehow, Sondra understood. "I felt it when she died. Something in me burned out."

"You were alone a long time?" Sondra asked.

"I don't know how long."

They didn't go back to sleep. Sondra asked more questions, and Sonya asked many of her own. By the end of that day, they were sisters.

Despite their name, the weredogs of the Antilles, also known collo-
quially as woo-woos, bear no connection to the domestic dog.
Their animal counterpart is a descendant of the African wild dog:
the only extant member of the genus *Lycaon*, which diverged from
Cuon and *Canis* 1.7 million years ago. Sondra's family descended
from the West African wild dog in particular, nearly extinct in the
wild and also in the human realm. An old magic had made them,
lost during the Middle Passage.

As with werewolves and the moon, weredog transformations
are linked to storm events. The weredogs are especially powerful
during hurricane season, able to change at will more easily than at
other times of the year.

Weredogs had endured, not through subterfuge like other
monsters in other places, but through proliferation of their stories.
Everyone on Sondra's island knew of the woo-woo even if they hadn't
seen one. A child, breathless in excitement and fear, could tell you all

about the woo-woo. "*Click, click, click,*" they'd whisper to each other during a storm or power outage, mimicking the sound of claws on walls, windows, and doors. "The woo-woo coming for you."

Sondra hated the way her kind was portrayed in these stories when she was a child, but as an adult, she knew that the stories were a blessing, a spell of protection. Stories of weredogs and woo-woos and other strange creatures known by many names existed on all the islands Sondra had ever visited. Most people outgrew true belief in monsters by adulthood, but even adults knew not to go outside at night during a power outage, go past a certain house, or answer to whispers in the dark. Monsters existed in the liminal space of half-belief and practical superstition. Even folks who claimed not to believe in God knew not to tempt devils. Superstition provided a certain kind of freedom, allowed a certain kind of power.

Which is probably why Sondra never remembered feeling fear for her family's safety. When her parents went on their trip to New York, she wasn't worried. Sonya and Sondra were staying by their uncle's place, and she remembered being happy that they were gone, at least for a little while.

A week passed, then another. Her uncle didn't seem worried, so Sonya and she weren't, either. In the third week, he pulled them aside and said, "We can't find your parents."

They spent months looking for them. On Sonya's fifteenth birthday—a birthday their parents had given her—Sonya asked Sondra for the blood. "Mom and Dad used to give it to me," she said. "To keep me from hunting."

Sondra knew that her sister needed blood, but somehow never knew that she fed on their parents. Sondra didn't want to know, but it was a little late for that. Sondra agreed to give her the blood. They were sisters, and now something more.

That first time Sonya unlatched her tongue, Sondra marveled at the gleaming black thing rolling out of her mouth, the thin, sharp tip curving up to meet Sondra at eye level. She'd never seen Sonya's tongue in this form before and wasn't prepared for its strangeness. She was dizzy already just looking at it. Sondra didn't see when it reeled back and stabbed into her neck, but then she saw the blood being pulled up through the organ into Sonya's parted mouth, into that deepest darkness. Sonya's throat undulated with wave after wave of swallowed blood. Sondra had only a moment to feel fear before Sonya unlatched from her and opened her mouth wide. The tongue disappeared back inside, but she couldn't close her mouth completely. Sondra shivered.

Afterward, Sonya asked to be held. "I need the blood," she said. "And the love."

Sondra didn't ask what the second part meant. Somehow, she knew. Sonya had been different once they adopted her. The love of family had been just as nourishing as the blood she fed on. Sondra let her sister fall into her arms.

They continued this ritual for a year without trouble. It was too easy to last that way forever. Eventually, though, something shifted, and little by little, Sonya needed more blood each time.

One night, the worst finally happened. The feeding started the usual way, but it went on too long. Sondra waited for the expected end but lost consciousness before it arrived. When she woke up, her head was a storm cloud raging, and Sonya was still on top of her, holding her, drinking her in. Sondra's skin felt . . . loose. She had the sudden thought that nothing would be left but her skin and bones.

There had been times in Sondra's life when she was afraid. But nothing before or since would ever come close to this terror.

Sondra hadn't noticed when she started screaming. She'd fallen into it and became aware only as the pit of despair stretched beneath her. It could have been minutes or hours before Sonya noticed and fell off her. Sonya's eyes were wide, Sondra remembered—a mirror of horror.

Many apologies followed. Sondra accepted them all, but it wasn't a thing one could mend that way. Neither of them brought up feeding again.

It became a wedge between them. Guilt, shame, and resentment filled that space—a tight knot that couldn't be unwound. Sondra could sometimes see the shame in her sister's eyes, despite any attempt to remedy it. In Sonya's eyes, Sondra could also see her own fear reflected back.

They grew apart, and then, a few months later, Sonya met Melku. Sondra never learned how, but she guessed that Sonya had been feeding on people again and had stumbled onto the tech mage. Melku started showing up with her to dinners and family gatherings. "A friend," Sonya said, but Sondra knew that it was more. And then, a couple of years later, Damsel and Cassie started coming around. Before Sondra knew it, Sonya's life was a revolving door of strange people, most appearing for a day or days at a time, only to disappear again. And Sonya was gone for days, then weeks, then months. Unlike their parents, though, she always came back.

"I want to know what you're doing," Sondra said.

Sonya seemed to be waiting for this. "Come to a meeting and find out."

And she did, but she could tell that these meetings weren't the ones where the real conversations happened. Monster solidarity wasn't the whole story. She was at the outer circle of something, far from the center of power and knowledge. She kept attending,

if only to keep an eye on her sister, protect her if needed, but then it became simple curiosity. As time passed, Sonya demonstrated the same elusiveness as the people she spent her time with. Sondra couldn't get anything out of her she didn't volunteer herself. But through Sondra's work in government and her ability to sniff out subtle magics, she proved useful enough to descend one rung deeper into whatever her sister had gotten her involved in. That was when she learned the organization's true name: the Order of Asha.

Little by little, she started to gather a sharper image, however incomplete, of a branching web of monster societies. The Order of Asha was a significant power. The Order of the Zsouvox was its counterpart, quietly influential and very dangerous.

And then there was the Fracture.

The official story from both orders was that it was an accident. Sondra knew that was bullshit.

Monsters fell into one of three categories. They belonged to the societies, which meant they were institutionally bound to secrecy. Or they were monsters with a deep family history of monstrosity, which meant they'd been taught over generations to hide well. Or they were rogues, whose only guarantee of safety from the societies and the wider world was their practiced cunning and low profile.

Sondra belonged to an old family. Sonya, before her adoption, was a rogue who would likely have been scooped up by an order if she hadn't been adopted by Sondra's parents first—and eventually the Order of Asha found her anyway.

But the monsters on the highway the day of the Fracture belonged to none of these groups. Those monsters were young and unaware of the monster societies, belonging to no one, having no history. They were just children in all this. Neither the Order of Asha nor the Order of the Zsouvox claimed to know anything

about them, which meant there was another player in this, turning vulnerable people into monsters.

In a sloppy attempt to put the mess back in its box, the Order of Asha had edited all the footage of that day, and the Order of the Zsouvox had used its vast connections to spin the official narrative. But a mess, once made, cannot be unmade. The laws of entropy will not allow it. Someone had leaked the video of the shooting, and they were still at work trying to tip the two sides into a war that would spill into the human world.

That was where Sondra hit a wall. She was at the limits of her knowledge, and too far away from the center of the Order of Asha to get more.

But now Sondra knows something else.

All those years ago, her parents didn't just disappear. They were taken.

46

Sondra comes home expecting her sister to be hiding somewhere in her apartment. But when she opens the door, the first person she sees is Damsel, sitting calmly on the couch, as if Sondra had let her in herself.

"What do you think you're doing?"

"It's okay," comes a voice from Sondra's love seat: her sister.

"I never invited her into my home," Sondra says.

"Well, aren't you cute!" says the witch, smiling. Sondra wants to punch her right in the face.

"Let's unpack this breach of personal space later," Sonya says.

Sondra sighs. "How are we getting to Mom's apartment?" There is a spark of magic, and the abdomens of Melku's little machines start to glow. "Oh," Sondra says. "Right."

"It'll be a quick in-and-out. Damsel's here for clean-up."

In the half-light coming off Melku's ants, Sondra finally sees it. Damsel is wearing her ritual shroud. "Oh, no," Sondra says. "You're going to wipe Mom's mind?"

Sonya doesn't say anything.

"Answer me right fucking now, Sonya. Are we or are we not bringing Mom with us?"

"We have to wait a little while longer, sis. Cassandra has divined it."

"I don't know what that means. I'm not a part of your little club, remember?"

Damsel shakes her head. "Look, I'll say it. Your mom isn't your mom, love. We're not going to risk the truce to rescue her."

Sondra wrinkles her eyebrows.

"Wow," Damsel says. "You really don't know shit about shit, do you?"

Sondra looks toward the empty spot where her sister should be, but before she can say a word, there is another flicker of magic, and the portal opens.

"You have to decide now," Sonya says. "Are you in?"

"This is fucked up," Sondra says, but there really isn't time to untangle all the conflicts between them, all the secrets. She'll have to see for herself, with her own eyes. "Fine. Let's go."

One by one, they step through the portal.

As Sondra clears the threshold, there is a whoosh of air, and the portal closes. The room they've entered is dark. Another living room, but smaller.

"Wait here," Sonya says, her whisper already moving away from Sondra. She waits as Sonya leaves and returns moments later. "She is in the bedroom. Down the hall."

They all head for the bedroom. The house is dark around them, all bare walls and minimal furniture. The air smells stale. Someone lives here but never opens the windows. Sondra doesn't like that Damsel is joining them, but the feeling she's getting makes her glad someone is with her, someone she can see.

The door to the one bedroom is open. Sonya enters first, but it is Sondra who elicits a response from the inhabitant. The older woman looks toward the doorway, and Sondra stops, breath held. Damsel is still standing behind her, gracious enough not to enter the room before Sondra. The bedroom is bare as well: a twin bed, a desk and lamp, a wardrobe. No pictures on the wall. No evidence that a person is living there at all.

The woman sitting at the foot of the bed doesn't move, her face obscured by shadow. Sondra doesn't move, either. This could be her mother, but she seems too small, too frail. She doesn't fit the mental image.

The woman's chest heaves, and she takes several sharp breaths. No, not breaths—she is sniffing the air. "Daughter?" she says, her voice so soft.

Sondra tries speaking. A nod is all she can manage. She is still unsure. It sounds like her mother, but it doesn't have the command she remembers. Sondra ventures farther into the room, her steps hesitant. The woman stands, which startles her, but she keeps going until they are close enough to reach out and touch. Neither of them makes any move. Sondra can see the woman's face now: gaunt, more cheekbone and sagging skin than she remembers, but her mother's nose, her mother's smallish eyes.

"Where is your father?" her mother asks. "Oh, no." She looks around the room, seemingly lost. "Oh, no."

Sondra feels sick. Something is in the air here, the same staleness as before, but more pungent in the room, in the space where her mother stands. "I don't know," Sondra says. "But we came to see you."

"Thank you," her mother says, tears in her eyes. "Where's your father?"

Somehow, her mother's pain feels fresh. Sondra doesn't know

where her father is, but she's spent years not knowing. The way her mother is asking, it feels like mere days. How can that be? Sondra pulls her mother in for a hug. "We'll find him," she says.

It is okay at first. There is something of her mother in there now that Sondra is close enough to smell her. But then her nose picks up what her eyes can't. "No," Sondra says. Something is not right at all. Her mother smells dirty, as if she hasn't showered in some time. But something else too. A sharp note of something at the heart of her mother. Muddy and sweet. Devotion, heart-deep and rich. Pungent and insane. A dark staircase reaching down forever.

And there, at the bottom of the bottomless: madness. She sees it in her mother's eyes, smells it on her, everywhere. It is not just in her mind. It is *under* her mind, playing like a song on a loop.

Sondra recoils, gasping. She can catch it, she knows. It is already in her, squirming on the walls, burning through doors, entering every room. She has to get out. Her desperation claws up out of her throat and into the world, on its way out tasting like oblivion. Sondra is screaming, but she is far away from herself. Sonya's invisible arms are suddenly around her, pulling her back through the doorway, back toward the living room and the hole in the world.

Sondra howls and struggles in her sister's grasp. There is a whoosh of air again as Sonya pulls her back through the portal. Sondra sees the portal close, her living-room wall replacing the scene of the distant living room as Melku's little machines quietly scatter.

When Sonya releases her, Sondra collapses to the floor and vomits.

Your mom is not your mom, love.

Guard your heart, child. Whoever you meet there won't be your mother.

This, she realizes, is the price of knowledge.

DEATH AND MEMORY

DRAGON
ST. THOMAS, USVI

NINE MONTHS AFTER THE FRACTURE

For the first couple of weeks since his escape, Dragon spends a lot of time in his bedroom inside Melku's house. A quiet woman lives in the house too. She doesn't talk, and Dragon rarely sees her. This woman is small and young-looking and speaks only when someone speaks to her. Dragon asks the woman her name, and she says, "Cassandra," but when Dragon asks her where she is from, she says she has never answered that question. The response confuses Dragon. He stops asking her questions.

Then Melku leaves with the quiet woman, and Dragon is sent to live in the Bordeaux Commune. Dragon meets a witch there. Her name is Damsel.

The Bordeaux Commune is more isolated than where Melku lives. The houses are bigger and spread out across the hillside. Dragon can go outside without running into people at all. The witch lets him play outside as long as he promises not to talk to anyone or do anything a human wouldn't do.

Dragon learns to climb coconut trees, to find and pull genip from branches, to follow stray cats into the bush. He spends a lot of time watching iguanas and birds, looking from one to the other, combining the two, comparing them to himself. He asks Damsel what these things are, and she tells him. Damsel is nothing like Smoke; she lets him do what he wants and seems to take little interest in controlling what he does. It makes him both happy and sad.

Dragon spends a lot of time in the bush. It is hot during the day, but he is a dragon, after all. The other creatures he finds are more of a curiosity than a threat. He has spent too long inside or underground. He likes being out. He wants to see things, be in the world. Dragon likes the trees and the animals, but he keeps his distance from cars, from people, from other children. He is afraid of them, but he is more afraid of himself, what he might do, what he might remember he's done. Dragon has the occasional urge to burn the tails off the iguanas he chases. He doesn't like that about himself.

One day, Melku comes to the Bordeaux Commune. Damsel brings Dragon into the living room, and Melku and Damsel have a conversation as he just stands there. He pays attention only to some of it. Something happened when Melku was away, and now Damsel has to perform a spell on both of them. Dragon is made to lie down on the floor beside Melku, and Damsel puts on a piece of cloth that covers her whole body in shadow; then she places her gloved hands over them. Something glows under the cloth in two places, on Damsel's arm and maybe her neck, and then Dragon feels something wiggling under his skin. He looks down at his chest and sees two glowing worms squirm out of him. He tries to scream, but Damsel glows again and his whole body goes stiff. The worms float up into the air, joining two more. One more spot

glows under Damsel's cloth, this time on her lower body, and three of the glowing worms explode into sparkling dust. The last one, Damsel places in a glass jar.

Dragon can move his body again, but he doesn't scream. The fear has passed. He sits up and looks at both of them.

"They're all out," Damsel says. "Soul worms are obscure magic. I need to meet her someday and exchange recipes."

Pointing at the jar, Melku says, "We'll need to keep that one moving. It'll keep Smoke and the Cult of the Zsouvox busy for a while, at least until after November fifth."

The mention of Smoke piques Dragon's attention.

"You sure about that?" Damsel asks.

Melku shrugs. "Cassie says it'll work."

Damsel looks at Dragon and gives him a smile. "So, the boy is staying at the commune, then?"

"She didn't advise either way. I'm sure it won't hurt."

Dragon has a horrible dream that night. It is formless and terri-fying, a smudged trail of ink that follows him into waking. He can't get back to sleep after that, so he presses his feet lightly to the cold tile and tiptoes to his bedroom door. Quiet out of habit, he inches the door open and slips into the hallway. Once he is out of the room, he snatches the tail of some conversation from the air. At the end of the hall, coming from the living room, Damsel is talking to someone. The other voice is pitched low in a careful whisper. By contrast, Damsel's voice is loud.

"Look, can't I just hex the both of you?" she says. "It's going to be crazy near the Commons, and Sondra's not going to like taking directions from me."

"You're not hexing me," says the other person, clipped and familiar. The invisible woman.

"You still don't trust me? Even after all this time?"

"I don't trust anyone."

As the conversation in the living room plods on, Dragon turns away and heads farther down the hall, toward the bathroom.

"Cassie says fireworks will start a little after noon. You'll need to be there by three minutes past at the latest." A beat of silence. "Come on, just one little hex."

"No."

Dragon steps into the open doorway. In a small window above the toilet, a tree limb moves with the wind, the sound a muted rustle. Darkness sticks to everything, allowing only the thinnest stream of moonlight into the room. Dragon takes a step and halts. Something makes a rattling sound from farther down the hall, where the shadow is thickest. Dragon loses interest in the bathroom. He backs out into the hallway and ventures slowly into the dark. Again something rattles, and his ears track it.

He has wandered very far down the stretch of hallway. As he goes, he tries each door. They are all locked. He should turn back. Damsel will be mad if she catches him. But there is the rattling again, and he can't resist. Now it is coming from a door directly ahead. Dragon reaches the door, tries the knob, and it turns. He nudges the door open just a little, making a gap large enough to peer through.

Dragon holds his breath. Inside the room, someone or something is sitting cross-legged on the floor as a tower of cards constructs itself from floor to ceiling. The creature has not moved, except for inky tendrils that sway rhythmically where its head should be. There is no open window in this room. No sound from outside or inside. Cards continue to float up one by one, taking their place in the tower. The thing's tendrils dance to a beat that Dragon cannot hear.

Without warning, one of the cards flies out from its position, and then the whole tower comes crashing down with a rattle like the tiniest animal bones. The tendrils wave back and forth uninterrupted, and then it starts again. Card by card, the tower remakes itself. Dragon can't hold his breath anymore. He exhales. The shadowed thing turns its head, and the light flicks on.

The light reveals them both. Looking up at Dragon is a child of similar age and height, with locks of long hair as black in the light as they were in shadow. By appearance, the child looks completely human, though its skin is pitch black and its eyes are wells of wet, glistening darkness. Dragon stands there in stunned silence until the child smiles, revealing a set of absurdly white teeth. The yell that spills out of Dragon startles them both. The child's smile cuts away, and the tower of cards flies into the air all at once, pointing at Dragon like a school of flat little fish, hungry as knives.

Damsel clenches Dragon's shoulder and jerks him back with one hand, while the other pulls the door shut. "What are you doing?"

Dragon's heart is thumping in his ears. "I heard something," he says.

"What did you hear?" Damsel asks.

"The thing," Dragon says. "The thing in there. What is it?"

"A Zsouvox," she says. Damsel leans down so that they are at eye level. Her expression is worse than anger. "Promise me you'll never speak of this to anyone." A perfect circle is tattooed on Damsel's neck, and just as Dragon sees it, the tattoo starts glowing the orange of live embers. Then a hundred tattoos shimmer to life on her face, her neck, her exposed arms. They cool at once, and then a tattoo on her arm glows to life: a sharp-toothed fish

with a large open mouth. "I can take the memory from you," she says. "Leave a hole there nothing can fill. But you understand me, right? You'll keep your promise?"

Dragon feels the sting of tears and a bone-deep shudder. He nods.

"Good." She lets him go and leaves him at the door.

Fear keeps Dragon nailed to the spot. He listens through the door but hears nothing inside. He doesn't dare try the knob again. The house takes a breath and holds it, all sound disappearing into the silence. The shadow stretches out, grows darker, deeper. The silence and the darkness of the moment remind him of late nights underground. For the first time, he wonders about the dangers of this new place.

He also remembers something he had forgotten.

It was years or months ago, Dragon isn't entirely sure. Something in the shape of a child, with skin the color of eggshells, visited him in his cell. Smoke was there too, standing in the corner.

"Will it be useful?" the thing asked Smoke.

"Yes," he said with deference. "He will grow into his power."

The thing in the shape of a child leaned down and cupped Dragon under the chin. "What are you?" the thing asked. Its voice was more air than sound. Its eyes were all white. Except for a thin outline around the iris, which was somehow a darker shade of white.

"I'm Dragon," he said, repeating the truth he'd been told for as long as he could remember.

"I'm the Zsouvox," the thing said, and it smiled.

Dragon repeats the strange word from his memory: "Zsouvox." Damsel said the same word, though she said "*a* Zsouvox," not "*the* Zsouvox." What kind of monster is a Zsouvox?

Featherlight footsteps approach the other side of the door.

Dragon doesn't move, only listens as the steps reach the door and stop. The floor creaks, and then he hears soft tapping on the other side of the door.

"Hello?" the thing on the other side of the door says. "Would you like to play?"

Dragon runs back to his room and shuts the door.

The next morning, Dragon is back to normal. He spends a couple of hours playing outside before breakfast. The witch makes him pancakes and smiles at him as he eats. He's never seen her eat a single thing.

A cat is on the windowsill. A pretty cat, bigger than the wild ones Dragon has seen in the bush near the Bordeaux Commune. It, too, is watching Dragon eat. Its eyes are orange-yellow and bright like the sun. Dragon feels fear at first, but then his healthy curiosity takes over. After he finishes his food, he inches toward the cat little by little until he's close enough to extend a hand.

"Careful, child," Damsel says, smiling. "Asha is the god of everything you know. If you upset her, she might erase you from existence."

Dragon watches Damsel, suspicious. "You're lying."

Her smile grows. "Am I?"

Dragon takes another look at the cat. He pulls back his hand.

"Let her come to you," Damsel says.

Dragon has to wait a long time before the cat stands and leaps from the windowsill. On soft padded feet, she saunters into the living room, and Dragon follows a few paces behind.

This is when Damsel turns to me. I step back and go completely still.

"The answer is yes, I can see you. Don't run. I'm sure you have questions. It's okay. Come over here and have a seat. Cal, right? Oh, don't look so surprised; you're not the only one that can read minds. Who am I? Well, I'm a tourist mostly. This place is beautiful, and I'm attracted to beautiful things. A living multiverse, the first and last of its kind. I'm learning as much as I can, feeling the craft of it, so I can go home and make one of my own. Oh, yes, I am a god. There are quite a lot of us, though there used to be many more. Calamity, of course. Be careful, you're getting dangerously close to things you don't want to know. The price of too much knowledge is madness, kiddo. And danger—so much danger. You've never been hurt, have you, out here, swimming around minding other people's business? There are things in this universe that can open you up like ripe fruit."

Damsel's lips curl just a little, and her eyes gleam with a spark of magic. "Oh, you're thinking about *her*. Abyssia. You'll meet her again and she'll be different, always different—what she knows, what she wants. Time, for her, is a tangled web. She must have recognized you, recognized your magic as her own. She gave it to you or will give it to you, or some other thing. I don't know; this stuff is stupid confusing."

Suddenly, her attention shifts away from me. "Oh, shut up. That wasn't in the contract. Well, you know everything,

so you should've stopped me. Look, Yuni, I don't take well to threats." She turns back to me. "Sorry, got to go. Call on the other line."

As she is walking away, I poke once more at her mind and find nothing there but a yawning void.

OTHER WORLDS AND THIS ONE

SUBJECT: HUGH EVERETT
LOCATION: MCLEAN, VIRGINIA
EARTH VERSION: 017

When I finally visit Hugh Everett, it's 1982.

We sit down, and pahnah pours himself a glass of sherry and lights a cig before asking me about the purpose of my visit.

We're in Hugh's bedroom. He's sitting on his bed, in full suit and tie, taking deep drags from his cigarette. I take a seat in a chair by the window.

I tell him I want to hear about his theory. This isn't true. I know his theory well.

"Well, not a theory," he tells me. "Not proven."

On the street outside the house, a car is stuck in time. A woman sings along with the car radio, her mouth open just slightly, frozen. In the back seat, a little girl sleeps, her lungs in the midst of a lazy inhalation. They both will be stuck like this for as long as I'm here.

I smile. "Tell me about it anyway."

• • •

EARTH VERSION: 001

It's 2008, and I'm on St. Thomas, sitting under the big tree outside the auditorium at Charlotte Amalie High. One of my boys comes up to me and tells me that Cory's gotten pantsed by some dudes from Ghettos because he walked through their hall without permission. They have the whole of Building B looking at my little brother's drawers and laughing.

When I get there, Cory's running around in X-Men briefs he got in sixth grade. Don't even ask me why he let Mom get him X-Men undies in sixth grade, or why this pahnah is still wearing them. The Ghettos crew is throwing his pants around. They're laughing as he runs to catch them. Real original shit.

I come up and immediately start taking these dudes down, and I mean hard. I clock a few before they really catch on, but when I turn to get the dude that's actually holding Cory's pants—*Wham!*

My legs turn to noodles under me, and I fall face-first to the ground. Later, people tell me I looked like that dude from *Punch-Out!!*

I wake up in a hospital bed, with a massive headache and a pulsing fire in my ribs. Cory's sitting by the bed, just staring through me. Known him all his life, and that empty look he gets still trips me out.

"I'm sorry," he says when he realizes that I'm awake and looking at him.

"What you doing wearing X-Men briefs in high school?"

"I like X-Men."

I'm not joking, that's what he tells me. "You can like X-Men," I tell him, "but that don't mean you have to cover your balls with them."

"Campus security had to pull them off you."

"They should've gotten their fat asses there when those dudes were messing with you. Who's gonna pay for all this?"

"Mom's pissed."

"*Duh* Mom's pissed." My jaw throbs through the words. My left eye is puffy and leaky. "Where she at?"

"Outside on the phone." Cory stares off at God knows what.

"You got to man up, B."

He nods.

"I'm serious."

He nods.

"Can't let these dudes keep punking you like this. And as you can see, I can't always save your ass."

He starts crying.

"You can't be serious, dread."

He tries to stop, but that just makes his body shake harder. "I'm sorry," he says, heaving through the words, drooling all over himself.

"That's what I talking about right there. You can't be doing that in front of people, mehson."

He heaves. He drools.

"Hey," I say. "Just promise me this ain't gon' happen again."

He nods. "I promise."

For a moment, I swear the room looks different. I close my eyes and rub at my temples, disoriented. Inside my eyelids is a light show of colors.

Mom is livid when she comes back in. Because of the concussion, they have to keep me overnight. "I'm tired of all these fights," she tells me.

"Don't look at me," I say. "Tell Cory to stop being a little girl." I feel as if I'd been rolled out by a rolling pin, my insides a flattened mush.

"Don't say that," Mom says. She gives me the don't-test-me look, and I shut up real quick. I glance over at Cory, who's quiet, his head lowered, staring into his lap.

"Remember your promise," I say.

In the late nineteenth century, J. J. Thomson does an experiment proving to everyone that electrons are particles, and they give him a Nobel Prize for his work. Thirty years later, George Thomson, the dude's son, does a similar experiment and proves that electrons are waves. They also give him a Nobel Prize.

"Ask some physicists and they'll tell you, that sums up the great mystery right there," Hugh says. "But there's also the two-slit experiment."

How it works, Hugh tells me, is, you shoot electrons at a slab with only one slit and a detector screen behind it. The screen ends up looking pretty much like what you'd expect; the electrons form a slit-like spatter on it.

But shoot at a slab with two slits, and the electrons go fucking nuts.

"It's as if the electron, faced with that extra slit, decided to

explore all options," Hugh says. "It superimposes. It becomes a wave of possibilities."

If you attach a camera to try to record which slit the electron actually goes through, the electrons become particles again. Two slit-size spatters show up on the screen.

"The act of observing electrons affects the outcome," Hugh says. "That shouldn't be possible."

It's not just electrons. Other subatomic particles also ignore Newtonian laws. They teleport, superimpose, and disappear. They run off cliffs and forget to fall.

Upon witnessing the complete lack of fucks given by the quantum world, physicists collectively lose their minds. How can they reconcile reality with what they are seeing? In desperation, many of them entertain solipsistic ideas. If the world of tiny objects can disregard Newtonian physics, then how can we tell for sure that reality isn't just a product of our imagination?

"Of course, what becomes the official explanation," Hugh tells me, "isn't far from just that."

Enter the infamous Niels Bohr.

Bohr won the Nobel Prize in Physics in 1922. He modeled the atom. He is brilliant and highly respected, and when he tells a room full of people his theory, they listen. They listen so hard that Bohr's ideas hold the field hostage for decades.

His idea is this: The world is separated into two: our physical macro world, which we pretty much understand; and the quantum world, where shit just happens. When we are not looking at subatomic particles, they exist as waves of possibility: wave functions. When we observe them, the wave collapses, and they become particles. It is pointless to try to figure out what subatomic particles are doing when we are not looking at them, and that is not our job as physicists.

"Another way of putting it is this," Hugh says. He's animated now. He has put down his glass of sherry on the nightstand next to the bed. His cigarette is resting in an ashtray. "When we observe subatomic particles, we are changing their very nature." He laughs.

"Not possible?"

"Complete bullshit."

It surprises me that Hugh curses.

From the 1930s to the 1980s, the Copenhagen Interpretation of quantum mechanics becomes dogma with a capital "D." Dudes crazy enough to question it—or, worse, come up with alternatives (ha!)—face the ridicule of the tribe.

"I didn't stand a chance," Hugh says. He closes his eyes for a moment, and the world is still as death. He's a painting of himself, quiet and tortured. Then he opens his eyes and looks at me. "Who are you, again?"

• • •

It's 2009, and I'm graduating from high school with a bruised body and a bruised ego. When I walk up on stage to get my diploma, someone yells out "KO Cally," and I have to pretend I don't hear the entire auditorium / basketball court erupt in laughter.

After graduation, I work at Kmart to try to save up for UVI, and then I stay on in the fall, deciding that I haven't saved enough, spending way too much money going clubbing and going to the office (me and my boys' code name for the strip club).

In tenth grade, Cory starts taking boxing lessons down at UVI, and before long he is running laps up and down Waterfront, punching the air like Apollo Creed. I'm hating, but the boy is actually pretty good. Starts competing in some local matches and actually wins a few.

"Don't think I can't still kick your ass," I tell him.

He just smiles at me, all cocky. "You mean like them dudes from Ghettos?"

What can I say? He has me mum there.

Around then Cory gets into girls, and I mean big-time. Surprises the hell out of me. Dude trades in his Marvel undies for Calvin Kleins, and girls seem to dig his weird mix of nerd and badass. I get jealous and start taking lessons, too, for a hot minute, but I don't climb the ladder like he does. That stuff is for some people, you know? But I would never have guessed it would be little Cory messing dudes up.

That isn't the only thing, either. I come home one night after a hard day at Kmart (fucking Kmart, man! Jesus . . .), and I smell Cory burning cahn in his bedroom. The weed's just wafting out into the hallway.

I knock on his door, and pahnah tells me, "Come in," like he's been expecting me or something. I open up and I see him spread out on the floor, smoking and watching *Sixteen and Pregnant* on MTV.

First of all, *Sixteen and Pregnant*? The fuck?

Second, this is the first time I've ever seen Cory do anything he isn't supposed to be doing, so imagine my surprise. I just stand there staring at him.

He looks up at me and says, "You gon' just stand there? Come and take a hit."

I close the door and sit beside him, and we pass the joint back and forth. We watch the show together and talk in the breaks.

After a while, I turn to him and say, "So this is how you moving now?"

He smiles. "Yeah." He passes the joint to me.

"I see you," I say.

I soon decide that I've had enough of lounging around in my mom's house with a dead-end job. I've finally saved up enough loot to really do something with myself, so I enroll at UVI and move out. I take up a second job at the school, filing and answering the phone in the financial-aid department.

By then, Cory is in eleventh grade and has made a minor name for himself. He's still a midlevel boxer, but he is stacked and intimidating. He starts cutting class and taking girls up to the house during school hours. Mom comes home sick one day and finds him in the house with some girl, and he has to run out half naked as she chases him around the yard with a belt.

"What about the girl?" I ask him later.

"Mom almost beat her, too," he says, and we laugh together.

A month later, Cory has a big fight set up with this dude named Antonio, from Croix. Cory is feeling himself way too much, saying all kinds of shit about the boy. I couldn't blame him. Up until that point, the Cruzan hadn't been doing so well. It seemed obvious that Cory would be taking home the win. Cory tells people to come out and witness the carnage. Tells me I should see how it's done.

Cory gets knocked out in the second round.

The haters descend quick. Cory becomes the butt of endless jokes. "Living up to the family name," one of his friends says. Cory doesn't take any of this well. He hides out in his room and lights up all day. He tells Mom to mind her business when she tries to intervene. He cuts class constantly. Spends most of his time running from hall monitors and hiding out in the back of the special-education building, smoking.

"Take it easy, baby bro," I tell him.

"Don't think I can't handle you," he warns.

"You mean like Antonio?"

Dude pounces on me, throwing punches. I can't dodge them, so I run. "Calm down, dread," I yell.

Cory doesn't listen to me. He spends the rest of that year driving his grades into the dirt. When I ask him how he's going to get into college, he tells me he's joining the military. And he does. After he barely graduates, he goes to basic training and is off to Afghanistan within a few months. Mom gives him the silent treatment up until he leaves, but it doesn't stop him. On his day of departure, she begs and begs.

"Don't worry about me, Mom," he says. "I'll be all right."

It's 1955, and young Hugh's hanging with friends, drinking and smoking at a cocktail party at Princeton. The room is thick with smoke and conversation. It's late, and Hugh is drunk, so he's talking loudly.

"You have to know what you're saying," Hugh says. "You must know how ridiculous this interpretation is."

"It makes sense to me," says Harvey.

"Me too," says Charles.

Hugh thinks. It is hard because his head is swimming and he feels as if he were underwater. "What if the wave doesn't collapse?"

"What?" Charles and Harvey say together.

"The wave of possibilities. What if it goes on forever, but we just can't see it?"

"Sit down, friend," says Charles. He looks at Hugh, concerned. "And put down your glass. It's doing things to you."

"What would that even look like?" Harvey asks.

"The other possibilities would have to go somewhere," Hugh says.

"Where?" Harvey asks.

"Somewhere else."

"Oh," says Charles, "you definitely sound like a physicist now."

They all laugh. I laugh, too, because the joke is corny as hell. None of them notice me.

Hugh steadies himself on his legs. He feels euphoric. "Schrödinger's cat!" he yells. He looks to his friends for confirmation, but they just stare incredulously. "Look, I am made of atoms! If atoms can be in more than one place at once, why can't I?"

"Please, Hugh," Harvey says. "Are you saying one of you isn't enough? Jesus, to even imagine a wave of you . . ."

They laugh again. I roll my eyes. They drink some more, and the conversation drifts on to other things.

The next morning, Hugh wakes up with a hangover and the answer. He pulls out a notepad and begins scribbling furiously.

"That's the night it first comes to me," Hugh tells me in his bedroom back in 1982. "The universal wave function."

I consider telling him that I know, that I was there, but it would only confuse him. He's already forgotten asking me who I am.

So I just nod.

Hugh smiles. He sips sherry from a glass that will never run dry—not as long as I'm here.

• • •

Cory doesn't seem that different when he comes back from overseas. He is quiet, but he has always been quiet when he's not pelting

you with sarcasm. Looking back, though, I find meaning in those silences. They seem dark and threatening.

For the first two weeks, he spends a lot of time in his room. I come by Mom's house to visit, and we hang out and watch movies. We talk a little, but he doesn't have much to say. I ask him what he did over there, and he tells me that they mostly built infrastructure. I ask him if he killed anyone, and he says no.

"It was boring. Can we watch this movie?"

After that, I stop asking.

During the next two weeks of his leave, he goes out every night. He meets a girl named Keren, and for that last week I see him out all the time with her. I catch them at the movies or over by Fat Turtle or at Starz Night Club on Friday and Saturday. He nods and I nod, and then I go about my business.

Then he is gone again. This time for a few months. When he returns, he tells me that he has been discharged.

"Why?"

"Medical reasons."

"You sick?" I ask him.

"No," he says. And before I can say another word, he says, "It don't matter, anyway. Now I can be around for my baby girl."

"Who? Keren?"

"No, my baby," he says.

"When the fuck did that happen?"

Cory looks offended. "What's that supposed to mean?"

I tell him that babies are expensive and he should have been more careful. He tells me he is a grown man and that he can take care of his responsibilities and who the hell am I to tell him anything about his life. When I tell him I am his big brother, he laughs at me.

"You haven't been that for a long time, biggest."

That hurts my feelings. I'm thinking: *After all the ass-whuppings I gave on your behalf, you gon' turn around and say something like that to me?* I tell him, "Well, I hope one a'you have an actual place to stay, because Mom's not gon' have you raising no damn child in her house."

I get up to leave, determined to wash my hands of the matter. When I'm at the front door, I catch a glimpse of myself still sitting on Mom's couch. "What?" I blink. When I open my eyes, there's no one there.

• • •

In 1955, Hugh begins his paper: "The Theory of the Universal Wave Function." The pages stack up. He shares the idea with his thesis advisor, John Wheeler, who is both excited and apprehensive. In its favor, the logic is sound. On the other hand, it will be very unpopular.

Around this time, Hugh meets Nancy, his future wife, at a physicists' party. He is charming, and Nancy is fun-loving and passionate, and they hit it off. Nancy helps him type up the final draft of his dissertation, and he submits it to Wheeler.

"Prepare to make waves," Wheeler says with a chuckle.

"I hope," Hugh says.

In the meantime, Hugh and Nancy get married. Soon after, Nancy's belly begins to swell. She gives birth to a baby girl, and they name her Elizabeth.

The waves do not come. Wheeler takes off to Copenhagen to get some buzz started on the idea. He comes back discouraged. He calls Hugh and tells him the news. Hugh listens quietly.

"Sometimes, it is like this in the beginning," Wheeler says. "It's not so bad."

"Yes," Hugh says. He cannot bring himself to say more.

A couple of years pass with nothing. Hugh begins work at the Pentagon—a big-money job with the Weapons Systems Evaluation Group. He makes a name for himself analyzing the possible effects of nuclear fallout.

"I did things at that job I still can't talk about," Hugh tells me.

In '59, Wheeler calls Hugh and tells him that he should go to Copenhagen himself.

"It's a shot in the dark," says Wheeler. "But maybe if they hear it from you . . ."

Hugh smiles reluctantly. "Maybe."

"Take the wife," he says. "It's a beautiful city."

So they go. Hugh meets Bohr, and they talk over the course of several afternoons. The conversations do not go as hoped. There is a lot of talk. Hugh explaining, Bohr listening. Bohr responds mumbling half-completed sentences before getting up sporadically to relight his pipe.

"You see, uh, the particles all continue to exist equally in other universes," Hugh says.

"Well, yes, yes, that makes some . . . I am sure that it could if these other . . . But again, this can't be proven, Hugh. We would need . . . and there's also space and time to consider, well, yes, if these universes are superimposed. You say the math is consistent— oh, give me one second while I light this. Terribly sorry. It's a novel idea, but—oh, why do these burn up so quickly? Just one moment. You're very smart, but like I said before. Impossible to prove."

"I was right," Hugh says defensively. "I was right!"

"You were," I say absently. And then I change the subject. "Tell me. Your wife and daughter. Do you love them?"

53

Mom does end up kicking Cory out, but not for the reason I thought. It is 2011, my last semester at UVI, when he calls asking if he can live with me. He is breathing all hard like he's in a panic.

"Mom finally kicked you out, huh?"

"You gon' help me out or what?"

"Why she kick you out?"

I hear him take in a deep breath before answering. "She found something in my room."

"Something like what?"

There's a pause, a heavy quiet. "Weed."

"Oh, yeah, dummy. That'll do it."

"You gon' help me?"

I want to say, "So now you calling your big brother, huh? See how you almost burn this bridge?" But I don't say any of that. I say okay, and the next day I help him move his stuff in. The semester before, I quit Kmart and started working at the university full-time,

moved out of the dorms and got a spot up Contant-side. I'm taking night classes to finish up school. The apartment is a one-bedroom, but I'm thinking about getting a two when the lease is up, if Cory plays his cards right.

Cory takes the couch for a few weeks. I start seeing this girl named Mona, an expat from LA I met down by Frenchtown. I spend a lot of nights over by her house and tell Cory he can have the room when I'm not around.

When I come home for a few nights, I have to kick him out of the room. His girl, Keren, comes by with baby Gina, and they lie around in the living room and watch TV. Sometimes, I overhear them arguing, but those first months it seems like normal couple bullshit.

One day I am cleaning, and I find a little glass vial in the crevice of the couch. I stare at it, bewildered. *What is this?*

I look at it a bit longer, and then I walk into the kitchen and throw it in the trash.

In that moment, the room around me shifts and gleams like sun hitting glass. Then I see another me sitting on the couch, staring at the vial in his hand. He places it on the table.

Moments later, Cory walks in. "Hey," Cory says, and it sounds like two of him speaking at the same time.

I feel suddenly dizzy, so I lean against the kitchen counter. I close my eyes, and behind the lids is a kaleidoscope of dancing colors. When I open my eyes again, the other me is gone, and Cory is staring at me.

"What's wrong?" he asks.

I wipe sweat from my forehead. "Nothing," I say, but I can't stop shaking.

• • •

It's 1974, and I'm watching Hugh's seventeen-year-old daughter, Liz, push lima beans around on her plate. She looks up at Hugh suddenly and says, "Would you fucking stop that already?"

"Elizabeth!" her mother says, and looks to Hugh.

Hugh doesn't look up.

"You," says Liz. "Hugh Everett the Third."

He looks up.

"Stop writing in that stupid fucking notepad."

There is a flash of surprise in Hugh's eyes. Is it interest? I can't tell. His mind is completely blank. "You're right," he says after a moment, and he pushes the pad and pen to the corner of the table and begins eating the cold food on his plate.

"So my day was shitty," Liz starts, looking at her father.

"Language," Nancy says.

"Ms. Rita gave me an F for my paper. All I said was that I hated *The Grapes of Wrath*. I was just being honest."

"Oh, really," says Nancy, suspicious. "What was it about?"

"Too boring to remember," Liz says with a wave of her hand.

"Oh, Liz," Nancy says, exasperated.

Hugh has lost interest in the proceedings. He has returned to a well-worn path in his brain. It's the most logical option. How could they not see it? Idiots, all of them.

Liz takes a deep breath and leaves the table, not even bothering to pick up her plate. "Maybe tonight," she says as she heads down the hall.

Nancy's eyes look down to Liz's plate. The macaroni has barely been touched. The meat loaf forms a depressing pile next to a scattering of lima beans. Liz could at least have eaten the meat loaf.

She could leave tomorrow, Nancy thinks. Leave this loveless marriage.

All the while, Hugh is still thinking, *It's perfectly logical. The fuckers. The fuckers.*

A few weeks later, Nancy finds Liz hunched up in a ball next to the toilet. She turns her over and sees an empty bottle of sleeping pills. I'm there, standing at the doorway unseen, tears in my eyes. I think of that glass vial, think of myself not saying anything.

Nancy calls the ambulance.

When Nancy returns home from the hospital, she sits in the car, her fist cupped under her chin, staring at the purple sky. For a long time, she just replays the scene of Liz lying on the floor. Then she notices that the living room light is on.

Nancy goes inside to find Hugh in his chair, reading *Newsweek*.

"Where were you?"

"Work," he says, and there is no hint that this is a shitty answer. "Is she okay?" he asks, a slight tremor in his voice that Nancy doesn't notice.

"They had to pump her stomach," Nancy says. She stares at Hugh. He isn't looking at her. His eyes are still buried in his *Newsweek*. She doesn't notice his trembling hands.

"I'm going upstairs," she says.

"Upstairs," he repeats.

Nancy walks to the stairs.

"Did you know?" he asks, stopping her.

"Know what?"

"That she was depressed."

Nancy is thinking *yes,* but she doesn't answer.

"I didn't know," Hugh says.

There is a universe where a bolder Nancy walks over and grabs

Hugh by the shirtfront and tells him that he is worthless and a liar, which he knew, of course. Of course he did, if he was fucking paying attention at all. But in this one, Nancy stares at Hugh until he returns to his *Newsweek,* and then she climbs the stairs.

Mom must be happy we are both out of the house because she starts seeing this corny dude named Daryl from Dominica. She ends up pregnant with twins. Twins in her midforties! But I'm happy for her because she didn't have much of a love life since our dad exed out when we were kids. You get your happiness where you can find it, even if it's with a corny dude named Daryl.

Me and Cory end up getting that two-bedroom. Cory's having a hard time holding down a job, but after graduation I manage to get a cushy one selling jewelry on Main Street, so I'm not giving him a hard time, at least. Every few months, though, he gives me a big wad of cash.

"What I owe you," he says.

And for the next couple of weeks, I watch him sideways.

Keren comes over a lot, and before long, it is like she is living there. I wake up in the middle of the night to the baby crying and Keren sitting on the toilet with the bathroom door wide open.

She looks up at me with sleepy eyes, and I back up and wait for her to finish.

Most weekends, I go over by my girl Mona and leave Cory and Keren with the apartment. I carry work clothes for Mondays with me and then go home Monday nights.

One of those Monday nights, I come home and hear yelling from Cory's room. He has some rock music playing—Metallica or some crazy shit—but I can hear Keren yelling and baby Gina crying. There is a loud crash, muffled in the music, and then Keren sobbing. I knock on the door, and Keren and Cory get really quiet inside. The door opens, and the music stretches itself, loud and menacing, into the hallway. Keren, in a shirt and panties, brushes past me, tears in her eyes, and goes into the bathroom and slams the door. Cory's sitting on the bed with baby Gina. He's drenched in sweat, and his eyes are bloodshot.

"Everything all right?" I ask.

He looks up at me as if just noticing me. "Yeah, we cool." And then he goes back to zoning out. Gina is still crying, but he doesn't seem to notice that, either. He just keeps rocking her.

• • •

"Parallel universes are troubling," Liz tells Hugh. "If any old universe can exist, then what is the value of this one?"

It's 1976, two years after Liz's overdose.

Hugh smiles at Liz, suddenly attentive. It is the middle of the night, and they both are having trouble sleeping. They are sharing one of Nancy's apple pies. Liz clinks her fork against her empty plate, unsettling bits of piecrust. She waits for Hugh's reply.

He loves to talk about his idea. She knows this. In these moments, she can be his daughter.

"All universes are valuable to the people living in them," he says. "They have to find meaning in the choices they've made."

"But how does choice matter if you can literally make all of them?"

He thinks for a moment. "Only the possible ones. Only the ones you would make in the universe you are in. Universal laws and human behavior still apply."

"Still," she counters, "what decides the choices I will make in one and not the other?"

Hugh cuts himself another slice of pie. He should stop—it's his third piece—but he can't help himself. "Different things. Some outside factors. Some bits of knowledge you have in one universe and not another. Whims. Crises. Luck. All sorts of things." He carves off a piece of pie with his fork and brings it to his mouth and chews.

Liz watches him intently.

"We're all blind," he says after swallowing. "Take solace in that. Choice comes first. Meaning comes later."

• • •

In 1982, Hugh is glaring at me. "What?"

"Do you love your wife and daughter?" I repeat.

"Of course I love them," he tells me. "Why would you ask me something like that?"

"Because we are alike," I say. "Men like us . . ." I stare directly into his eyes. "We are oblivious to our fuck-ups. With you, it is your obsession. With me . . ." I don't finish the sentence. I get up

and walk around the room. The light coming in the window illuminates the motes of dust in the air.

"I didn't come here to hear about your theory," I continue. "Not really. I thought it would help me understand what's happening to me. But it won't." I walk over to him. Hugh looks uneasy now. I'm close, so close he could reach out and touch me if he wanted to. "I'm here to tell you about things you won't get to see. I'm here to tell you how it ends."

It isn't the shakes or the strong chemical scent that clings to him, or the skipping of showers. It isn't the smell of something burning that I catch a whiff of when I come into the apartment. It isn't his insomnia or the sight of him pacing in the middle of the night. It isn't the bloodshot eyes or the weight loss. It isn't his inability to keep a job.

I think he's smoking. I think he's drinking. I think he's depressed and isn't taking care of himself, dealing with shit from over there he has never told me about.

But one night, I'm sitting in the living room, watching *Fresh Prince*, when Keren comes in with Cory. Baby Gina isn't with them. Keren has a split lip and fresh tears on her face. She keeps her head down, her body convulsing softly. That's when I know. All the signs coalesce in my mind as something solid and certain.

"What the hell?" I say. "Where you get that?"

It is the smallest glance over at my brother. He glares at her with wide eyes. I've known him since he was shitting his diaper, and I've never seen him look like that. Didn't know he could even make a face like that.

"Baby bro," I say, "where she get that?"

"Don't know. Bitches be clumsy."

"What!"

He grabs Keren by the arms and pushes past me.

"Are you on drugs?" I ask. At any other time in our lives, this question would be a joke.

Cory takes Keren into the room and shuts the door. No words. No answer to my question. Only the soft voices on the TV set, and the darkness. Will cracks a joke. The audience laughs.

I stay outside in the living room and wait for someone to leave the room. It is a long wait. The lights of the TV make long shadows on the walls. And then I hear the door creak open and someone slip into the dark hallway. Keren comes out and sits right next to me, as if she knew I was waiting for her.

"How long?" I ask her.

"Months."

We sit and stare ahead at the screen. It's one of those silly infomercials they play in the middle of the night. A woman in black and white struggling with her large oven, juxtaposed with another woman in color, smiling with perfect teeth, using one of those tiny rotisserie ovens with some person's fancy signature on it.

"You should leave him," I tell her.

"What if he doesn't let me?"

"Then you do what you have to do."

After that, I see Keren one more time in the apartment, and then I stop seeing her. Cory spends a lot of time pacing around the house, muttering to himself.

"It's for the best," I say. "Take it easy."

He ignores me. He listens to Rush so loud that the neighbors come by. He cries a lot. He has shouting matches with Keren's mother on the phone. A cop comes by the house to talk some sense into him.

"If you go by her apartment again, we will have to arrest you," says the cop, who is Keren's cousin.

More pacing. More muttering.

And then, out of nowhere, Cory takes a shower, irons some clothes, and goes out for the first time in forever. Gets himself a haircut, thank fucking God. Even starts looking for a real job instead of whatever the hell he was doing with his time.

One afternoon, he comes back with one. Guess where? Kmart.

It's looking good, though. Cory starts helping with the rent regularly. He keeps his hair trimmed. He puts a little weight back on. I feel confident enough to leave him alone in the house. I go over by Mona on weekends again. I come back, and the house is clean. Pahnah even starts cooking. Elaborate dishes he's seen on the Cooking Channel.

It's a beautiful couple of months. We sit and watch movies. We talk like the old days. He still keeps the whole military business to himself, but I'm fine with that. I feel like I have my brother back. He reads books again and goes on and on about society, the nature of humanity, and the concept of the soul. Every few days, I hear him in his room, muttering, but I'm

hopeful. He looks like he wants something better for himself, and I want that, too.

• • •

Three months after the whole Keren thing, I come home and there's Cory, on the couch, eyes bloodshot, a glass crack pipe on the table, burnt on one end. I know what it is now.

When I come in, he immediately starts yelling. That Keren is seeing some guy. That she has him around his daughter, and he doesn't want some random pahnah around his daughter, and so on. I throw the crack pipe in the trash and then sit with him, letting him rant and rave for a half hour.

And then I tell him, "Come on, baby bro. Get some sleep. We will deal with this in the morning when you calm down." I tell him that the worst thing he can do is go over there angry and get himself arrested. I remind him about the cop. I tell him that the only way he will get all this straightened out is if he focuses on himself right now, on getting clean.

He nods. "It's hard," he says.

"I know."

"I want my family," he says.

I look at him long and hard. "Then get your shit together."

I sit with him until he goes to sleep, and then I get up to go to my room. On my way out of the living room, I look back at my little brother. Cory is lying on the couch, but there's someone in the chair where I was sitting. I feel dizzy. I lean against the wall. I rub at my eyes, fractals of color dancing behind the lids. When I open my eyes, the person is gone. I take a deep breath, wait for the nausea to pass, and go to my room.

When I get up in the middle of the night, Cory is gone.

Later, I hear that he went down to Keren's house. He was high and angry and delirious. He called out her name several times, yelling this and that, hitting the doors and windows with a metal pipe he'd found, breaking a few. After about a half hour, the guy Keren has been seeing opened the door and shot Cory in the chest. When the ambulance arrived, he was already dead.

So it fucking goes.

Mom calls me up, and I listen to her cry for an hour. Then I go over by the house Cory and I grew up in, sit in the kitchen with her and Daryl and the twins, and I eat day-old johnnycakes and salt fish. Every few minutes, Mom looks up to the ceiling, her face filmed with tears, and says, "Lord, give me strength."

We bury him next to our grandparents on my mother's side. The service is long. Mom cries inconsolably. I hold her back from lunging at the casket. "Oh, Lord!" she screams. "Oh, Lord!"

Keren doesn't come to the burial. Mom tells her to stay away. I wait a few months, and then I go see Keren and Gina. I hold my niece for what feels like the first time, kissing her forehead. Before, I saw her as something separate from myself, not my business. But now she feels like something to keep close. She seems impossibly happy. She smiles and blushes at my kisses. After a while, she gets squirmish and I let her go. She runs off down the hall to her room.

The entire time, Keren is sitting by the door, head lowered.

"I am not judging you," I say.

This frees a well inside her, and she cries openly. After she's done, she looks up at me. I can hear Gina watching cartoons

in her bedroom, the sound of cheery music and voices with smiles in them.

"How could this happen?" she says. She recoils as if she has said something wrong.

"I don't know," I lie. "These things just do."

It's July 18, 1982. Liz is doing dishes, and her father is at the kitchen table. It is late afternoon. Liz is wearing a long-sleeved shirt to cover the needle tracks. It's been a few months since her last relapse. Her skin burns for it. Doing chores helps.

Liz looks up from the sink and tells Hugh she is thinking of getting a band together to record some music.

"You should," Hugh says, and it seems genuine. He has a smile on his face, his cheeks rosy from the sherry.

"Did you ever want to be a musician?" she asks him.

"Oh, no," he says, smiling. "That is not how I was made."

"Made?"

They laugh. It's just the three of us in the house. Nancy is out shopping.

"You should do it," Hugh says encouragingly.

That night, Liz and Nancy go to the movies. Before she leaves, Liz looks back for a moment to see her father lying with his back

to the TV. The volume is all the way up and blaring at the back of Hugh's head.

A universe exists where Liz walks back in and checks on her father, and a whole set of different quantum moments ensues. But in this one, Liz and Nancy leave because they don't want to miss the movie.

When they come home later, Nancy finds Hugh lying on the bed, in full clothes, one shoe on. His other foot is naked and hanging off the edge of the mattress. Hugh looks like wax, his cheeks empty of color. Nancy tries to wake him. She slams her fist down on his chest. She yells. But there's no life there. This Hugh is dead. Soon his atoms will displace and find new homes, and he will be lost to the other Hughs, irretrievable.

The paramedics come and cart him away in a body bag. Nancy stands in the doorway, shaking.

Liz doesn't watch this part. She sits at the table in her father's chair and idly flips through an issue of *Newsweek*. In another universe, Liz can think back and see many instances where she has touched her father, and the past, though painful to look at now, is filled with warmth. But you've sensed the pattern by now. In this universe, Liz can't remember a single moment in her life where they ever touched.

They cremate Hugh's remains, and Nancy keeps his ashes for a while before emptying them in the trash as Hugh wished. In the following years, Nancy dies of lung cancer, likely caused by second-hand smoke from Hugh's cigarettes.

Liz continues to struggle with depression and addiction. On July 11, 1996, she tries again to kill herself. This time, she succeeds. She leaves a note saying she wants no religious nonsense. She wants her body burned, her ashes sprinkled into a nice ocean or lake somewhere. Or the trash.

Maybe that way, I'll find the right universe to be with Daddy.

Only after Hugh is dead does he finally become famous. People excavate his life like a ruined cave. But they do not find him there. Only his absence.

• • •

After Cory dies, the episodes get worse. Throughout my day, I'm plagued with mirages of other worlds—cars appearing out of nowhere, buildings bursting into existence and vanishing again. Strange people in my kitchen, walking down the halls, shitting in my toilet. And Cory, lying on the couch, holding his daughter, watching TV with Keren, cooking gourmet meals in the kitchen, filling dishes with food I'll never eat again. And other me's, walking the halls at night, opening the fridge, crawling into bed beside me, crying in the dark.

I get all dizzy, and when I close my eyes I see spots of color, spinning and blurring together, and I have to sit down so I don't fall over.

In my dreams, I'm falling through an endless void filled with distant whispers and splintering constellations of rainbowed light.

It takes months to figure out what I'm looking at, and even longer to navigate it, to turn the pages, to descend into color streams and follow their currents, to run off cliffs and forget to fall.

I beat myself up for not figuring it out sooner, when it would have mattered. The regret is bottomless.

I learn the rules. I can visit people. I can stop time. I can listen to people's thoughts. I can ask questions and people can't lie about the answers. People can see me only when I want them to. I am like the shadow dislodging from the wall—an absence. I'm not meant to be a thing that makes sense.

What I can't do is change anything. I can't change the course of history. I can't make it so that things work out. Every universe exists complete from the start. It's all already happened.

When I tell Hugh what will happen to his family, he cannot speak. He murmurs. He sobs. He tries to put on his other shoe but can't. It is impossible for him to put on his other shoe. He is dressed to take himself to the hospital, but he won't make it.

In my universe, Hugh has two sons, but I can't visit them. I can visit other worlds only. Yet these parallel universes feel more real than the one I wake up to each morning. My waking life feels like short breaths alternating with vastness. The spaces between breaths are where I live now.

As Hugh reaches again for his shoe, I observe him with an expression of pity. For him and me and the ruin, we are helpless to change. "You won't remember me," I tell him. "It is probably for the best."

And then I disappear. I become the thing between things again. I watch time start again and I see him, confused for only a moment, return to where he was when time stopped, back to standing over his left shoe, the tears gone from his eyes. He stumbles for his shoe, but a pain catches him and he sits on the bed. And there his heart explodes.

There are universes where Hugh lives.

In one, he is in his house, remembering the night when his chest felt as if it would burn up inside him. Liz finds him and gets him to the hospital in time. The doctor tells him his arteries are clogged and that he has to make some changes. It is hard at first, and he is stubborn, but he reminds himself how it felt to be so close to death, and he climbs that hill.

He sits on the old couch with his granddaughter. Liz finally settles down with a guy too boring and too stupid for Hugh to really like, but he has a steady job and that's enough, Hugh thinks. So much better than what she was up to before.

Liz stops in and shares her music. Hugh thinks it's awful and melancholic, but it's his daughter, and he's proud that people call her "E" and show up to hear her play. Nancy had a cancer scare a few years back, but she pulled through. There's not a lot of time left for either of them. They're old and sickly from the years of bad

decisions. But they're here for now. He looks down at his grand-daughter, Helen. She's four, and she's staring at the TV with sleepy eyes that remind him of his mother's.

There's also a world where Cory doesn't die. Where I come home to find him high on crack in the living room, and I don't go to bed. A world where I don't wake up to hear that he went to his baby mama's house banging on the windows and threatening murder, where her new boo doesn't come outside and shoot him through the heart.

"I want my family," he tells me.

"Then get your shit together," I say.

I stay out in the living room with him. We talk. He's angry, but he's also tired, and before long we're both mumbling in the dark—him on the couch, me on the armchair—and sleep hits us hard. We wake up. He makes breakfast, some delicious-ass pancakes and scrambled eggs with the right amount of cheddar, and we hang out all day and play *Smash Bros.* and I utterly destroy him.

That night, we go out to the club and he meets a girl and he dances all night. I look across the dance floor and I see her tongue in his mouth. They leave together.

"You gon' be all right, baby bro?" I ask as he's heading out.

He just gives me that smile like *come on, B, of course,* and I let him go.

It doesn't last for them, but it is enough. His mind is off home-girl long enough to realize that he doesn't need her to be the one and only. Tons of fish in the sea. He spends time with his daugh-ter. He focuses on becoming a father. On her tenth birthday, he buys her an iPhone and he fights with her mom, but it is civil, like a dance they do once in a while to reconnect.

He doesn't pick up that shit again. Every once in a while, he

wakes up and he can feel lightning crackling under his skin, but he calls up his little girl just to hear her voice.

"Daddy, it's early," she says, annoyed and half asleep.

"Just calling my girl to give her a kiss," he says, smiling. "You too old for my kisses now?"

"I'm sorry," Gina and I say together, her voice bright and cheery, mine tinged with sadness.

He never hears me, though I've been here many times.

This is where I return: to my piece of heaven and hell, my always-open wound, my little snatch of infinity.

NIGHT MUSIC

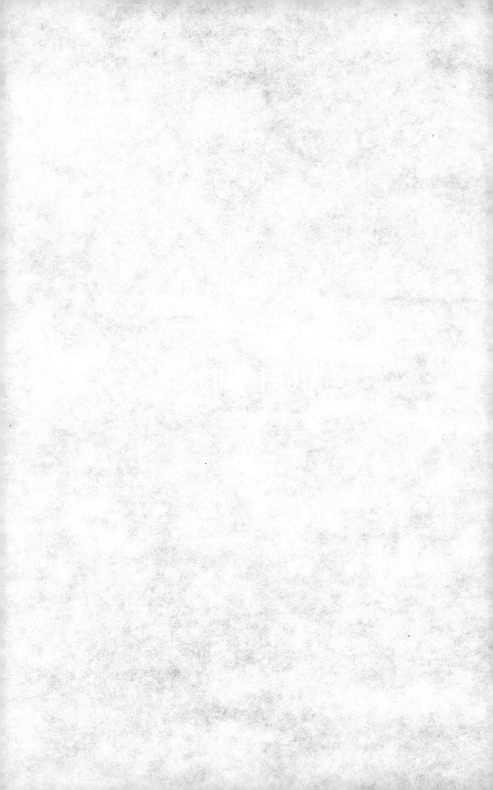

58

LAINA CALVARY
SOMERVILLE, MASSACHUSETTS
EARTH 0539

II MONTHS AND TWENTY-SEVEN DAYS AFTER THE FRACTURE

Laina has Ridley's birthday covered this year. She's messaged all their common friends and told them she is planning a surprise party. She's picked up several kinds of rum and gin, whiskey and vodka, fancy club soda, tonic water, and ginger beer. She's gone to a party supply store and bought a ton of Halloween-themed decorations, a happy birthday banner, paper garlands. She's dumped bags of candy and chips and nachos with dipping sauces into shopping carts. He is having a hard time, and Laina thinks a party will help.

Some people envy Ridley for being born on Halloween, but Ridley is of two minds. On one hand, he can dress up however he wants and no one can say a thing. On the other, he has to compete with Halloween festivities every year. There are so many parties to attend and, if he throws one, so many to compete with his. Usually, he doesn't bother with either and just stays home watching horror movies.

But this one, Laina won't let slip by. She takes the day off

work. There is still so much to do, and these things always take longer than expected. She spends the morning cleaning the house, straightening up their tiny living room, folding and putting things away, doing laundry.

Laina watches *The Americans* as she makes the chocolate cake. She mixes all the dry and wet ingredients in separate bowls. The recipe asks her to use a machine to whip the eggs, milk, and oil, but she uses a hand whisk instead. Ridley would laugh at her for her aversion to baking appliances. In this, too, he has her beat. Ridley, not she, is the baker. She has the idea of doing a layer cake but can't find two pans of the same size and shape, so she decides to do only one layer and see what happens. In the oven, it looks as though it will be fine—the cake looks full-bodied and beautiful—but after it cools, it looks more like a brownie sheet than an actual chocolate cake. Maybe she will make another layer after all. She looks at the time: four p.m. Two and a half hours until the party. Possible, if she hurries.

She orders regular and gluten-free pizza off an app on her phone, then realizes a half-hour later that she has requested the pizza from the shop in Brookline, not the one in Somerville. The one in Somerville won't be taking orders until six. She's done this before and had to call the app's help line to cancel the order and then make another one. But it is Halloween, and the pizzas are likely already made. She can't cancel now. She looks at the time and punches the distance into Google Maps. It will take a half hour to get to Brookline. Longer if she considers the rush-hour traffic. No time to sit back and think it over. She finishes putting up the last few streamers and runs out of the house.

"Halloween is going to be busier than usual this year," says the WGBH reporter as she pulls out of the parking spot. "Be careful out there."

What he isn't saying is that people have been buying up were-wolf costumes and running around in packs for at least a week already. On Twitter, #WerewolfAttacks has been trending for three days straight. Costumed gangs chasing people down empty streets, tackling joggers on park trails, harassing the homeless, and vandalizing buildings.

Even if the reporter mentions the attacks, he won't acknowledge the cause.

At first, Laina wondered how it could be so easy for so many people to dismiss what they saw with their own eyes. But she quickly realized her mistake. How had she reacted when she saw the video? The same way the cop did that night: with disbelief, a deep lack of understanding, and the desire to pull it all back into something she could name and fit inside her skull.

She has to remind herself what she saw, repeat it like a story so it would stick. She saw her brother die, and when he died, he wasn't human.

How hard must it be for everyone else, seeing a shaky video on their television? How deep was the release of pressure once the evidence went away? That terrifying weight, gone in an instant. What relief. Everything could go back to the way it was. Reality is a contract, after all.

Laina thinks of the flash drive, the unedited video still waiting there. She could do it again—disrupt this whole lie. But she'd need power, real power, to protect those she loves.

"It is going to be a dreary night," the reporter is saying now. "For folks rushing to get home, the traffic is worse than usual."

The words pull Laina from her thoughts. She looks at the clock: 5:07 p.m. *Fuck*.

Laina gets her first taste of traffic heading out of Somerville.

The sky is gray with rain clouds looking to burst. She is usually a bit intimidated to drive on the roads at peak hours, but she also knows she needs to be back at the apartment by six at the latest. She surprises herself with her aggressive driving. At a three-road intersection, she has to wait four turns of the light to squeeze her way through. She is behind an ambulance, which hasn't dissuaded anyone from blocking the way.

She finds the pizza shop but has to circle twice before parking illegally in the CVS across the street. It is five thirty.

"I came to pick up," she tells the guy at the counter. "Laina."

"Yeah, that's been here a while."

She tries on her best smile.

He goes in the back and brings out the pizzas, still warm to the touch. She smiles again and leaves the shop, running across the road, the three boxes shifting, horns blaring from both directions.

She types the trip back in Maps. Forty-five minutes. It is 5:37 p.m. She swears under her breath and tears out of the parking lot.

The way back is even worse now that she's officially been caught in the off-work traffic. She also planned to bake some cauliflower and chicken wings, but she won't be able to go to the store to pick up anything. She uses the food app again to get Korean chicken wings from another pizza shop in the neighborhood and curses herself for not getting everything from there in the first place.

At a traffic stop, she looks at her phone and sees a message from Ridley. *"Coming home at 6."* Shit.

It has started to drizzle, the splatter only barely enough for the lowest wiper setting. The way back is different from the way there, and Laina has to make sure it's Summer Street in Somerville and

not the one in the middle of Boston. That has happened before, and she has been paranoid about it ever since.

She gets back to Somerville by 6:15—a minor miracle—and picks up the wings and heads home. Ridley is walking his bike up toward the apartment building as she arrives, his silhouette recognizable even from several yards away. She runs over, gives him a hug, and then runs inside ahead of him.

"Can I come in," he asks.

"Yes," Laina says, and she gets to see his face light up at the banner and decorations.

"Oh, I love it, babe."

Laina is sweating through her shirt, but it all has been worth it.

People start arriving at six thirty. Laina leaps around, making sure everyone has what they need. She keeps her eye on the timer, to make sure she gets the cake out when it's ready. When it is done, she lays it out on the table, lets it cool, applies the icing.

Laina gets a few texts from people who won't be able to make it. An hour into the party, only four more people are in attendance, not counting Laina and the birthday boy himself. She was hoping for twice that number, but four people on Halloween, especially *this* Halloween, is a gift. People talk, drink, devour slices of pizza. Music plays softly from the Bluetooth speakers. Eventually, she brings out the cake and they sing happy birthday. Ridley is smiling, and it is so good to see him smile. They slice the cake, and as everyone eats, they go around the room and say nice things about Ridley.

"You're always so cool," says Roman, the bookstore's sole bartender.

"Your enthusiasm for politics is infectious," says Madeline, Ridley's friend and cofounder of the store.

"I've only known you a short time," Rebecca says, "but you've made me feel like family."

"You have nice hair," Sarah says.

Ridley does have nice hair. And great skin, too, bright amber eyes, and beautiful pink lips. Laina likes hearing the good things people have to say about the man she loves. Rebecca is smiling, too, and Laina feels a sort of comfort having them both there, in the same space with common friends and acquaintances.

"I love you," Laina says. "I'm happy we're on this journey together. I wouldn't have made it without you."

"I love you too," he says, and his smile is genuine and all for her.

The cake is okay. It still looks like a brownie, but she tries not to be hard on herself.

They drink cocktails and talk about television shows, movies, books. Laina goes on and on about *The Americans*. There is some business-adjacent talk about the bookstore, which Laina avoids participating in, and then some discussion of politics and recent news. A local Unitarian Universalist church recently declared its allyship with monsters, and then someone set fire to the church, killing three people. There's a moment of stunned silence, and then Sarah asks who is going to the monster march coming up in less than a week.

The room goes quiet, everyone staring into their lap or their hands. No one is answering. Ridley's eye is actually twitching.

"I'm going," Sarah volunteers. She looks at Ridley and Laina. "What about you guys?" Sarah's tone is friendly, in no way revealing her feelings on the matter.

More silence. More staring into laps.

Finally, Ridley says, "I don't know."

"You *don't*?" Sarah says. It isn't really a question.

"There are safety concerns."

"Safety," Sarah repeats. In an instant, her demeanor has changed. She leans forward. "You think monsters are dangerous? Or you think people who believe in them are? Which one? Both?"

"Come on," Rebecca says. "This is a birthday party. Now's not the time for a heavy discussion."

Sarah puts up her hand. "What are you saying? What safety concerns?"

Ridley's face turns visibly red. "I'm saying that people's emotions are heightened right now, and nothing good comes from that."

"Nothing good comes from emotion?" Sarah's veneer of pleasantry is gone. "I think emotion is a very good thing for creating change."

"What sort of change?" Ridley asks back.

"Equal rights under the law. So that monsters aren't gunned down in the street or get their churches burned."

"But that wasn't *their* church," Ridley says. "It was the people trying to protect the monsters, who were burned."

Laina stares at Rebecca, helpless. The horror on each of their faces is like a mirror.

"People need to be protected too," Ridley says.

The room descends into a deep silence. The space between two songs stretches unbearably long before "Natural Science" starts playing from the speakers. Everyone has pointedly started to look away from Ridley.

"Protect *people*," Sarah repeats.

Only then does Ridley seem to realize how far he's gone. "I didn't mean it like that."

"How did you mean it?" Angry tears fill Sarah's eyes.

And there's Geddy's voice, over a backdrop of lapping water and a lazy guitar:

> *"All the busy little creatures*
> *Chasing out their destinies*
> *Living in their pools*
> *They soon forget about the sea . . ."*

Laina tries to say something, but the words catch in her throat. Madeline and Roman are looking at Sarah. Laina can see the realization happening. Sarah is a monster. They are in the room with an actual monster.

"Yeah, that's right," Sarah says. "Anybody else got something to get off their chest?"

"Sarah, let's take a walk," Rebecca says.

"No. If they got something to say, they should say it."

Ridley stands up. He says, "I'm sorry," and leaves the room.

The party ends after that. Rebecca takes Sarah and leaves. Madeline and Roman wait a few minutes before leaving. And finally, the door closes and Laina stands alone in the living room. "Natural Science" is still playing, seven minutes into its nine-minute run. Jesus. Who even put this on the playlist? It could only be Ridley.

She finds him in the bedroom, head in his hands.

"Please, tell me what's going on," she says, standing in the doorway. "You've been holding back long enough."

"I can't."

"This isn't us. We don't do this to each other, ever."

He stares up at her with a look she knows but rarely sees on his face—defensive, combative. "Where did you get Lincoln's video?"

To her credit, Laina doesn't back away or flinch at the question.

The air sings with the accusation. "I told you, someone sent it to my inbox."

"Oh, yeah? And where is it now?"

"It disappeared just like all the other videos."

"Who sent it?" Ridley watches her, unblinking.

"I don't know," Laina says. "You're changing the subject."

"This *is* the damn subject!" Ridley says. "You're lecturing me about keeping things to myself. How much are you keeping to yourself? If you have a right to mine, I have a right to yours."

"I'm concerned, that's it."

"No. You're in the dark about something and you don't like it."

"Did you see what happened out there? This isn't about me!"

"So you invited Sarah for my sake?"

"Rebecca invited Sarah."

"Oh," Ridley says. "I suppose that explains everything."

"What do you mean?"

Ridley doesn't answer.

"Wait. Is all this about Rebecca?"

Ridley opens his mouth, the words lingering there. Laina sees them roll back in, sees sadness blanket all the anger that was there moments ago. "I don't know. I don't think so."

Now he looks confused, which is strange for Ridley. Of the two of them, he is the one most attuned to his feelings. She thinks he wants to say, *There's so much between us,* because she feels that, too, a painful lump at her center.

And she is right; Ridley is scared. In his mind, he is out in space being devoured by the Titan, Earth in the distance as the cold takes him.

Ridley lies back in bed, puts his hands over his eyes against the light. "I'm sorry. I just need to rest. I'll be better in the morning."

He relaxes his posture, and Laina knows they've reached the end of this particular conversation—nothing given, nothing learned. She has a gift she wants to give him, a new carving knife, but that will have to wait as well.

"Happy birthday," she says, and flicks off the light.

The living room is a mess of boxes and discarded plates and cups. Candy wrappers are strewn on the carpet. She gathers all of it and passes by the door to their bedroom on the way to the kitchen. Everything feels heavier than it should, her shoulders aching under the strain of gravity. There's a tangible pressure at the door, repelling her. She doesn't want to go in there tonight. She feels both shame and relief at acknowledging this. After cleaning the kitchen, she'll gather some extra pillows and a comforter from the linen closet and sleep on the fold-out in the living room.

She repeats a version of Ridley's words, tries to make them hers, tries to believe them. It will be better in the morning.

59

The air at Tomland Pool has that unmistakable smell of chlorine. All indoor pool facilities are like this, and Laina has been in enough to feel instantly familiar with this one. She walks quickly up the incline that leads to the top of the bleachers, the sounds of many voices and the loudspeaker echoing off the high ceiling. From here, she can see the crowd of people laid out before her on the descending bleachers, and the nine pool lanes and their swimmers. She is late, but Rebecca said it was okay to be late. She searches the half-full bleachers for Rebecca's head and finds her near the back. Laina inches past a few pairs of knees and sits down.

"Oh," Rebecca says. "I was looking for you."

Laina smiles and kisses her on the cheek. "Did I miss her?"

Rebecca shakes her head and points poolside. There's Sarah, standing in a line of women. Laina counts four people ahead of her, three behind. Sarah looks up at them, smiles, and waves excitedly. Laina and Rebecca wave back, and Laina feels a sense

of relief at how happy Sarah is to see her, despite the events of two nights ago.

"This swim meet is divided into heats," Rebecca explains. "By speed: slow to fast."

Laina watches the women at the head of the line. Some look older, some younger. As one group of women leaves the pool, another group steps onto the diving pads. The horn blows, and the next race begins.

"What category is this?" Laina asks.

"Hundred-meter freestyle."

"You go to a lot of these?"

"We all did. Lincoln and others too, when they were still around."

Laina is quiet until the race ends. "Were Lincoln and Sarah very close? She reminds me of him sometimes."

The horn blows again, and the next race begins. "Yeah," Rebecca says. "They were close."

Another heat starts and ends, and then Sarah takes her place on top of the diving pad. Even from a distance, Laina can see how strong she is. Compact but powerful. When the horn blows, Sarah leaps from the board in a clean arc. All the swimmers are under-water for a moment, their legs kicking like the tails of dolphins. The movements are so graceful, Laina forever abandons her belief that humans are not meant for the water. Almost at the halfway mark, Sarah starts using her arms, cutting through the water with long, even strokes. Laina watches the other swimmers and realizes Sarah is actually in second place, which surprises her. It takes her a moment to realize why.

Laina leans toward Rebecca and whispers, "Is she losing on purpose?"

Rebecca smiles. "She weakens her kicks and strokes. She also flexes her toes to create drag. Her coach gives her shit about it all the time."

When Sarah reaches the other end of the pool, she hinges at the waist and somersaults underwater. There is a yellow pad in the pool, under the water, and as Sarah completes her flip turn, she twists her whole body so that her feet touch the yellow pad at an angle. She bends her legs and then extends them, pushing off the pad. A burst of power sends her back down to the other end of the pool. The movements are practiced, clean. The first-place swimmer's lead vanishes in an instant. Within seconds, the race is over and Sarah has won.

"You think they know?" Laina asks.

Rebecca stares at her for a moment before recognition hits. "Oh, that. She's good at hiding it. No one cares, anyway."

"Don't you think some people might be upset?"

"She's slightly above average in this meet. Not going to the Nationals or the Olympics anytime soon."

Sarah is out of the water and fist-pumping the air in her excitement. She looks up at them with her mouth open in shock and joy.

"I think she beat her record time," Rebecca says.

"That's wonderful."

The next race isn't so interesting. Nothing has changed, only Laina's connection to the events happening before her. All the stakes are gone.

Rebecca has a serious look on her face.

"What is it?" Laina asks.

"I should tell you something, but it will have to stay between us."

"Okay?"

"Sarah and Lincoln were more than close." Rebecca says the

words plainly—a whole constellation of meaning, immense and terrible. It all makes sense now.

Laina can't tell how much time has passed between her words and her answer, only that she's nodded maybe twice in that time. And Rebecca has been watching her, silent and searching. A horn blows in the distance, and bodies splash into clear blue water.

"I wanted to tell you," Rebecca says, "but she says she wanted to do it. It is hard for her to share her emotions. I just wanted you to know."

Laina nods.

"I never met a partner of his."

"You did. But not one that loved him back."

Rebecca doesn't have to say anything, because Laina knows immediately who she is talking about. Tomas. The asshole she left him with that night, when Lincoln was crying and high out of his mind. Laina inches around that bit of shame, holds herself tight against her walls so she can't touch it.

"Sarah thinks we'll find other monsters at the march," Rebecca says.

Laina looks at her.

"Yeah, I know it's dangerous. I've said it over and over again: 'No further actions.'"

"And what does she say?"

"That this isn't our action. We can hide. We can say we were just curious."

And there's that same gleam in Rebecca's eye from a year ago. Laina knows it is already decided, with or without her. Sarah is going to that march, and Rebecca will follow. But what will Laina do?

All this time, she has been thinking she kept silent for Rebecca's

sake. For Ridley's sake. For the people she loves who need protecting. But the look in Rebecca's eyes tells a different story. Maybe Rebecca has been the one protecting her.

Laina wants to say she'll go with them. She's told no one about the unedited video. She wants to say this, too, which might have the power to change everything this time around. But a rock is in her throat and it won't budge.

"Don't worry," Rebecca says. "I'll make sure Sarah doesn't get into any trouble."

When Laina returns from drinks at Rebecca's, Ridley is already asleep, so she goes to the kitchen, makes herself a sandwich, and washes some dishes that have lingered in the sink since breakfast. Afterward, she sits in the kitchen and tries to finish *Dead Things*. The secret cabal has finally been revealed: a group of billionaires are trying to turn themselves into immortal monsters. Laina reads a few pages, but then her mind starts drifting. She looks up. A bird of happiness hangs in the kitchen now, gently spinning on its tether. Two are in the hall, and two more in the living room and office. A solitary bird also hangs in their bedroom. The population of birds has more than tripled.

Laina considers joining Ridley in bed, but she knows she can't sleep through the night if she turns in so early. Ridley sleeps early these days and stays asleep later. He's taken a whole week of wellness days from the bookstore. She tried asking him what's wrong, but he denies anything amiss. She has tried pushing and not pushing, with

the same result. They aren't talking, drifting away from each other little by little, and she has been spending a lot of time with Rebecca.

She doesn't want to join him in bed, but she closes the book and goes into the room. From the doorway, Ridley looks peaceful, but more than once she has woken up to the sound of him grinding his teeth. She takes off her clothes and throws them on a chair by the bed. Ridley will comment on it in the morning. She doesn't care. She wants to push him into a confrontation. She puts on one of her big T-shirts and climbs into bed. It is still early, just past ten. She puts on an audiobook and stuffs it under her pillow to muffle the sound. She puts thirty minutes on the sleep timer, but she's out before the halfway mark.

Laina isn't surprised when she wakes up a little after four in the morning. When the usual trick of keeping her eyes closed doesn't work, she sits up in bed. The room is dark around her, which is why she notices the little light go off on Ridley's phone. Someone has messaged him at four in the morning. She doesn't know what to feel about this. Though it has always been an option on the table, Ridley has shown zero interest in taking advantage of their openness. What could it be, then, at this hour?

The bed creaks as Laina gets up, but Ridley doesn't stir. Quietly she lifts the phone off the bedside table and leaves the room. Laina starts making laps through the apartment. Kitchen. Living room. Office. The floor creaks under her weight. The office window shines red, then green, as a traffic light outside the house changes. A car streaks by: some late-night wanderer like her. In the hallway, she steps on a loose floorboard and it groans like an old cat. She cringes. Any noise can startle Ridley awake. She turns to retreat back down the hall, away from Ridley's room, away from his nightmares and back to her own thoughts.

She has to know. Does she have to know?

Shifting her weight to go back into the office, she feels her knee

pop. The slow creep of age adds itself to Laina's worries. It occurs to her that her life has somehow been reduced to a series of ticking clocks hanging on every wall and sitting on every surface, counting down to moments known and unknown. Morning approaches, and she can see that clock ticking now, lost time that she could have used for sleep. And other things too. Death, that universal clock, its long hand slowly sweeping all before it. Her brother, dead already, and a clock measuring that loss in negative time.

Wait too long, and everything slips away from you.

With a series of swipes, Laina unlocks Ridley's phone. She almost thinks it won't work. He has so many secrets now. Maybe he changed the pattern. But the phone opens to the message.

> Goddamn it! Don't you have a
> conscience?

The message is from a woman named Ruth. Laina scrolls up to the beginning of the message thread.

> Please tell me what happened with
> my brother. I can meet in person if
> you're uncomfortable texting.

> He was very close to his niece, did you
> know that? She's been asking about him.

> All of you are fucking terrible.

> Please tell me what happened. I
> need to know.

And then the message Laina read first.

She finds twelve missed calls from Ruth. Ridley hasn't called her back, hasn't responded to any of her messages.

The keyboard opens up when Laina presses her index finger to the text box. She starts typing, stops, starts again. She hits send.

> I'm so sorry. Could you tell me
> what you already know?

Seeing her own words, her heart sinks with shame. She knows that she won't be able to get rid of the evidence. She has no idea what she's stirred up. A response comes almost immediately.

> What?

And then another text from her several minutes later . . .

> The officers that came by said he
> died in a car accident. They bought
> an urn with them, but why would they
> cremate him so fast, and without
> notifying us? They won't answer my
> inquiries except to say it is under
> investigation.

> I know he was there at the retreat.
> And you all have been ignoring me.
> That's all I know.

And again:

> Please tell me what happened
> to Nick.

Laina puts down the phone. The blinds on the other office window glow white from the streetlight. The shadow of a single tree branch dangles there, like the lure of an anglerfish. She listens to the house, the pounding in the walls (which she has never discovered the source of), the soft distant noises outside. Laina calls it night music, the way the silence brings the quiet sounds into sharp relief.

She shouldn't have done this. This was a mistake.

The phone glows, and it has been so long, Laina has to unlock it again. She reads the short message.

> I'm sorry. I promise not to contact
> you again.

Laina immediately starts typing, "Wait. Is everything okay?" But just as she is about to hit send, the phone shuts off. Laina powers it back on, unlocks it, and goes back into messages only to find that the entire thread of her and Ruth's conversation is gone. She searches the call history, and the calls from Ruth are gone as well. She checks the phone three more times to make sure, searches for Ruth's number in Ridley's contacts. Gone. She searches for Nick's contact information. Also gone. The same creeping panic and paranoia she's been having since she posted the video of her brother's death returns to her.

Up until this point, Laina had wondered why her family never connected the leaked video with Lincoln. The video had gotten the attention of some Black progressive groups before it was edited, and a few activists tried to identify the Black man in the grainy footage. They didn't find anything, but Laina always wondered why

the whispers about Lincoln's untimely end died down so quickly. If they hadn't, surely someone would have made the connection. But now Laina is thinking of Ruth's last text. She doesn't have to hear the words to know that Ruth is terrified—all that righteous frustration snuffed out in a matter of minutes. What happened in that time? What could scare someone so completely? And exactly how many people had been similarly silenced?

The same slab of wood in the hallway groans again, barely a whisper of a noise. Laina waits, and when Ridley doesn't appear at the entrance, her heart skips.

"Is that you again?" she asks the dark.

No response comes. If it is the voice, it has been several months since they last spoke.

"Please keep Ruth and her family safe," Laina says.

There's a couch in their office, right next to a short bookshelf. Laina doesn't see the woman sit down, but she hears the couch groan with the added weight. "And if I do, will you promise not to contact her again?"

Laina nods, says yes.

"We have a deal, then."

"But won't Ridley ask questions about the missing contacts?"

A short silence. "He won't. He knows a lot more than you think he does."

Laina sits with this new information. "Are you involved in this situation with Ruth?" Laina asks.

"You know I'm not," the voice says.

"And how do I know that?"

"Please keep your voice down."

Laina stops to listen. The apartment is as quiet as before. Her voice lower, she asks again. "How do I know you're not involved?"

"Because you still have the flash drive. If I was invested in silencing the truth, I wouldn't have given it to you in the first place."

"Please take it away from me," Laina says. She sighs, relieved. Now that the words are out of her mouth, she isn't surprised by them. She's wanted this all along.

"I won't," the voice says. "If you want to get rid of it, you'll have to destroy it yourself."

"I don't understand," Laina says. "Then why can't I contact Ruth if you don't need my silence to protect her?"

The voice laughs. It is a dry, gravelly sort of laugh, out of phase with the smooth quality of the voice's usual speech. "Your finger is on a bomb, Laina. I'm protecting her from *you*."

Suddenly, the bed in the other room creaks, and Laina can hear the heavy footfalls before Ridley appears at the doorway. "Who are you talking to?" he asks. His expression isn't easy to read in the dark.

Laina looks over at the couch. "Just to myself," she says.

"That's new," he says. "Have you seen my phone?" His head turns toward the couch. The movement could be nothing. Or everything. His phone is resting on the desk right beside her, but maybe he doesn't see it.

"I haven't," Laina says.

Ridley continues standing in the doorway while all the soft noises around them play their music. The couch is still, no subtle creaks or shifts to indicate another presence in the room.

"Okay," Ridley says, "I'll look for it in the morning." And he heads to the bathroom.

The next morning, Laina gets up to eat leftovers. She puts the cold pizza in the oven in a cast-iron pan and sits down to continue reading *Dead Things*. She forgets about the pizza until she smells the dough. She grabs an oven mitt, pulls the hot pan out, and sets it on the stove top, then turns the oven off.

Ridley walks in and begins making bread, as he does almost every week. He measures water in the bowl and moves around Laina. She doesn't see it happen, just hears the exclamation, the sound of something heavy dropping back down onto the stove. She turns and sees Ridley backing away from the cast-iron pan, holding his right hand open and hissing through his teeth.

Laina cycles through alarm, regret, and concern. He didn't know it was hot. She didn't tell him.

He is hissing still, staring at his red hand.

"Oh, no, baby," Laina says.

She takes the oven mitt and sticks the pan back in the oven.

Then she stands there, feeling helpless and anxious, as Ridley tries to pour the flour into the water and yeast. When he tries mixing them with both hands, he sucks in air through his teeth again. He tries with only the left. "This won't work," he says. "You'll have to help me knead dough."

"Sorry. Okay." Laina comes close to him and sticks her hands into the mixture, working it. The wet flour cakes on her fingers. She doesn't like this texture. It feels too alive, and Laina doesn't like most textures that feel alive, sticky and wet, and clinging. Laina was never interested in making bread. It always looked messy to her. But there's no way to back out without feeling worse.

Ridley nods as she works the dough, grabbing the solidifying glop and turning her hands clockwise. The dough has swirls like a cedar burl.

"I like your technique," Ridley says. "There's some dry flour there at the bottom. Get that too."

By now, the dough has taken full shape. Clumps of wet flour still cling all over Laina's hands, refusing to mix in with the rest of the dough. Her lips are tight in discomfort over this awful, awful texture.

"I don't know why it's so wet this time," Ridley says. He puts Laina's hands together and pours fresh flour into them. "Now rub your hands together."

She does, and the wet and dry flour bind through the friction. Little dough worms fall from her hands into the bowl and onto the floor.

"Put your hands in the bowl a bit more," Ridley says.

"How's your hand?" Laina asks.

"I think my middle finger will swell a little."

Laina looks up at him. "Babe."

"It'll be fine, love."

They put a cover over the dough and leave it to rise. Afterward, Ridley sits in one of the chairs in the corner of their small kitchen.

"You had my phone last night," he says. It isn't a question.

Laina comes over and sits down. She turns his hand over to see the swollen red blotch on his fingers. She resists the urge to touch the burn. It is tender and glossy, and she can feel the empathetic throb in her own hand.

"I was worried about you," she says. "I *am* worried about you."

Ridley's face doesn't express anger or betrayal. What she sees, to her surprise—and what she feels in herself—is relief.

"I'm scared all the time now," Ridley admits. "I don't want to filter everything I do through this fear. It'll change me into someone I don't want to be."

Laina can feel him on the verge of something, so she doesn't say anything. She waits.

"I'll be putting you in danger," he says, and winces again at the pain in his hand.

Laina looks at Ridley. "Well, how about an even trade? Danger for danger."

"Okay."

"And we should go to the protest."

"Wait a second. Maybe we should discuss—"

"For Lincoln. I want to do it for Lincoln."

It takes only one look at Laina for Ridley to know that it's an argument he will lose. "Okay," he says. "What day is it, again?"

NO GODS, NO MONSTERS

BOSTON, MASSACHUSETTS
EARTH 0539

ONE YEAR AFTER THE FRACTURE

On November 5, the trains are full. As early as eight a.m., groups of people stream out of the stops at Park Street and Downtown Crossing, wearing colored shirts over hoodies or under their jackets. They congregate at Boston Commons, a public park right off the Park Street T-stop. Microphones and speakers are set up in the Parkman Bandstand on the east side of the Commons. All morning, people speak on monster allyship. Protesters stand in the expansive open space, listening or talking excitedly with one another. They make speeches and read poetry and sing songs, with their signs hanging at their sides or bobbing in the air. "Monsters, we are with you." "Stop the Hate Crimes." "Monsters are people, too."

The march is scheduled for eleven a.m., from Boston Commons to City Hall, but people settle at both places. Small crowds make their way down Tremont Street or Washington Street or snake their way along Park via the Freedom Trail, or

they get off at the Government Center T-stop to save themselves the walk altogether. By ten o'clock, a large crowd has settled outside City Hall, cups of coffee and tea in their hands, huddling together to keep warm. By ten thirty, they've expanded all the way across the red-bricked plaza while cops look on quietly from the outside.

When the march starts at the Commons, Rebecca and Sarah are near the front. Marshals in orange traffic vests lead the crowd and cut off traffic as the protesters march down Boylston Street and up Washington, taking a slightly longer route.

As they march, they chant. "When monsters are under attack, what do we do?" a woman yells over a bullhorn.

"Stand up, fight back!" the crowd yells in response. This goes on for several rounds.

Rebecca watches Sarah scream with the crowd, and it makes her own latent defiance burn bright. For months, it has been just the two of them, monsters among humans, but it is different here. Even though she can't pinpoint anyone in particular, Rebecca can sense other shifters around them.

Chants and calls surge through the crowd like a current, changing as they go.

Ridley and Laina arrive late and join the tail end of the march, but the chants carry to them as well—a common language passing down the line of protesters like a massive game of telephone.

Near Ridley, a man yells, "No gods."

"No monsters," the crowd yells back.

The chant is an evolution of an anarchist slogan: "No gods, no masters," the original version meaning *no human above*. It is meant as a call against hierarchy. Ridley assumes that this

variation means *no human above, no human below,* or something like it. A call against hierarchy and discrimination. It has been quite some time since Ridley got close enough to a march to feel its infectious energy. Since those days with Marcus, the trauma has kept him away, but now he feels foolish for isolating himself for so long. He almost convinced himself that his work with cooperatives was enough. But he sees his error now. As he walks with the crowd, he understands what he had forgotten: that a march is not just a voice against violence and trauma, but also a reminder that even in a cause that is stacked against them, no one is alone.

He wants to tell Sarah this. He wants her to know that he gets it now and he is sorry. Laina has tried several times to call Rebecca, but the mass of people disrupts her cell service.

"It's okay," Ridley says. "We'll find them at City Hall."

They're on Washington Street, and the view overhead is all skyscrapers, their sharp edges cutting away the blue sky. There's something beautiful and devastating about the sight. Ridley feels small against it: the marvels of nature and human beings, intruding on one another; mass systems that existed before he was born and will continue long after he is dead. What can anyone do against them? The voices around him provide an answer. Like ants, perhaps enough human bodies can form a critical mass, becoming a marvel capable of great things, even against obstacles calcified through years of accumulated resources and power. Maybe. More often than not, Ridley has seen this fail to provide any change. But the effort has value for those fleeting moments when success can be snatched for the side of good.

Ridley doesn't know why all this is on his mind—the spirit of the moment, perhaps. There is an energy to crowds—a sort of

intangible thing, like heat, that finds its path all the way to the center of you. A feeling of power, as if anything can happen.

"No gods, no monsters!" the crowd yells, and for the first time, unselfconsciously, Ridley picks up the mantra with the crowd.

Farther behind Ridley and Laina, Dragon and Sondra stand at the edge of Boston Commons, watching dozens of people as they pass. By this point, the chants have evolved again. A woman with a bullhorn shouts: "No gods, no monsters! We will not be divided!" The crowd, signs in hands and fists to the sky, is a living thing as it repeats the call. It is a large creature made of many hands and limbs and voices.

Sondra isn't particularly interested in the protest. As people go by, she is sniffing them out, trying to detect monsters in the crowd. When she sniffs out a middle-aged woman in a red wool cap, she wraps a coil of magic around her, tagging the monster.

She quickly finds another monster—a Native American wolf-shifter variant, its magic old and very contagious, smelling of moss and tears and worn, bloodied feet—and tags him too. And then a European wolf shifter, a genetic variant that passes down only through the mother. It smells of old books with yellowed pages slowly turning to dust. Sondra tags her as well and quickly detects a Euro-American wolf hybrid—young, intensely contagious, and extremely volatile. She's tagged several more monsters in a matter of minutes. Three witches. An American bear-shifter variant, a coyote variant, a cougar variant that is as fleeting as the animal itself. Her nose is filled with the scents of monsters, dozens of distinct magics.

Here's how it works: When Sondra focuses on a person she wants to tag, she says Damsel's name in her mind. A hex is established, and a unique marker is sent through that hex to Damsel.

With Sondra acting as the conduit, Damsel sends a bit of subtle magic, which connects the witch to the person, and Damsel, now tethered to the individual, can track the monster herself even though her nose isn't quite as good as Sondra's. Indeed, no spell or hex has ever quite matched Sondra's peculiar skill. Magic, like many other things, resists being known so intimately, resists even being detected. Damsel explained once that it is in the bones of magic, the way it has been made, though she never fully explained what she meant. Sondra knew only her own magic and so couldn't speak to that truth or to why weredogs, of all creatures, should have such a unique ability.

The hex is a powerful bit of magic. Sondra has tracked monsters for the Order of Asha in the past, but never on this scale, never needing to use a magic such as this. But she reluctantly accepted the hex, obliging the order's stated objective of wanting to "track and protect as many monsters as possible." She didn't ask from what. She didn't need to. She knew enough to know that the time was coming. After Damsel hexed her, she had to sleep a full twelve hours.

She's still fatigued even now. Her body has this swimming feeling, as if she were superimposed on herself, syncing up only for brief moments. She has to fight through it to do her work.

There's a vampire in the basement of a nearby building, and two powerful witches and a sight mage up in a high-rise. Sondra's instincts tell her to leave those alone.

And then there is Dragon, who gives off a faint smell of something Sondra has difficulty describing—like tobacco smoke lingering on a coat after many years in a closed space. She has no idea why he is here. Cassandra, the sight mage, ordained it, and she's never needed a reason for anything.

And something else, too, though Sondra doesn't know what. Every time she homes in on it, her attention is pulled away and she forgets.

She thinks of her mother then, the image materializing in her mind's eye. The thought of her floods Sondra with a complicated mix of terror, yearning, and shame. She feels sick. "I suspect she was taken to track monsters for the other side," Sonya had explained. The other side. And what side had her mother been on? It occurs to Sondra that there must be many such casualties—monsters on no side, just in the middle, keeping their secret. And here she is, doing the same work, tracking them in the name of some greater good she barely understands. What a hideous thing to do: invade people's privacy and reveal their secret identities without knowing why, all for the sake of an organization that wishes to remain secret. Is this work even for the purpose the order claims? How would she know?

Sondra catches the scent again, and again she forgets. She looks around, confused.

Dragon isn't paying attention to Sondra. He's been watching the crowd too: the many colors of people's clothes, the chanting. All these people, all this noise. And in one place! How exciting. Dragon is looking everyone up and down, trying to take it all in, all this new information. This is what people wear. This is what people do. Dragon could do these things. It would be little effort at all to be just like everyone else, to live with them in their world.

It is because Dragon is paying such close attention that he notices a tall man in a long dark coat. The man, strange even among all these different people, is walking slowly through the crowd, a placid smile on his face. The top of the man's head is completely

bald, the sides messy and uncombed. Dragon feels a chill, a memory forcing its way up and through him, as if he were an open house facing a stiff breeze. He knows the man somehow. He looks around again, the creeping suspicion growing. He finds what he is looking for: a short woman in a long coat, her hair pulled back in a ponytail. Her expression is pleasant, an uninterrupted smile that is almost friendly. Except her eyes, which are fully open and unblinking. She is close enough that Dragon can see the single tear fall from her eye—condensation on a cold glass.

The woman hasn't acknowledged Dragon yet, but he can feel her shift of awareness, her attention slowly pulling toward him. Her eyes move first, so that they lock on him even while her head points straight ahead. She still isn't blinking, but her eyebrows wrinkle a tiny bit, a soft crease on the paper of her face. Her smile doesn't falter, but there's something in her expression that tips toward menace.

Dragon pulls on Sondra's shirt.

"What is it?" she says.

"I know that lady." Dragon keeps his eyes on the woman. She has stopped moving with the crowd. People move around her like insects around a puddle of water.

"Which lady?" Sondra asks, not seeing her.

"That one." Dragon points. "In the coat. The smiling lady."

Sondra shakes her head, confused.

The woman's smile creeps wider and her eyes widen. Her expression is a sort of happy surprise. Dragon sees the sleeve of the woman's coat, which hangs loose. The hand is missing. Dragon's head buzzes, filled with bees.

The woman places her other sleeve in her pocket, but Dragon can't see that hand since it's concealed by the large coat. She

rummages around briefly and pulls out something black that gleams in the sun. Sondra has stopped asking Dragon the question he can't answer, which is good. He will not be able to answer any questions for a while. The bees have drowned out the ability for language.

Dragon feels Sondra's touch just as the woman points the gleaming weapon.

It is the weapon that ignites Sondra's instincts. She jerks Dragon down to the ground. The gunfire cracks, the sound echoing off the tall buildings around the Commons. Two more gunshots come fast after the first, and the chatter and chanting unravel into a roar of human noise. Sondra picks Dragon up in her arms and starts moving. Even with his added weight, she is fast. The people around her, however, are much faster. Someone collides with Sondra from behind, and she tips forward. She does not want to fall on top of the boy, so she uses all her force to push him away from her. Her sight pitches toward the ground as Dragon sails through the air.

Sondra's head smashes against pavement so hard, her vision goes white. Two more shots ring out somewhere behind her, disturbingly close. It is difficult to see, but she tries scrambling to her feet. She turns her head and can see only a solid wall of people rushing toward her. Another collision sends her sprawling on her back, eyes to the blue sky, colors bursting in her vision like fireworks. Someone leaps over her, then another.

A fifth gunshot pierces through the voices, and a woman cries out a single long vowel. She falls on top of Sondra. Her flowing hair, like strands of silk, forms a shroud over Sondra's eyes.

Sondra tries moving the hair with her free hand, but the strands cling stubbornly to her sweating face. Spots of pain throb all over

her body. She grunts and groans, trying to push the woman off her. But then there's another gunshot. The woman's wailing is cut off at its root, and she goes limp on top of Sondra.

Frantic now, Sondra shakes free the hair obstructing her view. Finally, she can see the shooter standing over her, the sun framing her head in a circle of light, the revolver pointing down at her.

The next seconds are intimate: just Sondra, the dead woman on top of her, the woman with the revolver. Oddly quiet too. People are very far away. The trees rustle like faint white noise.

The shooter still has that strange smile. Sondra holds her breath, waits for the bullet that she knows is coming.

But something hits the woman from the side, and she falls away, revealing sharp sunlight. Sondra winces at the glare. Familiar magic fills her nose. She doesn't need to guess who this is. She feels the invisible hand touch her shoulder. The dead woman, as if on her own, rolls stiffly off her.

"Are you okay?" her sister asks. "Can you stand?"

Sondra tries a nod, fails, tries again, and manages something like it.

From within her pocket of magic, Sonya says, "Okay, I have to take care of this."

Sondra feels the magic ebb away from her. She takes a solid breath and then slowly, deliberately rolls over and pushes herself to her knees, then to her feet. She sways a little and has to widen her stance.

Now Sondra can look around. Besides the dead woman, two bodies lie nearby, one under a tree and another in the middle of the now almost empty street. Blood pools around the dead man's head.

As an afterthought, Sondra turns toward the woman who tried to kill her.

The woman is struggling with her invisible assailant, her smile gone, replaced with bitter frustration. She swings her gun hand, hitting nothing, and then swings her other arm, the sleeve rolling back to reveal a stump just above where her wrist should be. There's a loud smack, and the woman's head lolls backward from the invisible strike. She stumbles, but her head quickly whips forward again. She yells out in wild anger. Another phantom strike. The woman's trench coat crinkles at the midsection, and she falls to her knees. For a moment, she just rests there in a heap. Her head looks up to the sky, mouth open, her body heaving with exhaustion, her expression part human and partly some other thing. Sondra can smell the magic coming off the woman. The madness is familiar. Her head is clear enough now to smell all the places where this magic populates. This is not the end. This day has more blood to spill.

The woman is looking at Sondra again, a faint smile returning to her lips. She straightens a bit, still on her knees. Sondra can see the woman mustering the effort to lift her revolver again. But she doesn't get that far. A pair of phantom hands grip the woman's head. With vicious force, her head twists too far. The snap is terrible and final. The strange smile leaves the woman, along with everything else, the life cord that tethered her snapped and floating away. The woman sways in the direction it went, and then collapses to the ground.

Sondra listens to the wind. In the distance, it has begun. More gunshots. The sounds carry to her ears, mixed in with otherworldly noises of calamities past and future.

Even as things change, much stays the same, she thinks. Other tragedies are already queued up for their entrance.

A man comes out from behind a tree and makes his way to

NO GODS, NO MONSTERS 335

the woman at Sondra's feet. He doesn't speak, only leans over the woman, and cries silently. This woman who died right on top of her. She has no words for the grieving man. Nothing to ease what she knows will be a lifetime of pain and trauma. So, she just stands there, wordless.

It is only then that Sondra remembers. She looks around. Dragon is gone. She has lost him.

63

"Firecrackers?" someone asks.

The march is larger still as people find it along its path. They are now packed tight together, a solid line of unspaced human beings, on their ritualized course to their destination at City Hall. Because they are packed so tight, Ridley has difficulty pinpointing who asked the question. No matter, it is on everyone's face now. People are looking around. No one looks particularly panicked. Not yet.

The leap from firecrackers to gunshots is a tiny one, but the words are frozen on Ridley's lips. It is a dangerous suggestion. It might start a stampede. But he knows that isn't why he can't say the words. All he has seen, all those nightmare-filled nights, and he still wants to be polite. And the words feel impolite somehow—an intrusion on everyone's comfort and euphoria, an unwelcome dose of ugly reality. Ridley remembers how they all reacted when that man materialized in front of them on that day. They were alarmed, nervous, but no one seemed afraid for their lives. But

the man's intentions were written on his face from the very beginning. All of them, Ridley included, were just perfectly willing to pretend it wasn't happening, as if by consensus alone they could wish the reality away.

Three more distant pops. Ridley looks to Laina, and she is looking right back at him, searching him for confirmation. Did he know this would happen? He was worried about something that night when Sarah asked them all if they would attend the protest. Maybe. Though it was not a concern he had named in any concrete way. Only a generalized fear. The universe has legs, he might have been thinking. It can stroll through a barn or down a street, stare right through the gaps in you if you weren't careful. Those swirling eyes . . .

"Rubber bullets? Some protesters acting up?" says someone in front of them—a woman with a wool cap, one of those fuzzy balls hanging off the top. It has all the hope and desperation of someone trying to enforce normality on a situation that is far from normal. Police pelting protesters with rubber bullets. Normal, easy to categorize. But the crowd is turning away from that interpretation. They are starting to panic.

No one actually says the words *active shooter*—not within earshot of Ridley, at least. But they know what's happening. Ridley sees it, the precise moment when hysteria takes over.

"Don't push!" someone yells. "Stop!" And with that, the chanting finally gives out and a hectic chatter replaces it, restless and searching.

Ridley grips Laina's arm tight. A man in a long trench coat has stepped out of an alley ahead, and he's grinning at the crowd. A collective animal sense pulses through all of them.

"What is it?" Laina asks, but then she sees the man too. No need

to explain. The shooter lifts his revolver, and in the second before he fires, the stampede has already begun. The crowd surges, and Laina and Ridley move with it, carried on the current of sudden panic. The first gunshot is somewhat muffled by the screaming. Ridley gropes for Laina, pulls her toward him. Together, they push their way onto the sidewalk and run in the direction away from the shooter.

"Where are we going?" Laina is yelling.

Ridley has no idea. He dodges and weaves between people. *Away.* He is trying to get away, though he can't say what that means. Ridley hears the second shot, sees blood spray out of a tall man ahead of them. As the man falls, protesters skitter around him. Hand tight on Laina's arm, Ridley threads his way through the opening. A woman falls next, shot through the shoulder. Ridley finally looks back. The shooter, who is unbearably close, has his eyes on them. Even as dozens of people cross his path, he is tracking Ridley and Laina specifically. The man is taking his time to aim again, making some sound deep in his throat, like a frog trying to hum a tune. A shudder goes through Ridley's entire body.

Without thinking, he pushes Laina off the sidewalk and staggers backward just as a shot passes between them.

"Run!" Ridley yells. He spins around, heading directly for the shooter.

The shooter doesn't register alarm. He pivots, re-aims his revolver.

Laina is yelling, "No!" over and over again. Not running as she was told, but stumbling toward Ridley, helpless. She can't reach him, not in time.

Ridley slams into the man's side. The shooter sways slightly, but Ridley falls back as if he'd just hit a solid wall. He hits the ground

hard, and for a second he looks dazed. And then suddenly, Ridley is scrambling to his feet and fleeing just as the shooter re-aims his weapon.

Laina is still running toward Ridley, screaming. Her scream pulls Ridley's attention only for a moment, but it is enough. When he follows her eye back to the shooter, it is already too late. The shot comes a moment later than he expects. He feels where the bullet hits his shoulder—an explosion of tight, hot pain, the impact sending him wheeling, his back now to the shooter.

Laina is so close, an arm's length away. The look on her face— it hurts him to see her look like that. A final flash of memory. No, not a memory, but an image remembered: the Titan picking him up with cold hands, fingers flecked with stars, the waiting void.

"I'm sorry," Ridley says. He hears the second shot.

The first two shooters were far enough away from the police that they went on for some time without interruption. There were other shooters, and different things spurred them to action. Three took their cue from the frenzy caused by the first two, a couple more from some half-forgotten trauma. These were quickly subdued by a flurry of gunfire from the police. One shooter forgot where he was, and wandered off, away from the protesters. Another followed close behind the wanderer.

That made nine shooters. Nine out of twelve.

The last three shooters are clustered at City Hall, near the greatest number of officers and the highest concentration of monsters. The shooters are aware of these facts. They have developed a sense for their targets, matched with a certain degree of cleverness. Earlier, they took out their revolvers and dropped their coats before the first shots went off, hiding their weapons in the waists of their pants, letting their shirts hang over the bulge there.

They reasoned that they'd look less conspicuous without the large coats. Their clothes are threadbare, and it is chilly out, but they hardly notice the cold.

Their gamble has paid off. They've wandered through the crowd without raising any suspicion, placing themselves in strategic locations among the protesters. Properly positioned, they wait for some of the cops to taper off in response to the distant gunshots. This gamble, too, has paid off.

Two minutes passed between the first and the second shooter, only a minute between the first two and the following five, and in that time, there are sounds everywhere: gunshots, of course, and sirens, and people running, people screaming, people crying. When the three shooters point their guns in the air and fire, only seven minutes have passed since the first shooter started her rampage. The marchers, already scattered, quicken their pace. People go down into the subway, run into buildings around the plaza, or take off down streets, away from the gunshots.

Rebecca and Sarah are kneeling behind a short block wall near the Government Center Subway entrance when the closest shooter points his revolver in the air and fires. The shooter has the gaunt look of someone who has lost a great deal of weight over a short time, but his eyes are sharp, alive, like those of a predator that has found prey. The barrier would have been useful, but this shooter, unlike the other two, happens to be on the other side of it, with Rebecca and Sarah. There's a line of people with them, and quite rightly, they take off running at the sound of the gunshot. Rebecca does not, and she feels Sarah still there beside her. Neither of them speaks. They are frozen, in shock or some other close-by emotion. For Rebecca, it is something like wonderment, like gazing at a completed prophecy. The shooter sees them

there, but he isn't completely paying attention to them. Rebecca follows the shooter, sees what he is seeing. A silver fox has dashed out into the street. A big fox, not nearly as small as a fox should be, and there's still some semblance of a human face above the muzzle. Human eyes. The shooter takes aim and fires, striking the fox in the gut, and with a yelp it swerves into an alley, flecks of blood marking its passage. Sarah taps Rebecca's shoulder and says, "Come on," and they use the distraction to jump over the barrier and start running.

As they run, Rebecca sees a snake slither down a drain. The snake is large too, but not alarmingly so. The incongruity of seeing it here in the middle of the plaza convinces Rebecca that it, too, was once human. *Lucky,* Rebecca thinks, grateful to have witnessed its escape.

Another gunshot pulls her back to the shooter. He is calmly walking in their direction, aiming at them.

Rebecca sees the officer before the shooter does. It is as if he just appears there, weapon already drawn, but Rebecca thinks it is just the noise of the moment that is overwhelming her—too much information to filter out with her enhanced senses.

The officer doesn't waste time. He fires, and the shooter yells out.

Rebecca keeps moving, but she is slowing down, glancing back to observe the last bit of the altercation playing out: the shooter firing at the officer, the officer falling, and a second officer, from a farther distance, firing several rounds into the shooter until the man stops moving.

"Becca, what are you doing!" Sarah yells.

Rebecca turns.

She finds that a considerable distance has opened up between her and Sarah. And the more alarming fact that she is now in the

middle of the plaza, completely out in the open. Several people are laid out on the bricks around her.

When the bullet catches Rebecca in the side, she gasps in surprise, instinctively moving her hand to cover the wound. She has already stopped running, but the shock makes her lumber forward, her body halfheartedly following its last directive. Rebecca does not see the shooter renew his aim, but she senses Sarah's intent right before Sarah tackles her. A bullet zips above them as they fall, hit the ground, and roll, Rebecca sliding onto her belly. The pain pulls tears from Rebecca's eyes.

She blinks to clear her sight. She'd swear it was only a moment, but when she opens her eyes again, Sarah is sprinting away from her.

Rebecca has seen something like this before, and she is struck with the sudden sense of déjà vu. It was in the early fall, two years ago or thereabouts, when Lincoln was still alive. During the good times. Her pack was at the beach. It was cold, and the shore was almost empty, so they spent hours passing around a flask and getting drunk as late afternoon turned to night.

By nightfall, the beach had cleared completely and Sarah was out-of-her-mind drunk. "Who wants to swim?" she asked. Lincoln stood up and took off his shirt, and Sarah, not wanting to be shown up, took off her shirt and sprinted off, not waiting for Lincoln. She stripped the rest of her clothes as she ran, screaming into the change before plunging into the sea. Once Lincoln caught on, he followed her.

It was something that only Sarah could do—run off like that at a moment's notice. So natural was the connection between Sarah on land and Sarah in water, between Sarah the human and Sarah the wolf.

Sarah is doing this same thing now, sprinting into the change, and the memory of her on that long-ago beach and of her running toward the shooter is like water poured over oil. Rebecca can see Lincoln there with Sarah, screaming and plunging into the rough waves. Rebecca tries to blink the memory and the reality away but can only manage to return Lincoln to the valley of the dead. Sarah is still receding away from her. She is screaming a battle cry that, paradoxically, grows with the distance between them.

Sarah's body is almost completely covered in the beautiful gray-black coat of her wolf. She tacks toward the shooter at angles, making herself a difficult target. She tears her underwear off with one hairy forepaw. Even covered in fur, the muscles of her body show. Now that she is finally free of her clothes, Sarah lets the rest of her body complete the change. In the span of a heartbeat, the transformation is complete.

Rebecca tries to call out to Sarah, but it's no use. Sarah has gotten it into her mind that Rebecca needs protecting, and Rebecca is in no shape to dissuade her.

Sarah the wolf closes the remaining distance between herself and the shooter. She's on the man before he can shoot. She is very efficient. First, she places her front paws on his chest, then she buries her teeth in his neck. They fall together, she on top of him, and the muscles along her back ripple as she tears away everything her jaws encompass. No time to scream. He is dead already, his head dangling from the thinnest strip of skin.

Rebecca is losing a lot of blood. She needs help, sooner rather than later. She's tried changing, but the pain flares and her head spins. With the bullet lodged inside her, some sense of self-preservation within her magic prevents her from making the change. *You'll die for sure*, the magic tells her in its not-quite-language.

Sarah is still lingering next to the victim's body. The man's head is off to one side, so that Rebecca can see only his hair. A small miracle. Not a big one, since Rebecca can still see that terrible strip of skin. Sarah has no interest in the body. She is looking around and sniffing the air. For what? Rebecca's own wolf helps her put it together. Another shooter nearby, hiding.

She, too, starts looking for the second shooter, then notices that Sarah has gotten the attention of some officers. A solid line of them, hesitantly approaching from the Government Center stop, moving back the way they had come.

When Sarah also sees the officers, she jumps back, resting on her haunches. She growls, and it has a drag to it, like gravel on the bottom of a deep steel drum.

The officers falter.

The not-quite-language of Rebecca's wolf tells her that there is more happening in this moment, more to pay attention to, so she starts looking around again for the shooter. And there she is, peeking out from a row of concrete benches across the plaza. Rebecca knows this is the shooter, not through her wolf, but through human instinct. The woman's general features are hard to see from so far across the now-empty plaza, but one feature is horribly unambiguous. In a situation like this, no one would be smiling unless they meant to do evil.

When the shooter aims her weapon, Rebecca isn't surprised, but she gasps all the same. The crack of gunfire comes predictably after. Sarah twitches, a distinct ripple of impact starting in her hind leg and passing through her entire body. There's a delayed yelp of pain. With a limp, Sarah turns to follow the path of the bullet to its source. The woman is not hiding. She doesn't even lower her gun. Not even a flinch of surprise when Sarah takes off toward her.

What the shooter does is aim her weapon at the line of police. She fires one careful shot, striking an officer in his side. Then, finally, she ducks behind the benches.

Rebecca sees the result before she understands what's happening.

The officers unleash a volley of bullets at the shooter, only now Sarah is in the line of fire. Sarah cries out, struck twice in her side.

Rebecca knows the wolves in her pack almost as well as she knows her own wolf. They are all intelligent, all capable of achieving something near the reason of their human counterparts. A bit of the person always lives in the wolf, but the wolf is something else too, with its own brilliance, its own ideas on morality. Wolves appear impulsive, but that's not the whole truth. They make careful decisions, but these decisions often center on immediate threats and secondary ones. Here, now, the threat is apparent. Here, now, something needs to be done. A wolf comes to an easy solution where a human might hesitate, consider the ramifications. For a wolf, the answer can be nothing else.

Sarah could not know what Rebecca knows: that the officers weren't aiming at her. Sarah is already wounded, already in a state of self-preservation and rage.

"Oh, no," Rebecca whispers.

Sarah the wolf suddenly weaves out of the path of the bullets. Away from the shooter. She is turning again. Even wounded, Sarah is still astonishingly fast, her limp a mere suggestion as she runs. She's there before the officers can respond, leaping into the air and landing behind them. She pivots and lunges, grabbing one officer by the leg and with a show of her strength, tossing him into the

air. The next officer follows the path of the airborne officer with his eyes, and so he misses the opportunity to dodge Sarah's swipe to his face. The blow spins the officer's head violently, and his body goes with it in a backflip of gruesome beauty.

Rebecca quickly does the math in her head. First victim: hopefully not dead. Second: paralysis at best.

The third victim's fate is less ambiguous. Sarah has found his neck.

Rebecca adjusts her hopes. Now she wishes only that Sarah won't die. She doesn't know how strong the wolves actually are, because she's never had to push hers. But Sarah's wolf looks larger than before, larger than any Rebecca has seen. The wolf that bit Rebecca was the record holder. Until now.

Sarah pushes the fourth cop to the ground with her front paws, and the woman's scream is cut short as the air is pushed right out of her lungs. Then Sarah goes for the fifth, holding the officer's head in her huge mouth and crushing it. It is not a good way to die. His screams turn Rebecca's skin to ice.

It may have been over then if Sarah were more efficient with the fifth officer, or if the sixth had had a more active sense of self-preservation.

Two bullets pierce Sarah's side. The man's hand is trembling, so the other shots miss their mark. Sarah doesn't waste this. She turns and leaps, tackling the sixth officer and landing square on his chest. There is a crack, audible even at Rebecca's distance, and then Sarah goes for his face. This one is over in an instant. No screams.

Rebecca watches Sarah stumble off him, knows from the tired look in her eyes that she will not survive. If only she could just die here, now, on her own terms. But this tragedy has no capacity for such kindnesses.

Sarah's tired left eye explodes, the crack of gunfire echoing through the bloody plaza. Another bullet finds the center of her forehead. Sarah sinks to the ground almost as it happens, and like that, she is no more. The shooter has the grace not to smile now. She looks on solemnly, and when she is satisfied that the work is done, she turns the gun and fires the last bullet into her open mouth.

Harry is near the northern edge of Boston Commons, close enough to see the pale white walls, the gold top of the Capitol building, without having to strain. The sun is brighter than he remembers, or his eyes have changed after so much time underground. He is still wearing his coat; the left sleeve, hanging loose, sways as he walks. The phantom limb is burning. He can still feel the teeth biting down, the blistering heat. He doesn't remember who the mouth belongs to. Only the heat. Always that heat.

Something is weighing down Harry's right jacket pocket. Hard as stone, but deadlier.

Eleanor liked days like this, the way the sun catches on everything but is cool enough to lie outside. Today is too bright for Harry, but she would have liked it. It is too noisy here. Sirens are going off. And firecrackers? Is it July? He listens for music, parade sounds. Only sirens and firecrackers. Strange.

He should go home.

He tries to picture his house, but all he gets is a black spot, the distant ringing of bells, a woman with frail arms, whispering words from a heavy book.

He pulls the revolver out of his pocket and looks at it. Satisfied, he puts it back in. He keeps walking. He is hungry. He should get something to eat.

Someone runs past him.

Harry pulls out his gun and aims at the teenage girl. He doesn't think about it; the action is perfectly natural. "Don't run," he tells the girl, and fires the revolver. There's a kick, and the target is moving, so he isn't surprised when he misses. The noise is louder than Harry expected. He jumps, drops the gun. He leans down to pick it up, and when he stands again, he is alone. Harry is disappointed, though he doesn't know why. He looks around for more people.

He doesn't see anyone at first. The Commons is oddly empty. But Harry looks closer, and that's when he sees the child. Hiding behind a tree. Looking at him. The child looks uncomfortably familiar. Harry's phantom limb flares with pain. A memory rises from the muck of his mind. He can hear chewing in his ears.

What he is thinking feels natural too, not unusual at all. He is thinking, *that child is a dragon.* He is also thinking, *there are a number of abominable creatures in the world, and they all need to be killed, this one especially.*

"Please," he says to the dragon, not knowing why. He has to steady himself. "Please," he says again.

Now he is walking toward the dragon, his gun aimed. He fires twice, but the monster has slipped behind the tree again. Harry

screams in frustration, which feels like such childish behavior. It is embarrassing. He laughs and cries all at once—a trembling that rattles his teeth.

"Come out!" Harry yells.

To his surprise, the child does as he's been ordered—actually steps out from behind the tree and stands where Harry can get a clean shot. Now that he's done this, Harry's mouth falls open in astonishment.

"I'm going to kill you," Harry says, and it sounds to his own ears like the barking of a fenced-in dog.

The threat does distress the child, which Harry likes, but the child, this dragon, does not try to run or hide. *If he's this stupid, he deserves to die,* Harry is thinking. He aims the revolver right at the monster's head.

Thump.

The pain erupts at the base of Harry's skull, and then he is falling, the world going black again—this has happened before—the bright sun and the day turning to darkness. *No,* he almost says, but he is out before the words can come to his lips. Harry drops his revolver. His body and the weapon hit the pavement at the same time.

From Dragon's perspective, Harry looks like an unwanted toy, held upright and then discarded, allowed to fall to the ground. The woman behind Harry is wearing a gray shirt, no coat, but her left hand is missing, cut off at the wrist. The skin up to the elbow is discolored, crinkled in places.

Dragon knows her too. He wants to run but doesn't. He's decided to accept whatever comes of this.

"Can you help us get out of here?" the woman asks.

Dragon looks confused. "What can I do?"

"Can you shift?"

"That is a secret," Dragon says. He's never shown anyone before, except Smoke, and Smoke told him not to show anyone else.

"Please," she says. "There's no time."

Dragon has only to decide. He has only to say yes. Smoke is not here. And Smoke doesn't have to know.

"Don't look," Dragon says.

The woman closes her eyes, and Dragon takes off his coat and shirt. He's practiced this. He is very good at it now, the change. *After* the change will be the real challenge. He closes his eyes and goes deep into himself. He feels them first, on the inside, and then the wings burst from his back, obeying his command. It hurts, but he is a dragon. He takes pride in not making a sound.

"You can look," he says.

When the woman opens her eyes, he sees a little surprise on her face. She's suspected he could do it. She's read stories about dragons. But Dragon is not a story. Dragon is real.

He moves closer to her, extends his hand, and the woman takes it. He leans down and holds the sleeping man by his forearm. He has to turn his hands to claws to get a firmer grip.

"Where will we go?" Dragon asks.

"I'll show you," the woman says.

Dragon can feel his wings the same as his arms and legs. The wings are big in comparison to his body. When he flexes them twice, his feet almost leave the ground, and this gives him confidence. Dragon knows they'll do the needed work. He summons the power to lift himself into the air and finds a well of strength deep inside himself, hot and churning. It surprises him with so

much joy, he almost laughs, but he doesn't. This is not a moment for laughter.

"Ready?" he asks.

The woman nods.

With a beat of his wings, Dragon catches the wind.

THE WAKING WORLD

66

"There you are," Laina says.

Rebecca blinks a few times until the blur crystallizes into recognizable shapes. She smiles at the statement. Where was she before? Not dead, which is good. She groans and tries to sit up but can't.

"Easy," Laina says, and she is touching her forearm. Rebecca smiles again.

"Did they give her something?" someone asks. "She is smiling a lot." Rebecca recognizes the voice.

Laina leans over her and mouths the words: *Your mother is here.*

Rebecca clears her throat, trying to remember how to make human sounds. She says, "How long have I . . ." and loses steam.

Laina wrinkles her brow, and then she understands. "You've been out for a couple of hours." She leans in again, this time to her ear. "Will you be okay for a while? I have to step out."

Rebecca nods. Her eyes pinch shut with a throb of pain. A tear falls down the side of her face.

"We'll need to talk about things," Laina says, "but not now." Rebecca can feel Laina's presence move away from her, and when Laina speaks again, her voice is far away, though it carries. "I'll be back."

Rebecca listens to the retreating footsteps, and the silence that settles in afterward. Time stretches itself out, wide and empty. Rebecca can feel the fluorescent ceiling lights burning at her eyelids. Her heart is throbbing in her chest like a caged thing that wants out. More tears fall from her eyes, from a pain more terrible than anything physical. She's been hurt. She's watched people she loves get hurt. Someone has died, though Rebecca doesn't want to acknowledge it even to herself.

Her body convulses—one long spasm she is helpless against—and then her mouth opens in a long, silent scream.

She hears a chair drag and then can feel the warmth of her mother's body—can actually *feel* it. And then her mother's hand, coarse from hard work and age, touching her shoulder. Rebecca opens her eyes and looks at her mother. The relief she feels just seeing her mother's face and the uncomplicated concern written there. Just concern. Not anger or disappointment, or resentment. Only concern.

Rebecca's tears fall freely now, her face uncomplicated in its expression of terror and sorrow. She's come to think of herself as a mother, or at the least, she has molded that identity onto herself, like clay. An identity she used to protect her pack. *No more pack. All gone.*

"Mommy," she says.

Her mother makes a soft clicking sound with her mouth and rubs Rebecca's shoulder. She is crying now, too, and Rebecca realizes she's seen her mother cry only once, at Dad's funeral. Rebecca

lets it wash over her, all of it. She is shaking, and it is awful and it feels right too, as if the poison is leeching out of her body before it can kill her.

They don't say anything else. There is nothing to say. Her mother is there, and for the moment, this is enough.

The man is pacing around the living room. Dragon tries to take up as little space as possible, standing in the corner, but he can tell that his mere presence is upsetting the man, no matter what he does. Dragon still doesn't know his name. The woman is in the other room, going through a cupboard. Dragon inches his way to the space connecting the rooms. He can see them both but also be as far away from them as possible.

The woman is pulling out a small box from the cupboard pressed against one wall of the dining room. She opens the box and pulls out something Dragon has seen a few times. Something people use to talk to people who aren't there—people in other places. She plugs the phone into a wall and sits, watching it.

"I need to call my school," the man says from the living room.

"No," the woman says back—not quite a yell, though it has the power of one.

"Why not?"

The woman makes a funny face. "Because you've been missing for months and you are missing a hand and several missing people with missing hands just attacked a crowd of people."

The man says nothing to this but continues pacing. He is keeping an eye on Dragon the whole time.

Dragon looks away, to the woman's wrist where her left hand should be. He did that. He ate that hand.

The woman looks at Dragon, and he feels stripped naked by her stare. "None of this is on you, child," she says.

On that day when he hurt her, she watched him just like this, with a sort of surprised fascination, as if she'd lifted a rock and found him under it. She was groaning then, of course, and her mouth was creased from the pain, but she didn't seem scared like the others.

Dragon isn't sure he likes the woman, but he feels better paying attention to her than to the terrified, angry man in the other room.

The woman returns to the phone. She seems satisfied, picks it up. "I'm Karuna," she says, and for a moment, Dragon is unsure who she is talking to. Then she looks at him.

"Dragon," he says.

"A fitting name." She smiles, but Dragon doesn't return the gesture. Everything she does feels as if she were peeling the skin off him.

Karuna puts the phone to her ear.

"Please sit down, Harry," she says to the man in the other room.

The man, whose name is Harry, stops pacing. He spares an angry glance at Dragon, and then he sits.

"Hello?" Karuna says—not to Dragon or Harry, but to someone who isn't there. "Yes, it's me. Okay, there'll be time for that later. Not over the phone. I just wanted to know, how is she? Good. Stop. I said not over the phone. No, I need you to keep her a little

while longer." A short pause. "When we were kids, you stepped on the axle of a busted yo-yo and bled all over the carpet. You know anybody else who cut their foot on a *yo-yo*? Believe me now? Good. I should go. No, don't tell them. Just give everyone a kiss for me."

Karuna puts down the phone. She spends a moment sitting and staring at it, her breath coming in slow. Then she gets up and goes to the kitchen and pours out some water for herself.

"You thirsty?" she asks Dragon. "Hungry?"

Dragon imagines her fingers in his mouth and shakes his head.

"Okay," she says. "Go wait in the living room. I need a moment to myself."

Dragon obeys and goes to the living room. The man named Harry is still sitting, but his head is rolled back, his eyes closed.

Dragon finds another corner and stands in it.

"How did you get out?" Harry asks.

"Some people helped me escape," Dragon says.

Harry's eyes open. Dragon has said something wrong. "Who?" he asks. "Why?"

Dragon doesn't know how to answer the question, so he just stares at the man.

"Just you?"

Dragon shrugs. "I think so."

"But why?" he asks again. "Why you? Why not us?"

Dragon edges his way back to the kitchen.

"Who are they?" the man asks. He is getting louder now. He gives Dragon the same expression he gave when trying to kill him earlier.

"Stop scaring the child," Karuna says, laying a hand on Dragon's shoulder.

"He isn't a child."

"Either way, he wouldn't know how to answer your questions." Karuna nudges Dragon over to a chair and sits by the man on the couch.

"It doesn't make sense," Harry says. "Why didn't anyone come for us? Why didn't anyone help us?"

Karuna doesn't say anything, but she is clearly thinking.

"The child knows something," Harry says.

Karuna makes another funny face. "Please shut up," she says.

The man named Harry glares at Dragon but falls quiet.

"If there are malevolent secret societies, it makes sense that there would be benevolent ones. They've probably been in a secret conflict for a long time, only now the war has spilled over into our world," Karuna says.

Dragon doesn't know the words, so he says them a few times in his head. Malevolent. Benevolent. They both sound like the same thing, like sisters.

Harry says, "But why didn't someone rescue us?"

"We didn't matter. For some reason, he does," Karuna says in that way of hers, empty of surprise. She looks at Dragon again, and it is not easy to interpret (for him or me). "I need to make another call. Then we should get going."

Laina is sitting next to him when he opens his eyes.

"Hey, babe," she says.

"What happened?"

"You were shot. Twice. The second bullet ricocheted and exited right below your clavicle. You nearly punctured a lung."

Ridley can't remember anything that has happened. He is running, and then he isn't. He is falling and then he isn't falling. He doesn't remember the bullets—the one that grazed his shoulder or the one that hit him in the back. Can't feel them, either. He is all drugged up and can't feel much of anything.

He marvels at this information, at the wording of it. He almost punctured a lung. The second bullet ricocheted and exited. In this telling, the gunman is gone.

"Sarah is dead. Twenty-five people are dead," Laina adds. It sounds like reportage, except for the familiarity in how she says

"Sarah." Sarah is gone, but differently. Removed not just from mention, but from existence itself—a more final going.

Ridley considers her words, trying to find his own feelings. "I'm so sorry," he manages. "Rebecca?"

"Alive," Laina says. "Down the hall with her mother."

"I want to go talk to her," he says.

"Not yet, baby. A little later."

Ridley settles back. "Things will get worse now before they get better," he says. It is a plain statement of fact. He says it without alarm, just recognition.

"And what will *we* do?" she asks.

Nestled within the question is an entire conversation. This is the danger we were expecting, she is saying. Here it is, in the present tense. No more hypotheticals. So, what now?

What now, indeed. Ridley remembers the moment in the warehouse, Nick's severed arm in front of him, the vision of the Titan still fresh in his mind. He has never felt fear so keenly, never so fully understood the fear that others might have of monsters. He didn't like that story of himself. It wasn't honorable. The best he could do was package it in protecting another person. For him, that was Laina.

After the argument with Sarah, he stayed up, his eyes closed but his mind fully awake, trying to figure out a way they both could survive: the monsters and the humans. He went to the march because he needed to believe in that dream, and he wanted to be better than he was. It didn't occur to him until he stood in that crowd that there was no line between them. They'd been living side by side all along, only now they knew it. And for some of them, there had never been a line. They had never stopped being human. Sarah was fully both, monster and human, and now she was dead. Humans had killed her.

Ridley thought he needed protection, that he needed to protect the people he loved, through his complicit silence. It had made him uncharacteristically betray his principles, thinking he and Laina would be spared. But when the gunshots came, he lost that expectation.

That is the best word for it. *Lost.* He will never find it again, will never go looking. No one deserves protection over anyone else.

No human above. No human below.

"What will we do now?" Ridley says. "Well . . ." He clears his throat as if he is about to say a lot of things. But in the end, there is only one thing worth saying.

The cabin where they'll be staying the night is at the end of a long unpaved road. A friend of a friend, Karuna says. They will have to move again. Not just her and Harry. The monster will be coming with them. Harry will have to take care of the child before that happens.

It is nice as far as cabins go: hot water and electricity, a shelf of books if Harry is so inclined. The first thing he does, however, is take a shower. He lets the water run over him, washing the stink off and soothing his skin. He didn't shower often where he was living, and the water was always cold. This is better. The phantom hand burns, but it has been burning since that day. Nothing new. He keeps seeing himself inside his cell—the cold floor, the smell of dried blood and human waste. He keeps reaching for a gun that isn't there.

After his shower, Harry lies on the couch and is unable to keep his eyes open. For a while, there is noise around him, which he

half notices, trying and failing to keep himself awake. And then it is quiet, and his awareness lapses. He floats through memories and dreams, the two indistinguishable. Eleanor is with him, and she is explaining to him that Sir Arthur Conan Doyle was also an alleged member of the Hermetic Order of the Golden Dawn. Along with Bram Stoker. And Aleister Crowley. And then she is talking about L. Ron Hubbard and Cameron and the Black Egg. "Everything is connected. Every imagined world is real. All the underworlds and all the heavens. All the worlds within us and without." And then 6Alfred9 is there and Karuna is there, and somehow, it is difficult to tell who is speaking.

Harry wakes in the middle of the night to the door creaking open and shutting again. He lets a minute or so pass before hesitantly getting up and walking to the door. He is close enough to open it when a voice stops him in his tracks. He drops his hand from the knob and presses his ear against the door to listen instead.

"Did you come to get me?" the child is asking.

"If that's what you want," a woman says. "Do you want to stay?" Her voice is beyond human somehow, while also sounding ordinary. There is an authority in her voice, which she carries playfully, as if she might destroy the world on a whim. It sends a chill through Harry.

Another monster is right outside, a slab of wood between them.

The child hesitates for a moment before answering the woman. "The lady is nice, but the man is horrible."

Harry is too afraid to be offended. He doesn't hear anything from the woman. She must still be waiting since the child hasn't answered her question. Harry considers running, but where? He is inside. Nowhere to go but out. Hide, then. That's foolish too. The coin is already in the air.

"What will happen to them if I leave them?" the child asks.

"I don't know," the woman says. "You are under our protection. If you stay, they'll be under our protection too. You're safer with us. They're safer with you."

"Can they come with us?"

"No," she says simply. She makes no effort to elaborate.

Time passes, the thin separation between Harry and the monsters feeling thinner and thinner.

"I'll stay," the child says.

Harry's breath catches in his throat. The hand resting on the door has gone slick. He feels the ghost heat of his other hand, the one he no longer has.

"That's really grown-up of you," the woman says. Then, more softly, "Remember your promise."

Harry remembers to breathe then and inhales slowly. The monsters are quiet after that. Harry steps away from the door and goes back to the couch. He is lying back down when the child slips back inside. Harry makes his breath slow and even, listening for the gentle creak of the child returning to the bedroom where Karuna sleeps.

"Thank you for getting us out," Harry says, stopping the child at the doorway. He can't quite bring himself to sound grateful as he says this.

The child turns and stands there a while, so Harry can guess what might be coming. "I'm sorry. They made me," the child says.

They almost made Harry kill people too. He tries to understand that fact, their power over the will of others. It terrifies him still, the work they did to make him so pliable. Who is responsible when a person is made into an aimed weapon? Where is the line? Was there ever one?

Harry remembers all the little actions and inactions that led him here. Had he aimed himself, or had he simply followed the path always set for him? He tries to imagine 6Alfred9's answer to the question. He tries to imagine Karuna's.

"Go to sleep," Harry says, and turns away from the boy.

Without another word, the boy goes into the bedroom. Silence follows.

Harry will have to do something about the child or do something about himself. But his eyelids are heavy. He has completely exhausted himself again.

He'll give it another day at least. Decide then.

70

Laina could not have escaped on her own. She was holding Ridley in her arms, and the shooter was standing over them both. She doesn't remember how it all got to that point. She was already on her way to him, and the shooter approached sometime after that. He was staring down at her and had this look in his eyes. It looked like remorse, but he was also still sort of smiling, still making that odd croaking sound. When he lifted the gun again, it was after a considerable time. She could have run away in that time, but she would have had to leave Ridley, and she couldn't do that. So she just looked up at him. In hindsight, that seemed stupid.

Of course, she prayed that the voice would save her. The woman had a gift of showing up exactly when Laina needed her to. It was easy to imagine she'd been there the whole time, but since Ridley was shot and she had not saved him, doubt had set in.

Just like in those hero stories, when all hope was about to be lost, a fireball appeared in the sky right above the head of the

shooter. It came down like a slow-moving comet and then extinguished itself.

First, she saw his hair move against the wind. Not with the wind—that would have been expected. She didn't notice the slight breeze until the moment his hair moved against it. It looked very strange. Then she saw the compression of fingers on his face. She put this together later. At the time, his face just looked lumpy.

The snap was what did it. His head whipped around, beyond its expected range of motion, too quickly and powerfully to be of his own volition. That's when she knew for sure that it was the woman, just as the man fell over.

"I have to go," the woman said. And then she was gone. Just like that.

Laina hasn't told Ridley how they were saved. Not out of habit or to protect him, or anything. She just doesn't think of it. Her mind is on everything else that has happened. On Sarah being dead. On Rebecca and Ridley almost being dead. Strange to say it, but the invisible woman ranks fourth, maybe fifth, on her list of concerns. Even her gratitude is buried under layers of distrust.

Sarah is first. Her brother's lover. Killed in almost the same way he had been. It is as if a bullet went through him and didn't stop until it hit her. Laina doesn't quite believe in destiny, but this brings her close. What else but destiny could be so poetic and devastating at the same time.

Laina imagines an alternate reality where they are both memorialized together. The Lovers. In her reality, of course, no one knows Lincoln's name. No one knows who he was, how he died. He'll be lost in all this, his tragedy a deleted footnote. Unless someone says his name.

She is thinking this when she asks Ridley, "You want to go see Rebecca now?"

"If you think it's a good time," Ridley says.

Laina helps him out of bed, gets him into a wheelchair, and rolls him into Rebecca's room. It is the morning after the shooting. Rebecca sits up in her bed and watches them both. She is alone in the room. "Mom went home for the night," she says.

"I'm so sorry about Sarah. And I'm sorry about that night too," Ridley says immediately.

"I can't give you forgiveness for her. She's gone."

Ridley nods. They've both said what needed to be said.

Laina says, "We know that you're alone now, and we think you should stay with us. If you want."

Rebecca's eyes have the red, glossy look of fresh tears, but her voice doesn't tremble when she says she will think about it.

Laina doesn't press the issue. What she is offering has a lot of implications, and Rebecca needs time to consider them. Instead, she says, "I think we should put all our cards on the table," and over the next hour, Laina tells Rebecca about the voice and Ridley tells her about the SEN retreat. This sharing of information also has its implications, and so they wait patiently for Rebecca's response.

"I think the woman who killed Sarah was under a spell," Rebecca offers. "And I've seen it before. In the police officers at the highway protest, and the one that came to my apartment after." She looks at both of them. "Something really big is going on here, and I don't know where it is coming from. If I look at all this directly, if I'm honest about what I think this is, the truth terrifies me."

"Us too," Ridley says.

"Keeping our heads down isn't going to keep us safe," Rebecca

says. "Running isn't going to keep us safe. We're going to have to be smart. We're going to have to be visible."

"We're with you," Laina says.

"I don't have a pack anymore," Rebecca says, and looks meaningfully at both of them. "How much are you with me?"

Laina and Ridley look at each other.

"I'm asking the both of you," Rebecca continues. "You don't have to decide now. I'll respect your decision no matter what."

Ridley rolls over to Rebecca's bed and places his hand on hers. "We've already decided. We're with you all the way."

Laina doesn't need anyone to look to her, the confession already on her lips. She is tired of hiding.

"I have the unedited video of how Lincoln died," she says. "I want him to be remembered."

Sondra feels the tension in her body ease when Melku and Damsel enter the room. "Where is he?" she asks.

"He's with friends," Melku says. "Don't worry."

"Which friends are these?" Sondra asks. "And where are these friends?"

"Goddess on Earth," Damsel says, smiling. "I don't think she's going to let this one go, Melly."

Sondra fights the urge to lunge at the woman. She turns to her sister, who has been standing in the corner, flesh and all. "Will you tell me?" she says.

It has been at least a year since she saw her sister in her skin. She looks healthy but tired, her glow a dull luster. She was not an attractive child, but as an adult, Sondra must grudgingly admit that she's never seen anyone as beautiful. The smooth curve of her face betrays no lines of age. Even now, even with the slight wrinkle of her brow, she seems untouched by time.

"He's in Massachusetts," Melku volunteers before Sonya can speak. "Outside Boston. That's all we can say right now."

"I could have died."

Sonya takes a few steps toward Sondra. "I wouldn't have let—"

"This will affect my political career. You know that, right? What will people say when it comes out that I was there?"

If it was unclear before how utterly fucked Sondra is, the look on Sonya's face removes all doubt. There will be fallout from this. And they did it anyway. Everyone can be sacrificed as long as they get what they want.

"It must be nice to have my life so completely in your hands," Sondra says.

Sonya is looking at her with this desperate look on her face. Her mouth is trembling.

"Your mother is at the Bordeaux Commune," Melku offers.

Sondra keeps her attention on Sonya. "And our father?"

Sonya shakes her head. "We didn't find him."

"You mean you knew you wouldn't find him?"

There are tears in Sonya's eyes now. It has been so long since Sondra actually saw her sister cry. Not since they were teenagers. Sonya never cries in her presence, and in situations where Sonya might show strong emotion, she is always invisible. Sondra is too angry to care or feel sorry for her. Her mother is insane. Her father is probably dead, her career likely destroyed. All these years, and all Sondra has managed is to stand in rooms where everyone knows more than she. They have taken everything from her, and her sister, her own family, stood by as they did it, knowing everything and manipulating her at every step. Even now they are doing it, using her mother against her to get her to drop the subject. Every person, every little thing, is a pawn to them.

And that is how it comes together. Sondra's eyes go wide, and the guilty look on Sonya's face is enough to confirm it.

"You leaked the video, didn't you?" Sondra asks.

Sonya doesn't try to deny it, but she doesn't answer, either. She has that same expression on her face as that time she almost killed Sondra: guilt and horror and fear of what this new reality will bring.

"It was ordained," Sonya is saying. "Please understand." She is reaching out for Sondra. Her fingers graze Sondra's shoulder and Sondra knocks them away.

"Don't touch me." How long has it been since Sonya's actual skin has touched hers? She can't remember.

"It would've happened anyway. We had to control it. Please."

She doesn't ask again for Sondra to understand. She is begging for something else, which Sondra can't give.

"No," Sondra says. "I'm done. I don't care why you did it. I'm not going to participate with you in manipulating the whole world."

Melku and Sonya exchange a look, and Sonya lowers her head. She can see the invisible link between them.

"Fuck the both of you," Sondra says, and leaves.

After Sondra is gone, Sonya slumps in a chair. She wipes tears from her eyes, but they continue to fall. Melku reaches out tentatively and then pulls back. "I'm sorry."

Sonya sniffles. "For the greater good, right?" she says, her tone betraying nothing; her face, everything. She is hugging herself in a self-soothing way, uncomfortable in her own skin. Every emotion that flits through her is painfully transparent: frustration, shame, anger, desperation.

Melku looks helpless. "I wish I could do something to make this easier."

"You have a lot of wishes and wants neither of us can do anything about." She reaches out, grasps Melku's hand in hers, and brings their hand to her lips. Neither says anything, but I can see the painful yearning on both their faces.

Melku looks away first. "I hate to ask right now—"

"It's fine," she says. She pulls her face into her best attempt at a neutral expression. "The Cult has found some of the Order of the Zsouvox members that went underground. They've been shelled. I don't know why they didn't kill them. Maybe they're planning to use them for another attack, like the one today. Twenty-Nine suspects that we helped release the video, but doesn't know how or why. He won't act on his suspicions."

"What is the status of our relationship with the Cult?"

"They've declared war, but they'll do it quietly for now. And no more attacks for the time being. They want to manage the chaos they've caused—"

"Which gives us an opportunity to brew a little chaos of our own," Melku says. "What's the bad news?"

"I'm burned. They know what I did at the protest. They'll start covering their tracks better. I won't be as useful as I've been in the past."

"We expected this. Cassandra has been chattier recently, so maybe we'll be fine for a while. Anything else?"

"Twenty-Nine let something slip. I'm sure they have the Zsou-vox now, but I haven't been able to get to it."

"Do they know about ours?"

"No."

"That's all, then?" Melku asks.

Sonya is starting to cry again, her body shaking from the effort to hold it in. I remember Cory sitting next to my hospital bed.

"I'm sorry," Melku says again. "I really am."

Sonya wipes her face in an aggressive way that is as much rage as sadness. She stands, turns her face away from Melku's. "The world is waking up. Time to get to the real work." And with that, Sonya walks out.

It has all played out with such familiarity.

I step forward, completing the recurrence.

"Finally," Melku says. "An introduction."

"You shouldn't play games with people."

Melku doesn't seem surprised by my words. "You shouldn't spy on people," they say. "And I'm not playing games with anyone. I'm just following the script."

"What *script?*"

Melku gives a tired smile. "*Contract* is a better word. Answer one of my questions: why are you here?"

I stare at him. "I don't know. It is just something I can do."

Melku shakes their head. "That's *how,* not why. I'm asking you about your voyeurism."

I frown. I don't have a good answer to that question.

"Okay," Melku says, "Let's try it another way. What are you looking for? What do you want?"

I don't have to think about that answer. "Everything," I say. "I want to understand everything."

I don't expect Melku to know what I mean, but I see recognition in their eyes. "Give up," they say. "If you ever get there, you'll never know it."

Melku gets up and walks around their desk to get close to me. Their hair is a lion's mane that makes the rest of their person seem small, though when I see the arms corded with muscle, the illusion breaks. They could subdue a person twice their size if need

be. They get so close, I think they could touch me if they wanted, though I know that shouldn't be possible.

I feel a surge of something pulling at me. I am waking up.

"There is no armor strong enough to save you," Melku says. "Nowhere. Ever."

And with that, I am pulled back into the space between worlds.

EARTH 001

I open my eyes, and there she is. She is at normal height this time, her eyes glowing from the corner where she stands. I sit up in bed.

Seeing her there, I retrieve something I'd lost without knowing. A memory.

In that other time, a warm St. Thomian night like this one, I'm sitting on the living room couch in the house Cory and I once shared, pain throbbing behind my eyes, my throat dry. Four bottles of flavored Cruzan Rum are on the coffee table: raspberry, mango, coconut, and passion fruit. No chasers, because I need to keep myself in a fog. It is late and I haven't slept. I reach for the bottles and swear because they're all empty. I think of Cory, and the loss doubles me over and I can't breathe. He is only a few weeks dead. It takes me a moment to notice her there, standing in the shadowed corner of my living room, but when I do, I forget the pain behind my eyes, the ache of my broken heart.

Nothing can prepare you for the way she looks—those eyes,

spinning in the same direction, hurricanes made of stardust. She dislodges from the wall—so easy, so smooth—and I can feel my stomach tighten, then and now. She walks or floats over to me; it's hard to tell. There's a sense of vertigo up close, as if I'll tumble into her and fall forever. The little wisps of hair on my neck wanting to jump right out of my skin, screaming.

"Do you want to see?" she is asking me.

I can't tell when she is saying this. Again it feels like being in both times at once, and somehow I know what she means. I've always known. I remember those moments when Cory was still alive and parallel realities would bleed together right in front of me.

I nod. Yes, I want to see. Tears of shock and grief fall from my eyes.

She touches me with a silhouette of a finger, and the sensation is all heat and cold and vibration as the power enters me. Those brief moments of quantum splitting cannot compare to the whole of the power. I feel like a collision of atoms, pieces of me spraying everywhere, then hurtling back together.

When I close my eyes, it is all there. All of it. All of you.

And then, in both timelines, she is moving back into the corner of the room, melting into the shadows, the shimmering stars of her blinking out, cluster by cluster, until everything fades to black. Her eyes are the last to disappear.

I turn on the lamp. If what I saw was ever actually there, it has left no sign. I can't go back to sleep, not after that, so I just sit there on the edge of my bed, staring at my toes. My toenails are all ragged and untrimmed. I wonder how many signs of my general lack of interest in grooming are evident to other people. I try to keep up with things, but I forget often.

I pick up my phone from the bedside table. It rings twice before she answers. "Hello?" Her voice has the grogginess of sleep.

I must have let too much time pass, because she says it again. "Hello? Calvin?"

"Yes, it's me."

"It's late," she says, and all the meaning is there—the rebuke, the wish for an explanation.

I don't have one she'll like. I had remembered her just then, so I called before I forgot again. "I'm sorry," I say.

I can hear her shift in her bed—it makes more noise than I expect—and then I hear someone whispering in the background. "Who is it?" I think they say, or "*What* is it?" Either way, the intrusion is clear.

"Go back to sleep; I'll just be a minute," Tanya says, and gets up out of bed. I can hear this too: her footfalls as she leaves the room, the door creaking as she closes it behind her.

"I just wanted to call," I say.

"I told you to call when you land," she reminds me. "It's been three weeks."

It feels both longer and shorter than that. "I'm sorry," I say again.

"If you can remember, call me in the morning," she says. "I've been thinking about you."

She doesn't say this with longing. She sounds concerned, like a work colleague or an out-of-touch friend. She doesn't seem uncomfortable that I've heard someone in the background, either. All of it sounds very expected, and it occurs to me, then and there, that she really does expect this behavior from me.

"Okay," I say. "I'll call at ten. Promise."

"Right," she says. "Looking forward to it."

When she hangs up, I put an alarm in my phone. *Call Tanya.* I set it to go off at ten a.m., then get out of bed and go to the kitchen for some water.

As I pass through the living room, I check on Gina, who is fast asleep on the couch. She's spent the night twice this week. I drink my water quietly and go back to my room.

Five minutes later, I am out again because the room makes me anxious even with the light on.

I shake Gina awake. "Hey, want to go for a drive?"

She wipes the sleep from her eyes. "What time is it?"

I tell her the time.

"Um, okay," she says.

• • •

The Northside roads are all steep turns and sporadic streetlights. It is late on a Wednesday night, so we pass only a few cars, their high beams zipping by in the other direction. I have no idea where I'm going; I just follow the road.

"Mom still does that, you know," Gina says. "Goes to the bathroom with the door open."

It takes me a second to know what she's talking about. "Oh, I'd forgotten I wrote that."

Another lingering silence. I was waiting for her to mention the file, but for the whole week she didn't say a word about it. I try hard not to press. Gina has her head resting against the window. She is so quiet, I think she's fallen back asleep, but a few minutes later she says, "It is hard for me to imagine he was like that."

I keep my eyes on the road.

"He visited me again tonight," she says.

"Did you talk to him about it?"

"Yeah." She doesn't elaborate.

I slow the car a little, trying to catch a glimpse of her face. She is staring out the window. She may be crying or may have been crying, but it's hard to see in the low light.

"I can't defend anything he did or how he was in the end," I say. "But I loved him and I miss him."

"You blame yourself," she says.

"How could I not?" I say.

"Cory says you need to cut that shit out. His exact words."

"I'll try."

"You still visit him in other worlds?"

"No," I lie.

Somewhere along the way, I make a decision. I take the turn down Mafolie Road and descend into Charlotte Amalie. The streets in town are mostly empty. It takes me only a few minutes to reach Waterfront. I park in the empty lot by Scotia Bank, and Gina and I cross the silent street to sit on a bench facing the water.

Arriving at the bench, we find a stray cat in the spot where we would sit. Politely, we sit a little farther down, giving it some space, but not even a minute goes by before the cat saunters right up to us, stepping over Gina's lap and sitting between us. Some strays are like this, gods of their little realms, ready to be worshipped.

The cat's golden eyes are staring up at me like tiny suns. She is long and slender, her coat midnight black. None of these features are alarming, but others stand out. Her ears are too pointy. And her tail, long and bushy, is unusual for an all-black cat. She looks like many cats at once—a chimera of cats.

"She's beautiful," Gina says.

"Yes, she is."

The cat is looking back and forth between us as if she, too, has stumbled across a small marvel. All the same, I warn Gina against petting her, and the cat doesn't rub against us in that way cats do when they want affection. Not worship, then, but something else.

I don't disturb the cat. Instead, I stare out at Hassel Island, or what I can make out of it. Beyond Hassel, Water Island's shadowed back looms out of the dark water. I reenact my usual exercise and picture another Water Island, stripped of its trees, a skyscraper-size metal object sticking up out of it like a spear, and another Water Island that's on fire, and another with a spaceship hovering over it and emitting a soft light. I lay them one on top of another, a stack of negatives merging into a single image. How many Water Islands have I seen? How many more will I see before it is all done?

I look back at the cat and think, *I don't suppose you'd tell me what's going on, how this all ends.*

The cat doesn't speak, but I hear something in the chamber of my mind, echoing off the walls. An answer.

Nothing ends. It bleeds.

This part I can't explain. I am used to thinking about myself as both sane and insane simultaneously. When I dream, I can't prove where I go. I can't bring anything back with me other than what I remember, which is a lot, but again, not actual proof. I maintain a healthy skepticism. Even my conversations with Gina are held in a liminal space, between truth and some beautiful fiction. I don't believe she can see Cory. I don't believe I travel anywhere. Not truly. Not completely.

But Gina is looking at me, astonished, and I know before she says anything that this particular bit of fiction has somehow been shared between us.

"Did you hear that too?" she asks. And then she repeats the

words, as if they weren't frightening enough the first time. "What does it mean?"

I don't speak. I can't; the words simply won't come. My heart is thumping wildly in my chest, and my mouth is open, but I am incapable of communicating anything more than my own astonishment.

This remains for a long time: a thick silence with nothing escaping, nothing coming in.

And in the silence, the little god purrs.

ACKNOWLEDGMENTS

My list has gotten bigger.

Michael Carr, my editor, and slayer of my worst writing tendencies. For doing what he does. And for coming back for a second helping of my prose.

Ananda Finwall, my copyeditor and a gift in her own right. For saving me in more ways than I can count.

Nell Pierce, the most patient agent on the planet. For putting up with me and continuing to be the person I can turn to with my craziest ideas.

Martha Millard, my previous agent. For convincing Blackstone I had another book in me before retiring. And for seeing something in me the first time.

Haila Williams, Jeff Yamaguchi, Lauren Maturo, and the rest of my Blackstone family. For reading this thing and not running for the hills. Lauren continues to have my back. I am immensely grateful.

Kathryn English. For designing another gorgeous cover greater than my wildest dreams. I don't know how she does it.

My writer friends from Cohort-19. For reading and providing feedback for parts of this novel. And for general awesomeness.

My writer friends from North Island Workshop. For reading other parts, particularly the climax, with very little context. Why I did that to them, I do not know. But I am glad they helped me anyway.

Emma "Em-Dash" Osborne, for reading this early and giving me some much-needed feedback and encouragement. And for always being there with a hug and smile when I have needed it most. Special shout-out to my homie, Jess, for being the third and equally vital part of the Team Tuesday trio.

My fellow Cryptids from the Clock Tower: Mary, Heather, Janelle, DJ, Shirin, and Abby. For inspiring some of the weirder aspects of this novel, but mostly just for being so supportive of my writing. It means the world to me. Special thanks to Heather and Janelle for letting me subject them to interviews.

Which brings me to thanking all the people who answered my questions: the big, the small, and the strange.

Mary Salcedo. For access into the world of swim meets. And Jake Peters. For talking to me about wood carving and nest ventilation in honeybee colonies.

Wayne Daly. For talking to me about Ireland, particularly Monageer. And for putting me on to some great horror movies which certainly inspired parts of this novel.

Miriam Johnston. For educating me on horse riding, which became one of Ridley's many talents.

Paul and Kyra from the Silver Unicorn Bookstore. For answering my questions about the work of running an independent bookstore.

Jeremy Shenk. For every question he answered about political

activism and his native Harrisonburg. And for being one of coolest dudes I know.

Grassroots Economic Organizing Collective. For teaching me everything I know about solidarity economics and for welcoming me into a community of kindred spirits.

And even more people to thank, just for being who they are.

The entire La Roche Writers' Center crew (and all honorary members). For being my first family away from home.

My people at Clarion West. For inspiring this book in some truly weird ways. And for continuing to be such an important part of my writing community. Team Arsenic for life.

My MFA professors and peers. For all the lessons I learned there (and am still learning years after). And for welcoming me back with open arms.

My mother, brother, sister, and the rest of my family. The ones still in this world and the ones who have moved on to other worlds. For raising me and loving me and believing in me.

My best friend, Elliot. For listening to my crazy ideas since we were both aspiring writers at Charlotte Amalie High School. And for being one of the only people I can call up just to talk for hours about movies. So much of my appreciation for great storytelling came out of those conversations.

All my friends who have encouraged me with this writing thing and have graciously read my books and stories, often early and with generous enthusiasm. I'm truly grateful to all of them.

My new readers. For getting to the end of this crazy thing. I know I have too many characters. Much gratitude and many apologies.

My returning readers. For reading *The Lesson* and showing back up anyway. In my quiet voice: the references to *The Lesson* are meaningful.

My fellow writers. For their support and guidance. And for welcoming me into their ranks. Most of the time I still can't believe I get to call them peers.

My wife, Anju. For being there when I needed someone to hold my hand. For being my reading partner and putting me on to a greater variety of urban fantasy. For all those hours we sat together listening to audiobooks and making faces at each other. For telling me, "Yes, do it!" when I came to her with the idea for this book. But mostly, for being the realest person I know. With every year I understand more fully how lucky I am. I'll be understanding that for a long time still.